LETTERBOX

BY

P.A.DAVIES

First published in 2011 by MJD Publishing, 920 Hyde Road, Gtr. Manchester, M18 7LL, UK.

Paperback edition first published in 2012 by MJD Publishing.

ISBN: 978-0-9572639-0-1

Cover designed by Paul Davies.

Though certain events captured throughout this book are based on documented fact, the main characters portrayed, are of a purely fictional nature and not intended to represent any person or persons, whether living or dead. Likewise, the views expressed by certain characters throughout the novel are, again, written within a fictional context and are not intended to offend or indeed portrait the views of the author or any other persons.

FOR MADDY

THANKS TO:

My family, friends and colleagues who have all given their valuable time and input in one way or another during the writing of this book. I truly do appreciate everybody's thoughts, interest and patience ... Bless you all.

AND WITH SPECIAL THANKS TO:

Mark David Dunn. A true legend and someone I'm proud to call a friend. May I thank him for all his support and contributions throughout the writing of this book and for all his hilarious little ditties that define the man himself, some of which have been included in the book as my personal tribute. (You'll know which they are Dude!) ... Cheers Dunny!

AND FINALLY ... To the dedicated and professional staff of the Greater Manchester Emergency Services and Security officers who acted with great tenacity and selflessness to protect members of the general public. It was through their tireless actions in the face of such adversity, that any loss of life was prevented and I give you all my respect!!

###

PART ONE

At this time it appears that the two governments are intent on changing the basis of the peace process. They claim that 'the obstacle now to a lasting and durable settlement is the continuing terrorist and criminal activity of the IRA'. We reject this. It also belies the fact that a possible agreement last December was squandered by both governments pandering to rejectionist unionism instead of upholding their own commitments and honouring their own obligations.

We are taking all our proposals off the table and it is our intention to closely monitor ongoing developments and to protect to the best of our ability the rights of republicans and our support base.

The two governments are trying to play down the importance of our statement because they are making a mess of the peace process. Do not underestimate the seriousness of the situation!

IRA statement Feb 2005

Chapter 1

11.30hrs Saturday 15th June 1996

The first chilling images of devastation beamed relentlessly across the airwaves onto millions of television screens throughout the nation. Radio broadcasts became dominated by the incredulous story that no one doubted, would change the face of history ... not only in the United Kingdom, but throughout the entire world.

Many saw the terrorist attack on the City of Manchester, as nothing more than a cold and callous act of violence by a group of evil and cowardly thugs, whilst others, deemed it to be an unprecedented victory against a complacent and oppressive regime that hid behind the walls of Parliament under the guise of the British Government.

For one man, this was the day that had served to exorcise some personal demons yet paradoxically, had also rekindled a conscience that he believed to be long dead. For another, this was the day when the powerful voice of the Irish Republican Army had spoken ... and been listened to.

###

The Commander sat behind his desk gently stroking his thick beard as he watched with interest, the unfolding stories coming through live from Manchester. There would be much celebration this evening he thought, but for now, he needed to remain focused and consider his next move. "Set up a meeting

3

of the council for this afternoon," he instructed, without taking his eyes off the television. A man stood by his side, nodded silently and began to leave the room. "And Marty," he added sternly, before the man had reached the door. "Bring Joseph here as soon as he returns!"

Once the man had left the room, the Commander glanced down at the two phones on his desk and wondered which of the two would ring first. Would it be the one that brought a tedious dialogue from the sycophantic lapdogs of the Prime Minister, decrying this outrageous act whilst issuing veiled threats on behalf of John Major and his countrymen? Threats that they had neither the balls nor the power *to* carry out ... '*Small cogs in a big wheel*!' he pondered ... Or would it be the anticipated call to his private and secure line? A call that would be the focal point of their meeting later that day and would undoubtedly result in the extending of the proverbial olive branch. It was a call that would ensure a place for *Sinn Fein* at the negotiating table and take them one step closer to a free Ireland. But whichever one it was, it always amused this particular Leader, how the right hand of the British Government had no idea what the left hand was doing ... or capable of.

He continued to watch the television, quietly musing how today had undoubtedly shown the free world the capabilities and commitment of his comrades, dedicated in the pursuit of their beliefs. It was also the day, he thought with some respect, that Liam Connor had finally become a man.

When one of the phones began to ring, the Commander looked down at it and smiled.

###

Chapter 2

Ten hours earlier

Somewhere in Belfast

The three men sat in silence in the sparsely furnished living room of a high rise flat, a building that did little to promote their importance or standing within the powerful organisation to which they belonged. An underpowered light bulb hung from the ceiling, struggling against the blanket of cigarette smoke that enveloped the room, whilst old wallpaper peeled away from the sodden walls like skin falling from a rotting carcass. In another part of the building, Bob Marley's *'Buffalo Soldier'* pounded the structure, educating the residents with a lesson in Black History, whilst somewhere else, a baby was left to cry as its parents hurled relentless abuse towards each other. A fourth man entered the room carrying a bottle of Bushmills whisky and four odd tumblers; socialising was not on the agenda. He placed the tumblers on a wooden crate in the middle of the room, filled them with the drink and passed one to each of the other men. He then took his own glass and raised it high in the air. "Gentlemen," he began, glancing at the others. "T'Ireland and Home Rule!"

In unison, the other men stood, raised their glasses and repeated. "T'Ireland and Home Rule!" Each man drank the contents of their tumbler and sat back down.

One of the party, a thick set, tower of a man in his fifties, placed a cigarette in his mouth and inhaled deeply. His weathered but well defined face was temporarily masked by the plumage of thick unfiltered smoke as he exhaled. When he spoke, it was with an air of great presence and authority that left no man in any doubt that it was time to listen. "Is he ready gentlemen?" he asked, glancing at the three other men in the room.

The man who had distributed the drink, nodded slowly and replied. "Aye, sure enough. He's ready."

The thick set man shifted in his chair and leant forward, looking intensely at the man who had answered him. In a half whisper, half growl he said. "But will he do it Pat?"

Before he could reply, a voice from another part of the room interjected. "One things f'certain, we'll know either way for sure in about ten hours!"

0500 hrs Saturday 15th June 1996
Somewhere in England

The radio alarm sprang into life, causing the man sitting on the edge of the bed to jump slightly. He needn't have set it, he hadn't slept all night.

The voice of a female news reader reported on; *'Britain's first female Chief Constable being on the Queen's Birthday honours' list, job losses announced at ICI and how John Major was to get tough with social scroungers. There were no current problems on the road and it was going to be a clear June day with a high of 18 degrees centigrade.'*

He remained seated and still, hands clasped together and head bowed as if in silent prayer. Only the gentle sound of his breathing distinguished him from a display piece at Madam Tussaud's Wax Museum.

He had replayed the schedule over and over in his head until it ached. There were to be no mistakes, no second thoughts and no contact until the package had been delivered. The words of his peers from two days previous remained embedded in his mind, playing again and again as if on a continuous loop. *'Do your Dada proud son. Do yourself proud!'*

He *would* make his Dad proud and there *would* be no mistakes, *no* second thoughts. But for himself, it was retribution he felt, not pride.

He remained motionless for a few minutes longer before turning his head towards the radio, a thin trace of a smile appearing on his face. He reached out and pushed the off button sending *The Fugees* and '*Killing me softly*' into silence.

###

Chapter 3

0900hrs Saturday 15th June 1996
Manchester, England

Putting the keys into his jeans pocket and zipping up his green hooded jacket, the man strode off along the high street, *package* delivered. The passenger he had picked up at Knutsford Services on the M6 motorway, as instructed, had also completed his task and without so much as a nod, had headed off in the opposite direction and was soon lost in the growing crowd. Finding a phone box, the man rang a number that he knew would be secure. "It's done," was all he said, all he needed to say.

The silent recipient at the other end of the line nodded, smiled and replaced the receiver. He looked at his watch, turned to the only other man in the room and said. "Call them in one hour!"

###

Leaving the kiosk and keeping his head down, the man walked on with a good pace, not hurrying, but methodical and brisk despite his heart beating quickly and his mind telling him to run.

As he threaded his way through small pockets of pedestrians bustling along the street, he consoled himself with the fact that nobody would give him a second thought, too caught up in their own intimate worlds to notice him. In less than 5 minutes he would be home dry, gone forever without a trace.

At first he thought it was his mind playing tricks, a rush of adrenalin perhaps causing his ears to wrongly decode the sounds. But there it was again, louder and clearer. "Liam?" The man faltered a little recognising his own name being called and though he tried to ignore it, his pace slowed to a near stop. "Liam. Liam, wait. It's me!"

'*Shit!*' the man thought as he stopped in his tracks, his heart pounding so hard he thought he would have a seizure right there and then. Turning around he saw the source of the voice. A man no older than himself was heading towards him, smiling with a hand already outstretched to greet. Liam wanted to run but he couldn't, fearful that this would draw attention to him. He had no choice. Face this smiling man, exchange few words as possible and then go, quickly.

"Jesus!" the male exclaimed. "Liam fuckin' Connor. How are you mate? It's me, Sean. Sean Bevan!"

Liam knew who he was from the first time he heard his name called. This was, after all, the person he had shared most of his childhood with, the man with whom he had been best friends and inseparable from. "What about ya Sean?" Liam responded, shaking his hand whilst quickly scanning his surroundings.

"Whoa, nice accent," Sean began. "Proper Irishman eh? How long you been back? Are you back for good or jus' visiting? Where are you...?"

"What's w'all the bloody questions?" Liam snapped, surprised at his own intolerance. '*Calm down,*' he told himself. '*Don't draw attention to yourself.*'

"Sorry mate," Sean replied, slightly bewildered. "I only..."

"No Sean," Liam cut in remorsefully. "It's me that should apologise. I'm just a little ... well, surprised!"

There was a moment of awkward silence between the two men, neither sure whether to turn and walk away or ride out the uneasy pause. It was Sean that eventually broke the deadlock. "Hey, do you remember Louise Duffy?" he asked with an overly chirpy tone.

Liam thought for a moment. "Yeah. Skinny wi' glasses an' spots, always tellin' tales on ya. Got ya inta loads o' shite too if I remember right!" Sean suddenly looked to the floor and gave a nervous laugh. Liam became confused. "What?" he asked, curious as to Sean's obvious and sudden embarrassment.

"Well," Sean replied, "I'm going to meet the *future* Mrs. Bevan in a couple of hours for lunch, just across the road there and..."

"Aw shite all mighty!" Liam interjected, he himself now overcome with sudden embarrassment. "I'm sorry mate, I had no idea ... I ... you and Lou? ... Aw shite!"

Sean Laughed. "Don't worry mate, you weren't to know ... and she's not changed one fuckin' bit!"

Both men laughed and for Liam, this was an unexpected but welcome release. He found himself remembering why he and Sean had been such close friends, closer than brothers many said. They could, and would, laugh at anything and everything given the opportunity. Even taking the piss out of each other was not only acceptable but expected. The bond they had forged during their childhood and early teen years had seemed destined to keep their friendship alive, for always; it was *their* world. What neither could have predicted, was just how dramatically that world was going to change.

###

Chapter 4

June 1982

The first time the two boys met, Liam Connor was busy watching the effect that the sun's rays, when intensified through a magnifying glass, had on a worm that he'd just dug up from the soil.

"What y'doin'?" asked an eight year old Sean suddenly standing above him.

Liam looked up and saw a chubby, blonde haired boy staring back at him. He had the remains of a sandwich in his hand and Liam could tell, from the spillage on the boys tight fitting white *Umbro* t-shirt, that the sandwich contained jam. "What's it to you?" he replied.

Sean shrugged and pushed the remaining sandwich into his mouth. "You're from the family that's just moved in aren't you?" he said through a mouthful of bread and jam, spitting out bits of masticated food as he spoke.

"Did your mum never tell you not to speak with your mouth full?" Liam said, flicking pieces of bread off his own t-shirt.

Sean shrugged again and continued to stare at Liam whilst he finished the contents in his mouth. "D'ya wanna see a dead bird?" he asked casually.

"Where is it?" Liam asked, now rising to his feet. The hot worm had now lost its appeal to a greater scoop and Liam wanted in.

"Not far," replied Sean. "It's on Joey's Field near the school." Liam looked at him blankly. "Oh yeah, I forgot you're new round here," continued Sean. "C'mon then, I'll show you!" And with that, the two set off.

On that day, the boys learned a lot about each other and their respective families. Liam learnt how, like he, Sean was the second of two children, with an older sister called Karen. He had a mum called Angela, who stayed at home and a dad called Peter who was an engineer in a factory making stuff. Sean learnt that Liam had an older sister called Margaret and that they had all moved over from Ireland because of his Dad's job, although he had no idea what his dad did, only that he was away a lot and brought back ace presents when he came home.

"You don't sound Irish," offered Sean. "Well, not like my Gran. Now she's proper Irish!"

Liam explained that they had first moved from Ireland to London three years ago, stayed there for a year and then moved to a place called Birmingham before coming to Manchester. "Probably why I don't sound Irish anymore," he explained to an open mouthed Sean.

"Wow!" Sean remarked, genuinely impressed, though he frowned a little before continuing. "I've never been further than the Arndale Centre in Manchester with me mum, unless you count Butlins in Wales, but that was just a holiday." He paused a moment and smiled. "Everything's free though," he added excitedly. "Have you ever been?"

Liam shook his head but listened with great awe as Sean told him about the free rides, free food and free swimming pool with a diving board. As the heat of the day turned to a warm evening, the boys began to walk home, the introduction to Joey's Field, dead birds and the best trees to climb, completed. They had covered everything in their lives from favourite food to football teams, from best Action Man toy to why girls can't build a den. They had also discovered that, not only did they live on the same street, but, after the weekend, Liam would be going to Sean's school, St Michael's Primary

12

and that would be '*top*'. Despite their differing backgrounds, they had found so much in common and both knew that a friendship had been forged in the last few hours that would surely stand the test of time.

###

As they stopped outside the front gate, Sean looked towards his house and sighed.

"What's wrong?" Liam asked.

"My dad's home," Sean replied.

"So what? Don't you like your dad?"

"Yeah, course I do! But he's home early and that means mum's sick again!"

Liam looked at Sean, confused. "Is she gonna die?" he asked before he could stop himself.

Sean turned quickly towards Liam. "Don't say that!" he snapped, taking Liam a little by surprise. "She's just sick ok!"

"Sorry. I didn't mean..." Liam started, but was cut short as Sean continued to speak.

"She drinks stuff, lots ... and it makes her a bit, y'know, sick?" He shrugged, wondering if Liam understood then looked again towards the house. "But my dad will carry her up to bed," he said in a near whisper. "And tomorrow she'll be better again." Turning again to Liam he added. "She's not gonna die, ok?"

For the first time, Liam saw sadness in Sean's eyes and felt a genuine concern. That's when an idea popped into his head. "Hey, do you like Irish stew?" he asked, hoping to change the mood. Now it was Sean's turn to look confused.

"What?" he replied, frowning.

"Irish stew? My mum makes it and she's making it for tea!"

"So what?" Sean asked, not really understanding what his new friend was talking about.

13

"Well," Liam continued. "Why don't you come and have tea with us? My mum makes loads and she won't mind you coming!"

Once again, a pensive Sean looked towards his house and after a moment's silence replied. "I'll go and ask my dad."

A few minutes later, the boys were heading up to Liam's house for tea, a routine that would become commonplace for years to come.

###

Chapter 5

May 1984

"Sean Bevan. Get out!**"** Miss Jamison scowled at Sean from the front of the classroom, her reddened face accentuating her bright ginger hair. She was not in the mood for foolishness today and Sean's disruptive comments, likening cows '*teats*' to girls '*tits*', was above and beyond the excuse she needed to impose her authority and put a stop to the silly laughter now resonating around the classroom.

"But Miss..." began Sean, putting on his most innocent face.

"Save your explanations for Mrs. Gunnel," Miss Jamison continued. "I'm sure the Headmistress will be only too happy to deal with you in a manner befitting your stupidity ... Now go!!"

Sean walked out of the classroom trying hard not to chuckle as Miss Jamison turned to face the remaining pupils. "And if anybody else would care to join him, please, feel free, as I will not tolerate this kind of behaviour in my lesson. Is that understood?" Silence fell around the classroom. "Is that understood?!" she demanded again. In unison, the pupils acknowledged their understanding. Miss Jamison remained still, glaring at them, mentally urging somebody to fall out of line. It wasn't to happen. She had been victorious.

At the rear of the classroom, two boys had sat and watched the expulsion of Sean with great delight. Neither was impressed with him or his '*teat*' comment, but found the outcome of his actions very satisfying. Once the lesson had fully resumed, one of the boys looked up towards Miss Jamison and seeing that she was occupied, gave the other boy a nudge, gesturing with his head towards Liam now sitting on his own.

The second boy looked at Liam and then too at Miss Jamison and seeing his opportunity, turned back to Liam. "Paddy. Hey Paddy!" he said in a loud whisper. Liam glanced round and looked at the boy, knowing that whatever Matthew Walker was about to say, would not be pleasant. "Are you missing your girlfriend?" Walker continued, pointing to the empty seat next to Liam where Sean had been sitting fifteen minutes ago.

Both Walker and his friend began to chuckle, causing Miss Jamison to look up. "Is there something you want to share with us Matthew?" she asked, the tone in her voice still menacing.

"No Miss, sorry Miss. I was just asking Pa ... er ... Liam for a rubber."

"Then do it quietly please, or you will find yourself joining Sean," she added before looking down again.

"Yes Miss," Walker concluded, his face reddening slightly. He turned and saw Liam smiling triumphantly back at him and, in frustration, put two fingers up. Liam shook his head and turned away.

###

Matthew Walker disliked Liam Connor from the first time he had been introduced into their class almost two years ago.

"Liam's originally from Ireland," the class teacher had declared. "So let's make him feel welcome!"

Not that Liam had done anything against him personally, but Matthew bore the influence of his father, an ex military man with a hate of anything Irish. For years, he had listened to his dad rant on about the *'Bloody IRA'* and how the *'Murdering Irish bastards had let off yet another bomb'* and though Matthew didn't fully understand what was going on in

16

the world, he felt an overwhelming duty to share his father's views; a desire born out of the mind of a child who is desperate to help and console yet desperate to be loved. Over a period of time, Matthew came to realise that he could neither help nor console his father and love was a virtue reserved only for mothers and songwriters.

Nevertheless, his misguided yet deep seated hatred remained and here, in his own classroom, stood a boy who symbolised the root of that passion. A boy not differing in age, height or colour from himself, nor in the style of clothing worn. But even so, different. Wrong. In short, *'a stupid Paddy'*.

It was later that day, during break, when Matthew saw an opportunity to make his mark and show the Irish boy what was what in St.Michael's. Seeing him standing alone in the school playground, he beckoned to his friend Simon and the two of them walked over to Liam.

"Hi Ian," he said in an overly friendly tone. "I'm Matthew but everyone calls me Matty."

"Hello," Liam replied. "But it's Liam, not Ian."

"What is?" asked Matthew

"My name ... it's Liam but you called me Ian!"

"Oh sorry," Matthew began. "You're not going to blow me up are you *Liam?"* The boy standing with Matthew let out a loud cackle, which sounded more like a dutiful appreciation than a genuine laugh. Liam looked at the boy and then back to Matthew, confused. He opened his mouth to speak but Matthew continued. "'Cause that's what you lot do isn't it Liam? Y'know? Paddies? You blow things up?"

"I..." Liam started, but Matthew ignored him and carried on.

"That's what my Dad says and he should know 'cause he's a soldier, isn't he Si?"

The boy with Matthew nodded before adding, "Yeah. And he's shot loads of people."

"Y'see?" continued Matthew. "My Dad knows what he's talking about and he says that all Paddies are cowards ... Are you a coward Liam?"

"No," Liam replied, feeling very uneasy about the way this was going.

Matthew grinned and opened his arms. "Ok, prove it then," he said. "Let's have a fight."

"What for?" asked Liam. "I don't want a fight!"

"See. My Dad's right. You're all shitty cowards!" Matthew sneered, taking a step closer to him.

"No!" Liam retorted. "It's just ... we'll get into trouble and ... AAH!" Liam didn't know which was worse, the sting from the sudden hard slap to his face or the shock that it had happened at all. Either way, his eyes welled up almost immediately, sending the sight of a smirking Matthew into a temporary blur. As he desperately tried to wipe away the tears and regain his vision, he didn't see Matthew moving towards him intending to '*finish*' the job. But neither did he see Matthew hit the ground as he was suddenly side swiped and prevented from doing so.

"What you doin' Walker, ya mong?!"

Liam's sight returned to see Sean standing over a bewildered Matthew now sprawled on the playground floor. The other boy, Simon, was backing away, quietly.

"What's it to you Bevan?" Matthew asked, attempting to get to his feet. "Are you a Paddy Lover or something?"

Sean moved towards Matthew and pushed him back onto the floor before kneeling full weight onto his stomach. Matthew let out a heavily winded gasp before Sean stood back up and dropped on him once again. Now it was Matthew's turn to have tearful eyes. When Sean stood up for the second time, he pointed at Matthew, shouting. "Don't you ever touch my friend again ok? You wanna fight, then fight me, y' spaz!!"

18

Matthew didn't reply. He couldn't. He just sobbed, trying to catch his breath as Sean led Liam away. When he was eventually able to get up a few minutes later, he brushed the dirt off his clothes and looked around the playground, hoping nobody had witnessed the embarrassment of his defeat. He then caught sight of Liam and Sean heading back into the school building, laughing. "One day Paddy," he whispered to himself. "And fatty won't be there to help you out!"

Things hadn't gone to plan for Matthew that day and for nearly two years it seemed that wherever Liam was, Fat Boy Bevan was right there with him. *'Thick as Thieves'* he had heard them described as. More like *'Man and Wife'* he had said, much to the amusement of his friend Simon.

But today, it seemed that the Gods had shone down and given Matthew a long awaited chance to exact revenge. Today was the day that *'mouth almighty'* Bevan had said too much and was now on his way to be given lunchtime litter picking duty by Mrs.Gunnel. Today was the day that Sean Bevan's Irish girlfriend, Liam Connor, would be facing lunchtime on his own ... result.

As the lunch bell sounded, Miss Jamison ordered everyone in the room to pack their things away quietly and make their way out of the classroom to lunch. "And walk Liam Connor!" she added in a very military tone, although Liam was already out of the door heading towards Mrs. Gunnel's. As he rounded the corridor that led to the Headmistress's office, he saw Sean sat outside, swinging his legs and staring at the floor.

When Sean looked up and saw Liam approaching, a big smile appeared on his face. "Now *that* was funny," he said once Liam was standing next to him. "Did you see Jamison's face? ... classic!"

"Yeah, quality!" giggled Liam. Then, nodding towards Mrs. Gunnel's office, he added. "Have you seen her yet?"

"Nah!" Sean replied. "Well, she opened her door and stared at me all weird, but then she went back inside!" Sean pulled a face that was his idea of 'weird' and looked at Liam. Both boys began to laugh. At that moment, the office door opened, making the pair jump slightly as a stern looking woman appeared, her gaze immediately fixing on Liam.

Mrs. Margaret Gunnel was an immaculately dressed woman in her early fifties, though her short grey hair and glasses dangling around her neck on a gold chain, gave her the appearance of being much older. The whole school knew that she was not a lady to be crossed. "And you are here for what purpose Mr.Connor?" she asked Liam directly.

"Erm, nothing Miss, I was just..."

"On your way to lunch perhaps?" she cut in, more instructing than questioning.

"Yes Miss," Liam replied. "Just on my way!"

"Off you go then." She directed. Liam looked at Sean feeling helpless. "Now Liam!" she added loudly, making Liam jump again, about turn and walk off double time, back along the corridor from where he had first come. Head down, he turned the corner at the end of the corridor and walked straight into a pupil coming the other way. Liam looked up and his heart sank. The lanky frame of Walker stood before him, his squatter, uglier sidekick Boland, just to his left. "Well well. If it isn't Miss Paddy!" Walker said, grinning. Liam guessed that this wasn't going to be pleasant.

Having watched Liam's departure until he had turned the corner at the end of the corridor, the Headmistress fixed her gaze on Sean, let out a heavy sigh and began shaking her head. "Why is it always you outside my office Sean?" Sean shrugged his shoulders and looked to the floor. "Right. In you go then!" she instructed, adding another sigh.

Crestfallen, Sean walked into the office, closely followed by Mrs. Gunnel still shaking her head. She knew that a ten minute lecture followed by the punishment of litter picking duty for the remainder of lunch, was going to have little, if any, effect on Sean Bevan. Oh, she would give him the usual speech about *being disruptive* and about *self discipline* and then finish off with the *deeply disappointed and let's make a new start* routine, but in reality, she could think of no better solution than to thrash this little shit to within an inch of his life then drag him home screaming to his drunk of a mother and do the same to her. *'That's the trouble with Educational Reform,'* she had voiced many times to her colleagues. *'No place for good old fashioned discipline anymore!'*

And here she was again, looking across her desk at a supercilious young boy who just didn't give a sod and feeling powerless to do anything constructive about it. *'Why can't you be more like your friend Liam?'* she thought as she searched for her opening words to Sean. *'Such a nice boy ... But then he comes from a strong, Church loving family, not a dysfunctional drunken one!'* With one final heavy sigh, she began.

Sean listened to the Headmistress speak, grunting and nodding in all the right places but wishing she would hurry up and finish. He didn't like sitting here. Not because of the lecture, he had heard that so many times before, but because of the smell. It reminded him of dead people. Not that he knew many dead people, but his Uncle Eddy was an undertaker and he once went to his funeral parlour to drop a letter off from his dad and it smelled funny, like someone had used a bad air freshener to cover the smell of a wet dog. *'Wonder why they call it a Parlour?'* he thought to himself as the words of Mrs. Gunnel became no more than a monotonic sound. *'My Gran's got a parlour, but she doesn't keep dead people in it, just her best cups.'*

"... and you're only letting yourself down Sean, can't you see that?"

"Yes Miss," right on cue. *'God, it stinks in 'ere. Maybe they use this office for dead people ... maybe Mrs. Gunnel is really dead and she's come back as a zombie ... shit, that makes sense!'*

"... deeply disappointed that you are here again Sean ..."

'She's well old and she looks a bit dead!'

"... more self discipline and a little less disruption ..."

'Bet she lives in a funeral parlour full of other zombies, that's why it smells in 'ere!'

"... and this afternoon, we can make a fresh start, are we agreed Sean?"

'And I bet she doesn't have a husband ... or he's mysteriously vanished!'

"Sean! ... are you even listening?"

Sean's eyes focused on Mrs. Gunnel as he was jolted from his own world. "Yes Miss, I am Miss ... A fresh start, yes Miss!"

Mrs.Gunnel stared at Sean for what seemed like an eternity before adding. "You should take a leaf out of your friend Liam's book. Such a nice boy. I never see him outside my office. Why do you think that is?"

'Cause he never gets caught!' Sean wanted to say, but shrugged for the umpteenth time and remained silent.

The Headmistress let out a final sigh, stood up and concluded. "Ok Sean. Go and collect the litter bags from Mr. O'Leary and see me at the end of lunch time!"

"Yes Miss," Sean replied as Mrs.Gunnel opened the office door to signify there was nothing more to say. Sean walked out of the office and stopped in his tracks, open mouthed. "I think there is somebody here to see you Miss!" he said with great surprise.

Mrs.Gunnel peered around the open door into the corridor. "Holy God!" she exclaimed as she saw the two people sitting outside her office. The first of the two was a slightly smirking Matthew Walker. The second, a dishevelled looking and bloody nosed, Liam Connor.

22

Chapter 6

May 1984

Even before the black vehicle had come to a complete standstill outside the modest Manchester semi, Bridie Connor was standing at the open front door waiting to greet the expected guests. Inside, her husband Michael turned off the television, lit a cigarette and sat down waiting for them to enter the room. Never before had he felt so anxious, though never before had a meeting been conducted at his home. He already knew, from the phone call he received two days earlier, that it was of some great importance to the *cause*. But still.

"It's a matter of some urgency Michael," his brother Joe had said. "And with most of our usual places being watched, it was thought that a change of *scenery* might be best for all concerned. But the final decision rests with you of course Michael!"

"For God's sake Joe," he had protested. "This is my home, the home of my wife and our children. It's somewhere that should be a world apart from our '*cause*' and the shite it can bring, you know that!"

"I know, I know Michael." Joe replied softly, but then continued with a slight patronising tone. "But hasn't your home always been provided for you by fighting for that cause? I'm sure our superiors would never suggest that your living '*gratis*' came with a price, but when it's about loyalty and commitment, well!"

"Don't start that shite Joe!" Michael retorted, feeling his anger rise. "And don't *ever* question my fuckin' loyalty again

... I have fought and fought hard in the campaign for our Country's freedom and no man, not even our fuckin' *superiors,* can ever doubt my commitment!"

"Ok Ok Michael, calm down. I just meant..."

"Y' meant what Joseph? T'try my patience? Well ye are doing a fuckin' good job of that!"

There followed, what seemed like, an eternal silence between the two brothers, eventually broken by a more humble sounding Joe. "So can I tell them it's on? ... I promise t' wipe the shite off my shoes before I come in!"

Reluctantly, Michael had agreed and now, two days later, he was about to discover just how important this meeting really was.

###

Chapter 7

Michael Connor was born 24th May 1946, the second of five children to parents Thomas and Elizabeth Connor. He was raised in an overcrowded house in a poor area of Belfast where everybody seemed to know everyone else's business. It was a community filled with unprecedented support and loyalty for '*their own*', but a community also consumed with a hate for the British regime.

From a very early age, Michael would listen with awe as his father recounted stories of the struggle for freedom against the British, of the battles won, and lost, and of the many 'soldiers' that gave their lives in honour of the cause. With feelings of pride and excitement, he would never tire of hearing about the Easter uprising of 1916 when a group of heroic men came together in the hope of overthrowing the British in one of the greatest battles Dublin had ever witnessed. Michael saw his father's delight with every telling of that story and understood his passion. He didn't understand why every time he told it, his mother would raise her eyes and offer to make a cup of tea.

Over the years, schooled mostly by the elders of the community, Michael learned that a fair and just British Government was a concept thought up by tiresome and overpaid politicians who spent endless days sitting around in Cabinet offices talking of plans for peace.

"*Hoping* for peace," his father had said, "is for fools who sign petitions and trust that a British Government is interested enough even to acknowledge them. *Fighting* for peace, Michael, is for the men 'n' women of this land with enough pride to stand up for what they believe in, with strength to say enough is enough. It's for all the people of our great country with the conviction to fight and lay down their lives for what is their right by birth. That of freedom!"

Michael was to hear that speech on many occasions and at 14 years of age, spurred on by the love for his father and his country, became a fully paid up member of 'The Belfast Patriots', an all boys marching band whose founders and patrons were openly sympathetic and supportive to the cause of the *Óglaigh na hÉireann* ... The IRA.

At fifteen, Michael had risen up through the ranks of *The Patriots,* achieved mainly by his role in running 'errands' and relaying messages for his peers during the *Border Campaigns,* an IRA initiative to break down the British administration in the occupied areas of Ireland. Although menial tasks in the grand scheme of things, it brought him a certain amount of respect from the community, a great deal of pride from his father and a little jealousy from his older brother Joseph.

"He's just a glorified lackey," Joe had said bitterly when he overheard a group of local girls going on about how '*wonderful*' Michael was. "But if it's a real man you're after ladies?"

"And you fit that bill do you Joseph Connor?" said one of the girls through the sound of giggling.

"More likely he'll be passing on somebody's address to us!" said another, turning the giggling into full laughter and Joe a shade of crimson.

"Fuckin' gypsies!" he retorted, before walking away ... quickly.

Joseph Connor was born 4th June 1943 in the midst of two bloody wars; the world against a Nazi Germany and Irish

Republicans against an intrusive Britain. Only the former would conclude a few years later.

When Joseph's mother announced that she was pregnant, the father sat down next to her, looked her straight in the eyes and sighed heavily. "Are you sure?" he asked. "I mean, could there be a mistake?"

"Of course I'm sure!" Elizabeth replied, a little hurt at his reaction. "And before you ask," she continued, "yes, it is yours!" Elizabeth took hold of the man's hand and placed it onto her stomach. Her excitement diminished with the look of worry on his face. "It'll be alright," she said softly. "We'll manage."

"How?" he replied, a slight quiver in his voice. "Your man Tommy will kill us both if he ever finds out!"

From that day on, nobody other than Elizabeth and her quick to flee lover, knew that Thomas Connor wasn't Joe's real father, yet she couldn't help thinking that deep down, Tommy knew the truth and was just biding his time before confronting, then disowning, her and the child. But he showed no signs of suspicion or doubt, only love and support towards her and *their* first born. That said, Elizabeth always felt that there was something missing between *father* and *son*, a niggling instinct that a piece of that bond was absent and it was to be a few years later, following the birth of her second child Michael, that it became all too apparent what that was ... Pride.

Joseph hadn't been blessed with handsome features and what he lacked in looks, he more than made up for in weight. With a thick head of jet black hair and small grey blue eyes set above chubby pale cheeks, Tommy had often referred to him as the 'baby cannonball'.

"Jesus, Elizabeth," he'd said, on one of the few occasions he had picked him up. "The lad gets heavier by the day! Ya wouldn't be feedin' him extra portions when I'm not lookin' would ya now?" Elizabeth would just smile and hope that the subject of where Joseph's looks came from didn't ever enter the conversation.

In contrast, his younger brother Michael was a beautiful infant with fair hair and deep green eyes that had the appearance of constantly smiling. From birth, Michael was the one who would receive most of his father's attention and though Tommy never ignored or neglected Joseph, it was clear from the outset where his heart really lay. He would pick Michael up, cradle him in his arms and in a soft whisper, promise him the world. "Y'have your dada's Irish eyes for sure young babby," he'd say smiling. "And the girls'll love y' for that!"

In the years that followed, neither Joseph or Michael ever left Tommy's side, though it would be Michael who was to be the centre of attention and receive adoring comments from the older women of the community. It would be Michael who always sat on his father's shoulders whilst Joseph walked slightly behind and it would be Michael who, in later life, caught the eyes of the local girls.

At eight years old, Michael ran into his house looking for Joseph, flushed with excitement. He found him in their bedroom lying on the bed playing with a model plane. Joe looked up briefly as Michael entered the room and then turned his attention back to his to toy Messerschmitt. "Joe Joe come see what Dada's got me!" Michael said, slightly out of breath.

"Nah," replied Joseph uninterested. "I'm busy."

"Please Joe, please. It's a bike, a real bike. C'mon and see!" Michael begged.

"*Please Joe Please*," Joseph mocked. "Please come and see what Dada's done for his precious Michael!"

Michael starred at Joseph, confused and slightly hurt. He walked over to the bed and sat next to Joseph who had now turned to face the wall. "What's wrong Joe? Why ya angry wit me?" he said softly.

"Go away Mikey and leave me alone. Go play wit your precious bike," Joseph replied, making Michael feel more confused.

"But I don't understand. I want you t'see it Joe. You're my brother and..."

"Just fuck off won't ya!" Joe cut in angrily. "I don't wanna see the stupid thing!!"

Michael jumped at Joe's angry outburst and, getting off the bed, started to walk back towards the door. Before leaving the bedroom he turned toward Joseph again, his eyes welling slightly. "I'm sorry for makin' y'angry Joe," he said, his bottom lip quivering as he spoke. "But ... but I still want to share it wit ya ... if y'like?"

For a few moments, Michael stood in silence hoping for a change of heart from his brother. Then, as a tear rolled down his cheek, he turned to go back out of the door.

"Wait!" Joseph called and sat up on the bed. Michael stopped in his tracks and with a faint feeling of hope, turned back to Joseph. "Ok Mikey," Joe continued with a sigh, "I'll come see your bike."

"Our bike," Michael said, a smile appearing on his face. "It's *our* bike now!"

At only 11 years old, Joseph came to realise two things on that day. The first was that Michael's love for him was, and would continue to be, unconditional and real. The second, was the all too hurtful fact that his father's wasn't.

When Thomas Connor passed away some years later, Joseph had long since given up trying to win his father's affection and grieved only for the sake of his mother and siblings. He had already resigned himself to the fact that Michael would supersede Tommy as head of the family; a process reinforced on the day of the funeral when hundreds of attendees made it their business to offer Michael their respects and continued support.

Michael, however, felt that a huge void had entered his world. He had spent his childhood, youth and early adult life in the powerful shadow of his father. He had listened, learned and developed his knowledge of the struggle for a free Ireland, never thinking that one day, *this day,* he would be expected to step into Thomas Connors shoes. It would be a great responsibility, he thought, but also a great honour. Yet, as he stood in the cold and misty church grounds shaking hands with mourners promising their loyalties, he knew that his acceptance of taking on this role rested solely on receiving the full blessing of one man ... his brother Joseph. Without it, Michael thought, the journey ends here.

Six days earlier, Michael had been at his ailing father's bedside, trying desperately to sound positive and talk of a future when Tommy would be better.

"Michael, Michael," his father had said in a frail voice. "We both know that I'm not getting out of this bed again, but I need to give you something before it's too late!"

"Don't talk like that dada. You'll be up and about in no time, you'll see," Michael had offered, but hadn't even managed to convince himself.

Tommy patted his son's hand and smiled, appreciating the words but knowing that his time was coming to an end. With a great deal of effort, he removed a chain that held a key from around his neck and passed it to Michael. He then looked and pointed across his bedroom. "Go to my drawers," he instructed quietly. "Move them aside and look under the carpet ... bring me the book!"

Michael went over to the drawers, moved them to one side and pulled back the threadbare carpet but saw nothing else. He looked back at his father, confused. "Try the floorboards," Tommy urged, smiling slightly.

Michael knelt down and saw that two pieces of the floorboards were loose. He pulled them up revealing a black metal box nestled in between the joists. He took the box out, unlocked and pulled back the lid and stared open mouthed at the green book lying inside it; a book that he knew was regarded by many as second only to the Holy Bible itself in terms of importance. A book so secretive, that to reveal its contents to anybody outside the organisation it was meant for, would result in certain death.

Michael removed it from the box and caressed it gently, turning it over and over in his hands. He opened its cover with both excitement and trepidation, knowing that this green book was *the* 'Green Book', a secretly published guide of philosophies, strategies, techniques, objectives and weapons. A book that was *the* training manual of the IRA. Smiling, he looked up from the book to his father's bed. His smile quickly faded when he saw that his beloved dada, at only 56 years old, had just passed away.

On 15th November 1966 and at just twenty years of age, Michael Connor was one of the youngest people in the IRAs history to possess the Green Book and over the years, in the continuing struggle against British rule, it would prove to be his greatest aid and guide ... it would become *his* Bible.

###

Chapter 8

May 1984

Michael stood up as Joseph and two other males entered his lounge, followed by Bridie.

"What about ya Mikey?" Joe asked as he gave Michael a hug and patted his back.

"A little apprehensive if truth be known Joe," Michael replied. "An' yourself?"

"Aye, Grand ... you're not still pissed at me are ya little brother?" Joseph asked laughingly as he sat down on the couch.

"Not at the minute, but there's still time," teased Michael before turning to the two other men in the room. "Robbie, Patrick ... how are y'boys?"

"Grand!" they replied in unison as they shook Michael's hand and sat down either side of Joe.

Robbie O'Neil was the brother of Bridie and a tower of a man. His swept back black hair, chiselled features and impeccably tailored suits, gave him a look that women adored and many a man envied. Bridie had once joked that when he and Joseph were together, they looked like Irelands answer to the Kray twins, a simile that wasn't a hundred miles from the truth. Although a quiet man, Robbie didn't suffer fools gladly and had developed a particular expertise that the organisation liked to call upon when certain members needed '*guidance*' with their loyalties. As such, his reputation grew within the ranks and earned him the title of '*An Sagart*'... The Priest ... a confessor that no member would willingly choose to receive absolution from.

Robbie had liked and respected Michael from the first day he met him, seeing the same dedication to the cause that he himself had but with much more vision and flair. When Michael and Bridie had announced their plans to marry nearly 15 years earlier, Robbie could not have been happier as he truly saw it as gaining the brother he never had.

Patrick McGinley, in stark contrast, was a skinny unkempt individual with a mop of curly red hair that sat above a pale, gaunt face. His thick rimmed glasses and ill fitting clothes would, in any normal world, make him the object of ridicule. But his wasn't a normal world and his penchant for whisky fuelled violence, had seen bigger men than he regret their outspoken opinions. Patrick had been 'drafted' into the organisation in the early 70s and brought with him a great knowledge of schematic diagram reading, communications interception and an unprecedented skill in explosive device manufacture. His commanders, however, were all too aware of his escalating 'problem' with the whisky but for now, his qualities when sober, served a greater purpose to the cause and thus, blind eyes were turned ... for now.

"Right, I'll leave you boys alone," said Bridie to the group. "Drinks are on the side and tea will be ready at five." She started out of the door but stopped and turned round, remembering something. "Oh, and make sure your business is finished by four thirty. Liam and his friend Sean will be home by then and I don't want them overhearing anything said in this room, ok?"

"Bridie," said Joseph holding out his arms. "What d'ya take us for?"

"I'm not sure Joseph Connor," she replied. "But as big as y'are, you'll have me t'deal wit' if your great pie hole isn't shut by four thirty!" The four men laughed as Bridie closed the door behind her, smiling.

Michael turned to Joseph, his face becoming sombre as he

spoke. "So," he began. "What is so important that it couldn't wait till we reconvened in Dublin next month as planned?"

Joseph shifted uneasily on the couch and glanced at Robbie and Patrick, looking for moral support.

"Joseph!" Michael said forcefully, wanting a response to his question.

Joseph cleared his throat and began, clearly nervous. "Firstly Michael, the Commanders want to reiterate their gratitude and praise for the Harrods campaign last November. It was a well executed oper..."

"Yes Yes I know all that," interrupted Michael irritably. "They have told me many times. That's the beauty of planning and timing Joseph, it gets results ... But they didn't send you all this way to blow smoke up my arse did they, that's not how things work. So what's the real reason for this visit?"

Once again Joseph looked at Robbie, who nodded his encouragement. Sighing heavily, Joseph reached into his inner pocket, pulled out a sealed envelope and passed it to Michael. "Remember, I'm only the messenger Michael," he said, getting up from the couch to go and pour himself a drink. "Anyone else?" he added, holding up the bottle of whisky.

"That'll be grand," said Patrick immediately. "Large one if you would Joe!"

Robbie nodded his head, now fixated on Michael holding the envelope, waiting for his reaction to the contents.

Michael turned the envelope from side to side in his hand, looking for a clue as to what would make Joseph so nervous but could find nothing. '*Best just to open it then,*' he thought and tore the end away. He pulled out the single page letter, read it, and then re-read it, not being able to believe the wording before his eyes.

There was a long tense silence in the room before Michael finally looked up to the other men. "Answer me this gentlemen ... How long did Harrods take to plan?" he asked, looking from one to the other. "How much manpower, time and effort did we use for that one operation? ... nearly a whole fuckin' year, that's how long ... and now they want us to carry this out in just over five fuckin' months!" Michael waved the letter furiously, his temper rising. "Have they lost their God given minds or are they turning our organisation into a bunch o' fuckin' amateurs?!!" He threw the letter onto the floor as Joseph handed him a drink. He downed it in one, composed himself slightly and continued. "These targets are untouchable at the best of times, but to plan and execute this in five months well, it's fuckin' madness!"

"But is it do-able?" asked Robbie, looking for his mentor to shine.

"Of course it's do-able," interjected Patrick. "We got Mountbatten and he's fuckin' royalty!"

"Aye, in open fuckin' water and with only a tenth of the security that will be at this place Pat," replied Michael. "They were lax and we got lucky!"

"Well," started Joe. "Maybe we can get lucky again!" Michael put his head into his hands as Joseph continued. "Look Michael, *your* decision is final on this one, otherwise our superiors wouldn't have sent this request direct to you ... but think about it. If we could pull this off, even if there is only a small chance, then this is our opportunity to show those British bastards what we're capable of. We could, *would*, make history and possibly rid our country of that scum once and for all ... so, wha' ya say Mikey, will we do it?"

Michael looked from Joe to Robbie and then to Patrick before picking up and reading the coded letter for a third time. Joseph refilled Michael's glass as he focused on the highlighted text within the letter, his mind decoding the script as he read.

He emptied his glass for a second time and looked up as his wife Bridie entered the room in time to catch his expression. Having seen that look on Michael's face several times before, she simply asked. "When are y'leaving?"

"Not till I've had at least two helpings of that stew of yours!" he replied smiling, hoping to hide his anxiety. With Bridie, it didn't work. She gave him an understanding look and returned a faint smile, knowing that her anxiety *couldn't* be hidden.

"I'll go and pack your bag," was all she added before leaving the room again.

This time, Joseph recharged everyone's glass before standing in the middle of the room, raising his own. "Gentlemen," he began, looking at them all, smiling. "I believe it's just become *do-able* ... Lord protect us as we fight in your name!"

"Amen!" they all responded, and downed their drinks. All, that was, except for Michael.

Robbie saw the look on Michael's face and was saddened by the lack of enthusiasm. He had expected more from his teacher and was genuinely concerned. Was he just tired or was it something more? Had Michael lost his passion for the cause or just a little faith? Whatever it was, Robbie had too much respect to brooch the subject directly with him and so, for the time being, remained silent. It would be a few days later when Robbie, without malice, would mention his concern to another. The listener would raise an eyebrow, thank Robbie for his concern and assure him that it would be addressed compassionately. Unbeknown to Robbie, the Chief Commander would then be informed.

Outside the lounge, Bridie stood in silence, holding the rosary beads around her neck as if in prayer. She sighed heavily, kissed the crucifix on the Holy necklace and went to prepare her husband's things, a duty she had performed so many times in the past.

###

Chapter 9

Bridie O'Neil first met Michael Connor in November 1966 on the one occasion she would have chosen not to; the funeral of his father.

At the time, she had been visiting her brother Robbie, who had moved from their home town of Dublin a few years earlier, to find work in Belfast and probably, she thought, to escape the strict regime of their Uncle's household.

Robbie had written to her regularly, giving vivid accounts of his successes, and failures, in his new life and how, with a stroke of luck, he had eventually found employment with a man called Thomas Connor. He described how Thomas was a local hero and a legend in his own right, a man with very strong views and even stronger connections both in and out of the community. Robbie often included Thomas and his son Michael in subsequent letters and though he barely touched on the details of his actual role, she was left in no doubt of the respect he had developed for both men in such a short time.

It wasn't long, however, before Bridie discovered what it was that Thomas and Michael Connor were actually respected for and she wondered if Robbie, from his reluctance to expand on his job description, thought she would disapprove of his chosen *profession*. He needn't have bothered, as she was both proud and pleased that her brother appeared to be doing well. '*And*,' she thought, '*who likes the British anyway?*'

When one of Robbie's letters told her that Tommy Connor had passed away, she sensed that he needed her and took the first available train from Dublin to Belfast. Robbie was more than pleased to see her but could do nothing to hide his sadness at the death of his mentor. He appeared genuinely morose that the 'Great Man' had gone and when he asked if she would attend the funeral with him, Bridie couldn't find the heart to refuse, though deep down, she wanted to say no. Having lost their own parents at an early age, she hated funerals and the painful memories they brought and so, whilst offering Robbie her support, she had made him promise that they wouldn't stay too long.

On the day of the funeral, standing in the cold church grounds, she witnessed an unprecedented amount of mourners paying their respects and thought that the whole of Belfast must surely be there.

"Is that the bereaved family?" she said, pointing to a group close to the Church doors.

"Aye," replied Robbie. "The stocky man is Joe, next to his sisters and Ma, and the taller man with the blond hair, stood away to the right, is Michael ... fine man that!"

"Why is he?" enquired Bridie. "And why is everyone lining up to shake his hand?"

"'Cause he's Tommy's son," replied Robbie. "And the man destined to carry on the fight with the British. He's a man wit' vision Bridie, wit' hope!"

As they too walked over to pay their respects, Bridie didn't know or particularly care about the vision and hope of Michael Connor but was suddenly taken unawares by one thing; how incredibly handsome she found him.

As Robbie shook his hand and offered his condolences, he turned towards Bridie saying. "An' this is my little sister, Bridie. She's up here visiting for a few weeks."

Michael looked at Bridie but she could see from the sadness in his deep green eyes that his mind was elsewhere. *'Understandable on the day of his father's funeral,'* she thought, but from somewhere deep inside, felt a surge of unexplainable and selfish disappointment, that he appeared to look through, not at her.

"Good ... well, thank you both for coming!" was all he said in a soft voice, before turning to greet the next people in line.

As Bridie and her brother walked away, she couldn't help but glance back at Michael, an action that didn't go unnoticed by Robbie. "Aye aye!" he remarked.

She turned swiftly back to her grinning sibling. "What?" she retorted, a little embarrassed at being caught.

"Let's just say that you're not the first woman to be in awe of him," he replied. "Was it the eyes?"

"I'm sure I don't know what you're prattling on about Robert O'Neil," she said feeling her cheeks flush. "I was jus' admirin' the Lord's house before we left!" She quickened her pace, so as to be ahead of Robbie and left the Church yard without daring to risk another glance at Michael. The second decision that day she had regretted. The first was making Robbie promise that they wouldn't stay long.

It was to be four years later, in the summer of 1970, when Bridie met Michael Connor for the second time. Robbie had invited her to a fund raising ball he had organised in honour of *The Belfast Patriots* and despite her initial misgivings, she was quickly convinced to go when her brother mentioned that a 'still single' Michael would also be there.

The evening had been perfect. Bridie was reminded how handsome Michael was, but this time, Michael had noticed how attractive she was. "Robbie mentioned he had a sister," Michael began, when she was introduced for a second time. "But not one so pretty!" He smiled as he took her hand and softly added. "Would y'promise me a dance this evening Bridie O'Neil?"

Bridie was at a temporary loss for words, captivated by his eyes, now void of any sadness. She tried to pull herself together but it was proving difficult. "I was at your Father's funeral!" was all she could manage and immediately felt

39

annoyed with herself for bringing up such a sad occasion.

Michael looked at Robbie for confirmation and then back to Bridie. "Then not only am I rude, but a blind eejit too," he confessed, looking sheepish. "Can you ever forgive me?"

Bridie, having regained her composure, thought about making him work for her forgiveness, but then he smiled and absolution was immediate. "I just hope you're a better dancer than you are observer Mr.Connor!" she replied and returned the smile before walking away. This time, she didn't need to glance back at Michael, she knew he would be watching her.

What became clear to both Michael and Bridie over the next few hours, was that neither of them had talked or laughed with anybody, let alone a relative stranger, as much as they had done with each other that evening. When it came to the last dance, Michael took Bridie's hand and led her to the floor. As the music began, they held each other closer than they had expected, but a closeness neither would correct. Bridie looked up at Michael and smiled. Feeling his heart pounding, Michael seized the moment and kissed her, hoping he wasn't acting too quickly. Bridie responded, wondering why it had taken him so long.

Just over a year later and much to the delight of Robbie, Bridie became Mrs. Michael Connor. Within a year, she had given birth to their first child, a girl whom they called Margaret, after Bridie's mother. They felt their family was complete when, on 31st July 1973, Bridie gave birth to their second child; a boy they named Liam.

###

Chapter 10

May 1984

Liam Connor felt around his eye and winced, wounded from a battle lost. Sean looked at Liam's face and took a sharp intake of breath. "That's gonna be one hell of a shiner tomorrow mate," he said with some concern. "What will y' mum say?"

"She'll probably give me the speech on 'thou shalt not use your face as a punch bag for dicks," Liam replied. "And then smother me in love, which means shit loads of Irish stew on my plate!" Sean laughed as Liam continued, "Don't know why your laughin' eejit, you're round at mine for tea tonight, remember?"

"Aw no," replied Sean. "Now she's gonna be on my case saying I should have been there to protect you or whatever it is she says. Still, it's worth it for the stew!"

Both boys laughed as they made their way out of school, home time at last.

"D'ya fancy a kick about on Joey's?" Liam said, as they walked towards the school gates.

"Dead right I do Connor," replied Sean. "'Cause if you won't let me batter Walker for ya, then at least I can batter you at footy!"

"In your dreams Bevan. Who is the reigning champ of keepie uppies, eh, eh?"

"Yeah, for one day but who was ..." Sean broke off and stopped in his tracks, before adding, "Aw shit!"

Liam looked up to see what Sean was starring at and began to chuckle. "It's not funny Liam, I have to do something quickly!"

"Too late," Liam replied still chuckling. "She's seen you!"

At the school gates stood Louise Duffy, a girl of ten who was besotted with Sean. She was a slim girl with bobbed red hair and a pale freckled face that might have been seen as pretty had she not constantly been wearing oversized brown rimmed glasses, supplied, no doubt, by the NHS. Louise's show of fondness towards Sean, however, took the peculiar route of seemingly always trying to get him in trouble with the teachers. *"Miss, Sean's talking!"* or *"Sir, Sean's distracting me!"* she would say, even when he wasn't doing anything. This always had the desired effect in that Sean would then rebuke her (a kind of talking) which is something he wouldn't normally do and that, she thought, was a good result.

The previous year, on one of the rare occasions that Sean was alone, Louise had presented him with a Valentine's card, half expecting him to laugh at her and tear it up. But he hadn't. He had just looked at her, shoved it in his bag and gave her the faintest of smiles before walking off. A moment in time that only one of them would forget. And now, seeing him approach with his friend, she still had hope that one day, maybe this day, he would be *her* friend too.

"Hi Sean," she said when the boys arrived at the school gate. "What you up to?"

"Err, what do y' think, going home of course," Sean replied trying to hurry past her.

"Are you going on to Joey's field first?" she shouted after him.

"Yeah," replied Liam before Sean had time to speak. "Come along if y' like!"

Sean stared, open mouthed, in total disbelief at a now grinning Liam. "Huh!" was all he could manage to say.

"Aw, let her come mate, she's not that bad and she'll be with her friends," said Liam seeing the way Sean was about to react.

"What?" was all a red faced Sean was able to offer before shaking his head and stomping off towards Joey's. Liam followed, smiling. Louise followed, also smiling but for a completely different reason.

Joey's Field was *the* place to go after school. Situated in between St. Michael's itself and the local housing estate, it was a large area of council owned grassland, that housed a small playing area with two swings, a roundabout and a slide, one uneven football pitch and a clump of trees that, to the kids of Sean and Liam's age, was a large forest. A place to explore and a place to be invisible from nosey adults. It was also a place that you never went into if it was dark.

The 'forest' had, over the years, played host to numerous episodes of children's lives and had seen many a child develop from imaginative adventurer into a young carefree adult. It had witnessed the rudimentary stages of their growth, from playing war one year to nervously scanning through a found porno mag the next. From the innocence of sweets and crisps to the first ciggie and taste of cheap cider and from a first kiss to the awkward and fumbled sexual encounters between teenage lovers. It was also the place rumoured to be hiding the rotted corpse of "Joey" himself, a missing shop assistant believed murdered by a mad axe man and buried deep within the forest; a story, however, only believed and known to be true by people under the age of fourteen.

Liam and Sean had once decided to go hunting for Joey, not long after Sean had told him the complete story of Joey's disappearance. "Well," he had started. "Joey use to work at Tesco ages ago as a shelf stacker and once dropped some boxes or tins or something, all over a bloke who was in there and the bloke was well pissed off and threatened to get Joey

43

back. So when Joey left work he came across this very field in the dark and the bloke was waiting for him with an axe."

"What was he doin' with an axe?" asked a spellbound Liam.

"Well," continued Sean. "He was a nutter that had escaped from the loony bin and stole one of them axes ... y' know, like a fireman's axe?"

"Oh, yeah. And what did he do to Joey? Did he chop him up?"

"Yeah, and cut his 'ed off. And then he hid the body in the forest but nobody ever found him!"

Liam remained silent for a moment whilst he thought the story through and then said. "How do they know he was chopped up if nobody's ever found him?"

"'Cause," replied Sean, already armed with the *facts*. "Micky Butler said his dad knew a bloke who was walking his dog one night and his dog went into the forest and when it came out, it had a *Tesco* badge in its mouth covered in blood!"

"So?" said Liam, still confused.

"So," continued Sean. "The badge said *'Joe is here to help'* on it ... that proves it!"

"Shit," replied Liam and after a short pause added. "Let's go an' look for him, I've never seen a dead body!"

And with that, in the late afternoon sun, the boys had gone to the 'forest' to search for the dismembered body of Joe the Tesco worker.

An hour later, the sun had fallen significantly enough to make the light within the forest seem a lot darker than it actually was, a factor both boys had not failed to notice, especially as they had split up to 'widen the search'. Sean, who had been checking the undergrowth for clues, was now standing still, looking around to see if he could see Liam. He couldn't and realised that the only thing he could hear was the sound of his own heart beating. His thoughts had suddenly gone from wanting to find Joey's body to wondering if Joey's rotting body might find him, rising from the dead to seek revenge ... like a zombie.

Liam had also stopped his search and stood frozen in front of a mound of uneven earth, *definitely* six foot long by three foot wide and *definitely* looking like a grave...or so his mind told him. He jumped at the sound of a twig snapping somewhere in the forest and knew, beyond all doubt, that the Axe Man was back, looking for witnesses to slay.

Sean heard the same twig snapping and knew, beyond all doubt, that Joey was about to pounce and sink his teeth into his neck. *'Hang on a minute,'* Sean's mind began. *'What's that dark figure lurking in the shadows?'*

'Hang on a minute,' Liam's mind began. *'I can't hear Sean ... maybe the Axe Man's killed him first!'*

Another twig snapped in the near distance followed by a rustle, much closer. Simultaneously, two nine year old boys, no more than fifty feet apart from each other, but hidden by a few trees, shouted out. "Shit!!"

They moved a few steps, saw each other and with looks of terror on their faces shouted again. "Run!!"

Both boys began to run back to the entrance of the forest, wondering why their legs felt as if they could only manage a slow walk. It was like everything was happening in slow motion, which wasn't good 'cause *Joey* and the *Axe Man* were 100 meter sprint champions and would catch up in no time. In his bid for freedom, Liam tripped over an exposed tree root and fell to the floor, his mind now telling him that the Axe Man was gaining fast. Seeing his mate down, Sean diverted from his escape route and went to help. "Get up Liam, shit, get up quick!" Sean encouraged and grabbed Liam's shirt, his mind now telling him that Joey was only seconds away and very angry. Liam scrambled to his feet, his knee grazed and sore, but determined that he wasn't going to die here. The boys continued to run, not looking back and not stopping until they fell into a heap on the grass just outside the entrance to the forest, safe at last.

They lay on their backs for a few minutes catching their breath and looking to the sky, wondering how it had suddenly become so bright. Neither of them spoke as their brains took over from their imaginations, bringing them back to a kind of normality. A sudden noise from the forest made the boys jump again and look back towards its entrance. They stared open mouthed as *Joey* and the *Axe Man* came out from within the darkness ... cleverly disguised as an elderly man and a Golden Retriever, carrying a stick, *not a badge*, in its mouth.

Liam and Sean looked at each other and, after a short, silent moment of mutual understanding, began to laugh, loudly and uncontrollably. It would have been a story worth telling, had they not vowed to keep it to themselves.

The match played between Manchester United (Liam) and England (Sean) on a sunny May afternoon at Joey's field, had ended in a draw. Ten goals to ten was the final score, but in this match, drawing wasn't an option. There had to be a clear winner. It was the rules.

Sean placed himself between the two evenly spaced school bags on the grass that had been used as goal posts. Liam stood some yards away holding the football under his foot, waiting for the ok from his friend. A quick nod from Sean and proceedings were under way. The penalty shoot out had commenced.

Liam took a few steps back from the ball, put his hands on his hips and looked at Sean, readying himself to deliver the shot. Sean watched Liam very closely and assumed the half crouched position, waiting for the shot, ready to spring into the save. Liam took a couple more steps back and one to the side before advancing at speed towards the ball whilst Sean stood rigid, trying to read Liam's body language and predict which way the ball would be kicked. Left? Right? Straight on? It was difficult, but the decision in that split second after the ball had been kicked would be to dive right ... no left ... no right ... aw shit!

Liam struck the ball with the inside of his left foot and watched it fly towards the goal, curving slightly. Sean, his mental decision made, started to dive to his right, arms outstretched to prevent the goal. It was too late. The ball whizzed past his finger tips and through the crude goal mouth, making the score eleven to ten in United's favour. Liam's arms shot into the air in celebration as he ran towards Sean.

"Hughes shoots and he scores and United have taken the lead ... the pressure is on for England ... can they pull it around?"

Liam took his place in the goal, smiling, whilst Sean went to retrieve the ball and make his way to the penalty spot, an equaliser in mind. "You're gonna need to be better than Peter Shilton to stop this one Connor," Sean said as he placed the ball carefully on the ground. "It's Lineker time!" Sean stepped back from the ball, quickly reviewed his options and set off to take the shot. As he positioned his body and swung his leg forward to kick the ball, disaster struck.

"Go on Sean!!" a female voice shouted loudly. The sudden, unexpected outburst momentarily distracted Sean mid shot causing his foot to scuff on the grass and his leg to lose momentum and power. Contact with the ball was poor and it rolled off towards Liam at a slow, easy to save pace.

Liam scooped up the ball chuckling. "What the hell was that Bevan?" he asked a bemused looking Sean. "My gran could do better!"

"No ... Wait!" Sean began to protest. "That doesn't count!" He turned round and glared at Louise Duffy sitting with a group of friends watching the game and pointed accusingly. "She put me off!!"

Louise quickly bowed her head, turning her attention to the bag of chips she had bought on the way to Joey's, which now lay on the grass before her. She wasn't about to look up again for some time.

"You can't blame her," Liam continued. "She was just cheering you on, like a *fan* does. But you ... well ... you were just crap. Louise could probably do better!" Liam laughed, knowing that his comments would wind Sean up. He wasn't wrong.

"What? ... No, piss off!!" Sean began, frustration and anger rising spurred on by embarrassment. "I'm taking it again ... it doesn't count!!!"

"Course it counts," Liam replied still laughing. "It was shit, but it definitely counts ... and United still lead eleven to ten!" Liam raised his arms and waved around the imaginary stadium, imitating the sound of a cheering crowd as he did. Sean shook his head and looked to the floor dejected. Suddenly, an idea popped into his head and he looked back towards Liam, smiling.

"OK, what about this?" he proposed. "If you think *she* could do any better," he pointed again at Louise, "how's about she takes your next shot?"

Liam suddenly stopped laughing, looked at Louise and then back to Sean. "What? ... why you being a dick? ... How's that right?"

"Well," continued Sean, "if you're sooo confident that she is better than me, let her take your shot and prove it!"

"Sean y'mong. It was a joke, a wind up. I was jus..."

"Oh," interrupted Sean. "A joke, right ... it's not that you're chicken then?"

"What are you on about?" Liam asked slightly confused. "I'm not chicken!"

"Let her take your penalty then?" Sean pressed. "I dare ya!"

Liam stood silently for a moment. The dare was on, the challenge had been laid down. He turned to Louise, now watching open mouthed, as were the girls sitting with her, and appeared to be studying her, contemplating the situation. For what seemed like an age, Liam looked back from the group of girls to a still smiling Sean. "Deal!" was all he said and walked over to Louise, who suddenly looked up from her empty chip paper with horror on her face. Had she heard right?

Sean's smile quickly faded. He was about to protest again with the old *'girls can't play footy'* line, but thought better of it and stopped himself. This was, after all, a chance to pull things around and if Liam wanted to waste his turn by using a girl, then so be it. He shrugged his shoulders and headed off to take his position in the goal. *'Your funeral Condor,'* he thought. *'Your funeral!'*

Sean watched as Liam spoke to Louise for a while and then led her from her group to the penalty spot. "Pep talk Ladies?" he said sarcastically. "I hope you remember that this counts as one of your shots Connor?" Liam shook his head resignedly and, after another quiet word with Louise, stepped away from her and the ball. Louise looked at the ball, then at Sean, who was grinning sardonically and then to her group of friends who were shouting words of encouragement. Louise put her hands up to her mouth trying to stifle a nervous giggle before looking back at the ball and then to Liam, who gave her a supportive nod. "Get on with it," shouted Sean, clearly bored with the situation he had created. "We've got school again tomorrow!"

Louise took several steps back and one to the side just as Liam had told her. *"Try to hit it with the inside of your foot and as hard as you can,"* he had also said. *"But don't take your eye off the ball!"*

Armed with her new knowledge, she took a deep breath and set off at speed towards the ball. Sean assumed the half crouched position for the second time that afternoon, still grinning, confident of scooping up a *pea roller* of a shot, laughing and then getting on with the proper game. Louise drew back her leg mid run and, with as much strength as she could muster, fired it towards the ball. In true *toe bunger* style, contact was made. The ball left the spot and rose from the ground with an unprecedented *and* unexpected amount of force that caused Liam to gasp out loudly and Sean's eyes to widen in a moment of utter disbelief. The ball cut through the air like a bullet, heading towards Sean and the goal at breakneck speed. *'Jesus,'* Sean thought in a split second. *'I actually need to try and save this!'* Seeing the ball heading slightly to his right, he made his move.

Now. Maybe Sean dived a little too early, or maybe it was just that little twist in the balls flight path, but whatever it was, Liam saw the end result coming way before it had actually happened and he could do nothing to stop it. As if in slow motion, he watched as the ball reached its penultimate destination with a resounding smack. "Aarrgh!!" Sean cried out loudly, as the ball hit him clean on the bridge of the nose just before he landed with a thud onto the ground. Louise let out a small yelp and covered her face with her hands, her watching friends gasped in unison.

"Shit!!" Liam shouted, running over to his friend. "Are you ok Sean? ... Sean!!"

Sean looked up, his face covered in dirt, his nose covered in blood. "Do I look ok?" he replied angrily, tears now starting to run down his cheeks. "Shit my nose hurts ... what does it look like?" Liam knelt down and studied Sean's face carefully as if making an important medical decision. After a few moments, he offered his diagnosis.

"Looks more or less the same!" he said. "'Cept for the blood, it's no different!"

"It's probably broken," said Sean dramatically. "It feels broken to me!"

"How do *you* know what a broken nose feels like, you've never had one have you?" quizzed Liam

"Well I have now haven't I?" Sean snapped. "Anyway,"

he continued, looking at Louise who was now standing behind Liam. "How did *you* kick the ball that hard?"

Louise looked at Sean open mouthed, not really knowing how to respond. "I'm sorry!" was all she could say and quickly bowed her head. Seeing that Sean was about to have a go at her, Liam quickly decided that a compliment was now the best route to follow.

"Nice save though mate ... thought that was well going in ... How did you manage to get across so quick?"

Sean wiped his face on his shirt and looked at Liam, composure returning and pride beginning to show on his face. "They don't call me 'Cat Bevan' for nothing y'know Condor ... quick as hell me!" Liam wanted to remind Sean that they called him '*Fat* Bevan' but thought, under the circumstances, he best leave it.

"Actually," Louise started, causing the boys to look up at her.

"What?" Sean asked tiresomely.

Louise felt a little nervous with the sudden captive audience but carried on regardless. "Well ... I was just thinking ... 'cause the ball hit your face ... and I am really sorry, I didn't mean ..."

"Get on with it!" Sean interrupted loudly, making Louise jump a little.

"Well I wanted to know," she continued. "Seeing as the ball hit you, does it not count as a goal ... even though it went through there?" She pointed to an area just behind the boys. As they looked round, they saw, much to Liam's surprise and Sean's horror, that the ball was sitting there, mockingly dead centre, just beyond the goal line. They looked at each other confused and speechless, both knowing that a goal had indeed been scored but neither knowing how. Sean looked at Louise dumbfounded and could have sworn that he saw the faintest of smiles on her face. She let out a breath and raised her eyebrows, seeming to savour the moment. "So that makes it twelve ten I suppose!" was all she said ... *all she needed to say*. Allowing herself a little time to watch Sean's face as the penny dropped, she turned and walked back to her group of friends, leaving a defeated and still speechless Sean in her wake.

Sean looked at Liam who was now trying to his best to stifle a laugh, not knowing which was funniest, the ball in the back of the 'net' or the look of complete exasperation on *The Cat's* blood stained and dirty face.

"Didn't your mum want us back at half four?" Sean said angrily, rising to his feet.

"Er, yes mate," was all Liam could manage, trying to disguise a chuckle with a cough.

"Then let's go before you wet your pants ... *Mate!*"

Sean picked up his school bag and set off at a fast pace, desperate to leave his hell. Neither eye contact nor speech was made when Louise shouted, "See ya Sean!", though he could think of plenty to say.

###

The boys walked most of the journey to Liam's house not speaking, though it was Sean who eventually broke the silence with a totally unexpected comment.

"She's alright that Louise isn't she?"

"What?" Liam replied with a look of total surprise on his face.

"Louise Duffy ... the girl with the mean right foot!"

"I know who you mean Sean," Liam continued, still shocked. "But I thought you hated her and after what just happened on Joey's ... I don't get it!"

"What's there to get?" asked Sean calmly. "I never hated her, she just winds me up at times. But, any girl with a shot like that is alright in my book!"

Liam stopped in his tracks, gob smacked. A few steps later and Sean also stopped, before turning to Liam.

52

"What?" he asked, holding out his arms and frowning as if he had said something wrong.

"Nothing Sean ... Nothing at all!" was all Liam could find to say before he and Sean set off once again for home.

The rest of the journey was pretty uneventful but as the boys turned onto their road, Liam's heart sank.

"Hey," Sean remarked. "Whose is that black car outside yours?"

"Dunno," replied Liam miserably. "But I bet it means my dad is going away again!"

Sean saw the disheartened look on his friend's face and tried to cheer him up. "He might not be ... maybe it's a friend just visiting or a neighbours' or something ... you never know!"

"Tenner says it's not?" Liam replied, not convinced by Sean's theory.

The two boys entered Liam's house by the rear door that led into the kitchen and were immediately hit by the smell of Irish stew simmering on the cooker. Sean walked over to the pan and inhaled deeply. "Aw, that smells ace!" he said and added, "I'm starvin' now. Where is everyone anyway?"

"Dunno," replied Liam. "I'll go and see ... get yourself a drink if y'want!" As Sean routed in the fridge for his fix of *Sunny D*, Liam walked into the hallway and put his schoolbag down, intending to shout out and let his family know he was home. Hearing voices coming from the lounge, he walked up to the slightly ajar door and stopped outside, listening.

"This campaign will make fekkin' history gentlemen," a voice said from behind the door, though Liam didn't recognise the owner. "The bastards will have no choice but to listen after this one!" Liam frowned, wondering what they were talking about and found himself compelled to eavesdrop just a little longer. The next voice he heard was one he recognised immediately. Though he hadn't seen him for some time, there was no disputing that loud and course Irish twang of his Uncle Joe.

"Aye, for sure," he said. "An' it'll be Ireland's voice that they'll be hearing come the twelfth of October!" There was a ripple of mutual agreement from the people in the room and then a further man spoke. The male's voice was quiet and Liam was finding it difficult to hear what he was saying. He needed to get closer to the door. He quickly looked around to check the coast was clear, thankful that he could hear Sean searching for a glass in the kitchen cupboards, too concerned about his drink to notice the prolonged absence. Satisfied, though a little nervous, Liam took a further step towards the lounge. As he did, the floor board beneath his foot gave out a loud, tired creak that seemed to echo throughout the whole house. *'Shit!'* he thought and froze part step.

Inside the lounge, Michael raised his hand at Robbie, who was mid conversation, then put a finger to his mouth signalling for quiet.

Liam stood rigid in his track as the voices within the lounge suddenly went quiet. He could hear his own heart, now beating so hard that he felt his temples throb. For a split second, he held his breath, convinced that the people on the other side of the door would hear his heavy breathing and discover him.

Michael glanced at his watch and waited for a couple more seconds before getting up off his chair and making his way to the lounge door.

'Jesus ... someone's coming!' Liam thought as he heard the sound of his father's movement. Panic began to set in. He needed to move away now, quickly, but his legs had suddenly become like lead, holding him to the spot, refusing to work. He was going to get caught *snooping* and that would mean serious trouble ... a grounding, a leathering maybe, or even both. He saw the handle on the lounge door move slightly and mentally prayed for redemption.

On the other side of the door, Michael had placed his hand gently onto the handle whilst the other occupants of the room looked around at each other, confused, wondering what was occurring. "What the hell are y'up to now little brother?" quizzed Joseph, just as Michael was about to pull at the lounge door.

Michael turned round and gave Joseph a look that left him in no doubt that silence was required from here on in. Joseph frowned, looked at Robbie, then Patrick and shrugged his shoulders. All remained silent. Turning back to the door, Michael took a short breath and yanked it open hoping to catch whoever it was listening in. He was met by the sight of an empty hallway and frowned. *'I could have sworn!'* he thought, convinced of what he had heard. He leant his head out of the doorway and looked down the hall seeing Liam and Sean standing in the kitchen. Liam looked up, a *moustache* of bright orange across his top lip, remnants of the drink he was holding in his hand.

"Hiya Dad," he said casually. "You okay?"

"Hi Son," Michael replied, suspicion lingering in his mind. "How long have you been in?"

"Just got in now," Liam replied. "We've been playing footy for a bit on Joey's ... we're not late, are we?"

"No no," Michael answered, but then stared at the boys for a few silent moments, wondering. "Y'haven't just been stood outside this door have y' boys?" he added, studying them closely.

Liam looked at Sean and then back to his dad and as innocently as he could, replied. "Us? No. We've just come in and got ourselves a drink ... why?"

Michael, certain of what he had heard but with no proof, resigned himself to the fact that it wasn't going to be resolved. "It doesn't matter," he answered and after a short pause added, "Your Uncles Joe and Robbie are here. C'mon and say hello ... you too Sean, they'll be glad t'see ya both!"

With that, Michael went back into the lounge and Liam let out a heavy sigh, grateful of the divine interventions that had just saved his neck. He looked at Sean and chuckled when he saw the look of cheated confusion on his face, unsure of what had just happened. Liam made a mental note to say an extra prayer later that night, as he truly couldn't have been more thankful to the Lord. Thankful for the fact that his Uncle Joe had spoken when he had, distracting Michael just enough to allow Liam time to flee from the lounge door. Thankful for the fact that Sean was too stunned to pass comment when Liam had run into the kitchen and snatched his glass of *Sunny D* off the kitchen table, drinking most of it. But above all else, he was most thankful for the fact that his dad had not looked down towards the hall floor when he had leant out of the front room. If he had done so, he would undoubtedly have seen, within inches of the lounge door, the incriminating evidence in the form of Liam's school bag.

###

Chapter 11

Despite the absence of his Father, Liam could not remember having had a better summer holiday than the one he had just had.

They had broken up from St Michael's primary school for the last time in July 1984 and though it was initially quite daunting that in just over six weeks they would be taking their place as '*newbie's*' at St Monica's High School, Liam and Sean decided that they were going to make the most of the break. That said, the last day at primary school was quite a sombre affair, with teachers bidding farewell to the pupils, wishing them luck and randomly hugging whoever was closest, and friends saying their tearful goodbyes to each other as if they would never meet again ... ever!

The day seemed to have affected Sean more than Liam would have expected and though Sean would probably never admit it, Liam suspected it was due to the fact that he wouldn't see Louise Duffy again until they began their new high school term some six weeks later.

Since the *penalty shoot out* fiasco back in May, Sean had not only become more tolerant of Louise, but decidedly more pleasant towards her. Of course Liam would wind him up by stating that he was '*in luuurve*' with her, but this always resulted in Sean expressing his denial by giving Liam a *dead arm*. Despite this, Liam definitely saw a spark between them and he himself wondered if Sean would cope when Louise went away to her family's holiday home for the entire summer break, as normal.

On the way home that afternoon, Sean's depression became more apparent when Liam had asked him if he wanted to go and have a kick around on Joey's. A rather glum looking Sean had declined, making some feeble excuse about having to go shopping with his mum. "Mate," Liam had said. "You never go shopping with your mum, what's wrong?"

"Nothin's wrong," Sean had replied quite defensively. "Why should anything be wrong?"

"'Cause you've had your head up your arse all day," Liam pointed out and decided, quite bravely, to add. "Is it 'cause you won't see Louise all summer?"

There was a long pause and Liam waited for the barrage of abuse followed by the obligatory punch to the arm. He could have been pushed over by a slight breeze when Sean replied. "Yeah, a bit!" He looked at Liam and then quickly turned away before softly adding. "Well, a lot actually!"

Liam stared at Sean and genuinely felt sorry for him. But how was he to play this one? Should he rib Sean and make fun of his confession at missing a girl or, like a true friend, should he treat Sean's feelings compassionately and try to understand how he felt. It was a difficult call for a ten year old, going on eleven, to make, so Liam opted for normality. "Bevan y' puff!" he started. "It's Louise Duffy we're talking about here, not some well fit space alien woman about to go back to Mars forever ... you will see her again in a few weeks!"

"Six actually!" interrupted Sean, clearly not fazed by Liam's *empathetic* approach.

"Ok, six then," continued Liam. "But it's not the end of the world, it'll fly by ... now snap out of it you big mong and let's go to Joey's!"

Sean looked back at Liam and after a short pause, gave a faint smile and replied, "Ok, let's go!"

Liam smiled and clapped. Sean's depression had temporarily left the building.

###

The boys started making plans for their summer break on the way home that evening and were still discussing the agenda as they sat down for tea at Liam's house a little while later. Liam's mum, who was serving up egg, chips and beans as the boys talked, intervened with some news that was to change their plans dramatically.

"Sean," she began. "I'm taking Liam and Margaret away on holiday in a couple of weeks, nothing fancy, just to a caravan in the Lakes!"

"Oh, right," said Sean reddening slightly, the sudden news rekindling his earlier depression.

"What?" interjected Liam. "I didn't know about that ... why? ... I mean, when will I see Sean? ... we ... but Mum!"

"Now come on Liam," his mum continued. "A break will do us good, what with your dad being away an' all and besides, you will have plenty of time to see Sean."

"Oh yeah!" Liam said bitterly. "Like when?"

Bridie looked at the two boys, their heads bowed, and gave a little smile before answering. "Well, probably every day, seeing as he's coming too!"

Simultaneously, Liam and Sean quickly looked up to a now chuckling Bridie, then to each other and then back towards Bridie. "But how? ... But who said? ... but!" stuttered Liam, not really knowing what it was he was asking or in fact how to speak. Sean remained speechless, shell shocked.

"Thought you might like that," said Bridie grinning widely, pleased with her *little joke*. She turned to Sean and placed her hand on his shoulder, tenderly. "And I've been round and sorted it with your Mum and Dad Sean," she added. "So there's no need to worry. That's if you want to come of course?"

"Me?" Sean replied excitedly. "'Course I do, yes please!"

"Right," she said. "That's settled then!"

Bridie watched the boys, enjoying their excitement, but wished that Michael could be there to witness it. She felt a moment of sadness at his absence and her smile faded slightly. She couldn't be certain if the boys had noticed this or not, but almost immediately, she was to be pleasantly shocked by two things. The first thing, was that Liam got up off his chair, gave her a hug and then kissed her on the cheek ... Liam! ... in front of Sean! *'Miracles never cease!'* she thought.

"Thanks Mum," was all he said before sitting back down. The second thing and even more surprising for Bridie, was that Sean then did exactly the same.

"Thanks Mrs. Connor," he said shyly. "No one's ever ... well, thank you!"

Bridie remained temporarily stunned and lost for words as she watched Sean sit back down and tuck into his food. "You're both very welcome," she eventually managed, genuinely overwhelmed by the appreciation. "Now finish your tea before it gets cold," she added, before quickly turning around and walking out of the kitchen, hoping that the boys had been too pre-occupied to notice the tears in her eyes.

A couple of weeks later, Liam was standing in the lounge in his pyjamas, hair ruffled, a smile beaming across his face. Though 8am was an unearthly hour to be up, especially during the school holidays, today it didn't matter. Today, he didn't even have to be woken up by his mum because if truth were known, he'd already been awake for an hour waiting for the sounds of his family stirring in the adjoining bedrooms. Liam's smile remained constant as he waited for his mum and sister to finish the resounding tune of *'Happy Birthday'*, a tune, that when on the receiving end, seem to take an age to come to its conclusion and allow present opening to begin.

31st July 1984 and Liam had reached the grand age of eleven. Bridie gave Liam a hug that seemed to extend longer than usual and when she finally released him, he could see sadness in her eyes. "What's wrong Mum?" Liam said concerned. "Why you cryin'?"

"I'm not crying darling," Bridie replied, smiling warmly. "I just can't believe that my little baby boy is eleven already!" Liam's sister Margaret let out a laugh making Liam's face redden a little.

"Mum!" he started defensively. "I'm not a baby anymore, I'm eleven!"

"Eleven you may be Liam Connor," Bridie said softly "But you will always be my baby till the day I die."

Bridie hugged Liam once more and kissed him on the cheek. For a moment, Liam smiled tenderly at his mum but quickly frowned when his sister interjected. "C'mere *baby* brother and give your big sister a hug!"

Liam shook his head in dismay, but, encouraged by his mum, walked over to Margaret and graciously received a hug. It was not something Liam was comfortable with but what certainly helped was knowing that, for today at least, Margaret would have to be especially nice to him. It was, after all, *his* birthday.

Liam needed no such encouragement to start opening his presents. He was thrilled with his new Man. United football shirt and Adidas sports bag, content with his Transformer action figures and *special edition* Super-car Top Trump cards yet slightly disappointed with the usual knitted jumper from his Gran. '*It's flippin' summer,*' he thought, but sensing his mum looking on, maintained an appreciative smile.

"Ooh that's lovely," she said. "You must phone Gran later and thank her Liam."

"I will," replied Liam and quickly moved on to the present from his sister hoping his Mum wouldn't ask for his thoughts on the sweater gift. He hated lying to his mum.

As he pulled the remaining present out of its gift wrapping, he discovered it was a T-shirt with psychedelic wording emblazoned on its white front. He frowned as he read the script; '*George Orwell was wrong!*' He looked at Margaret puzzled, looking for a clue as to what it meant.

"Have you not read the book yet?" she asked, slightly disappointed that he didn't get the joke.

"What book?" Liam asked, still none the wiser.

"Nineteen eighty four ... It's a book by George Orwell ... About the way the world was meant to be? ... this year??"

Liam looked at her with a blank expression, not really knowing what to say but thought he needed to say something. "We've read Charlie and the Great Glass Elevator!"

Margaret sighed and shook her head, looking towards her mum. "Wasted," was all she said and the pair laughed, even more so as they looked back at the birthday boy, now wearing the oversized t-shirt looking more confused than ever. It was to be a couple of years later before Liam finally got the joke.

Though it had rained for most of the summer break, it hadn't mattered much to Liam and Sean. The holiday on *Fell End* Caravan Park in the Lake District had turned out to be better than they had expected, mainly due to the number of children their age also staying at the site, willing to partake in endless games of football.

Their caravan which, Sean reckoned, was at least 100 feet long, was located immediately next to a forest that made the one on Joey's field look like a small bush. When not playing football, the boys would spend hours deep inside the woods making dens, building traps and whittling twigs into spears with their penknives bought from the site shop, bearing the legend, '*A souvenir from the Lakes.*'

Despite their differences in appearance, the boys were often asked, by other kids on the site, if they were brothers, to which the stock answer would be '*yes*', a scenario that pleased Sean no end. "It would be great if we *were* brothers," he had said to Liam whilst sitting in one of their many dens. "Cause then your mum would be mine too and she's ace!"

Liam was genuinely flattered but felt a little sorry for his friend who, he remembered, didn't have the most reliable of mothers. "We sort of are brothers," responded Liam and seeing the puzzled look on Sean's face continued. "Well, you're at my house most days and my mum thinks you're top so there's not a lot of difference really." Sean smiled and looked at Liam for a short time, not speaking. "What?" asked Liam, wondering what Sean was thinking.

"Nah," replied Sean, looking away. "It doesn't matter. It's stupid."

"No, go on, what?" pushed Liam, intrigued as to what Sean was going to say.

"Well," started Sean. "It's just that ... well you, saying that about your mum ... it's nice and I'm dead happy to be here with you, on this holiday and ..." he paused, shaking his head. "See ... told you it was stupid."

"That's not stupid mate," Liam replied. "I know what you mean ... I'm glad you're here too 'cause it would have been well boring on my own ... without my *brother!*"

Both boys smiled, knowing that they each possessed a friendship that seemed unbreakable. What the boys didn't know is that, later on in their lives, that friendship would be put to the test.

September 1984

Liam and Sean walked towards the gate of St.Monica's High School amongst a sea of children their own age, each clothed in a slightly oversized, all new, school uniform.

Liam thought back to how his Mum had wept that morning stating that he looked *all grown up* and how she wished his dad could have been there to see him. Liam had wished that too. He missed his dad and though he had gone away on many occasions before, Liam couldn't remember feeling like he did now. Maybe it was the absence of his dad on his birthday or perhaps on the holiday they had just been on or maybe it was just that he had gotten a little older and felt intimidated by being the only *man* in the house. Whatever it was, Liam felt empty without his dad around and found himself praying more at night for his quick return.

Liam had been given two things by his mum that morning. The first was a fifty pence piece that she slipped into his blazer pocket *for luck.* "You have to give silver to someone in a new suit," she had said. "It brings luck apparently." Liam had tried to reject the offer, claiming that it was a school uniform not a suit, but the concept, she insisted, was the same and the coin had remained in situ.

The second thing Bridie had surprised her son with, was an item that made Sean chuckle as soon as he saw it. "What the hell is that?" he said laughing and pointing to the shiny black patent leather briefcase in Liam's hand.

"What does it look like y'dick?" Liam retorted, a little annoyed at his friend's over reaction.

"Yeah," replied Sean. "I know it's a briefcase, but why the hell have you got one? ... we're going to Monica's not the CIS insurance building!"

"At least it's new," Liam snapped. "Unlike your charity bag uniform!" Liam regretted his words as soon as he had said them and saw the look on Sean's face change immediately to embarrassment. He knew that Sean's family were struggling a little since his dad was made redundant and a new school uniform was not on top of their list of priorities. This had forced Sean's parents to use the school's *good as new* box, a large supply of used uniform donated to the PTA of St. Monica's by the parents of ex-pupils. Though saving a great deal of money for the parents of children just starting the school, it brought no end of shame to the recipients unlucky enough to be wearing them. "Mate," started Liam. "I'm really sorry ... I didn't mean ..."

"It's alright," interrupted Sean. "I know you didn't mean it ... it's shit, innit?"

"No it's not!" Liam replied, trying to sound convincing. "It looks alright ... like you've been at the school ages. Not like me, I will stand out like a right polished dick!"

Sean smiled a little before looking again at Liam's briefcase. "You need to get rid of that Connor or you will get seriously bullied!"

As Liam was about to reply, a familiar voice from behind made them both stop and turn around quickly. "Nice handbag Paddy. Is it your mum's?" Matthew Walker said, as he walked up to the boys with his sidekick Simon Boland in tow.

"No," replied Sean, stepping slightly in front of Liam. "It's your sister's ... she gave it to Liam after she'd finished noshing him off!" Liam let out a laugh but more surprisingly, so did Walker's friend Boland. Walker turned to his friend and glared at him, making him look to the floor. He then looked back at Sean and studied him for a moment.

"Like the uniform Bevan," he began. "Looks like your mum was sober enough to stagger down to the pauper's shop then!" This time it was Liam who stood in front of Sean, holding him back, stopping him from punching Walker who had very wisely, taken a step backwards.

"Leave it Sean. He's not worth it ... you'll just get in shit from the teachers!"

Sean relaxed a little but didn't take his eyes off a smiling Walker for one moment as he strolled away. "I swear to God," started Sean angrily. "One of these days I will seriously smack that dick so hard, he'll wish he never ..."

"I know, I know!" interrupted Liam. "Just not today mate eh?" He glanced at his watch and added. "Come on, it's nearly nine o'clock. Let's get inside and find our form room. Can't be late on our first day!"

St. Monica's High school was a large, fairly modern building that housed almost a thousand pupils and was one of two schools in the area that took children not academic or rich enough to go into private education. There were two sections to the school both housed over two floors and divided into east and west wings. Liam had suggested that it sounded like a prison more than an educational facility; Sean had suggested there was no difference.

The east wing of the school was set aside for fourth and fifth years where, amongst other facilities, the sports hall and gymnasium were held. It was also the location for the prefect's common room; a room that was designed as a privilege for students entrusted with the power to enforce school rules. A room that students without such authority, would only visit when reporting to a particular prefect to receive punishment for a minor misdemeanour. A room that would become well known to Liam and Sean during their *incarceration* at St.Monica's.

The west wing was where years one to three were placed and besides the numerous classrooms, three science labs and a music auditorium, it was the home of the most feared room in the school. A room that no pupil ever wanted to visit, even when merely tasked with delivering a message. A room that was the office of Mr. T. McSweeny BSc, MEd, Headmaster; a room that unfortunately, would become very well known to Sean.

As the boys entered the school, they were met by the smell of freshly painted walls and newly polished floors, courtesy of the caretaker's efforts over the summer break. They stood for a while, silent and transfixed by the sheer length and width of the corridor before them. Doors upon doors leading into who knew what, lined the edges, their uniformity broken only by the occasional junctions with other corridors leading off to who knew where. There were children of Liam and Sean's age everywhere, impatiently walking to and fro, going in and out of doorways hoping to find the classroom that corresponded to the number allocated on their enrolment letters. Liam mused that they looked like lost sheep and was grateful for the information supplied to him by his sister Margaret the previous day, telling him exactly where his new form room, numbered 212, was located. Margaret had attended the school for the last 2 years and was only too happy to help Liam with directions, but issued a stern warning when doing so.

"And remember Liam," she concluded after going over the schematics of the school with him. "Just because I'm your sister and love you when we are at home and all, don't be approaching me in school with Sean or any of your other nerdy mates and embarrassing me in front of my friends!"

"Like I would ever want to speak to you and your girly girlfriends," replied Liam. "I don't wear enough makeup for one thing!" Liam pouted his lips and continued in the best girl's voice he could muster. "Ooo Margaret, what do you think of my new lipstick ... ooo Clare that's lovely but what about my new eye makeup ..." Liam would have continued had Margaret not thrown a magazine at him, promptly ordering him to get out of her room.

Liam and Sean were standing in the same spot as the school bell rang out loudly enough to make them both jump. As the last remaining pupils filed into their new classes, a door to the left of the boys opened, allowing a stream of teachers to transgress from the room within and filter off, like an army of synchronised soldier ants, into their respective form rooms. The boys jumped again when a loud male voice boomed out from behind them. "You boys ... what are you doing?!" Liam and Sean turned round quickly and saw a tall well built man in his forties, watching them intently. Dressed in a smart dark suit covered by a black gown and possessing a stature that was, at best, intimidating to children of *any* age within the school, the boys were left in no doubt that this was *the* Mr. Terence McSweeny BSc, MEd, Headmaster and supreme ruler of St. Monica's High School. Sean gulped, a gulp so loud that it sounded quite comical, making Liam chuckle.

"Do you find something amusing boy?" demanded the headmaster.

"No Sir," replied Liam. "Nothing ... sorry sir."

"Then may I suggest that you make your way to wherever it is you should be?"

"Yes Sir," the boys replied in unison.

"Good," the headmaster added before concluding. "And get a move on, the first bell has already sounded, in case you hadn't noticed!"

"Yes Sir," the boys repeated and turned around before quickly walking away to find their form room.

The Headmaster watched the pair as they left and sighed a little. *'Another school year begins Terence,'* he thought. *'What joy!'*

"Jesus," started Sean as the two of them walked off. "He looked seriously hard ... don't wanna be visiting his office anytime soon!"

"Then try to stay out of shit," replied Liam. "For this week anyway!" He laughed and clapped Sean on the back, before stopping outside a battered looking blue door.

Above the small panel of safety glass that was the doors window, a plastic sign, not much bigger than a standard business card, indicated that they had arrived at the correct room. *'She's good for some things that sister of mine,'* thought Liam as he took a hold of the door handle. He paused before opening the door, feeling a tad nervous. He looked at Sean for support, who gave him the necessary nod of encouragement. Taking a deep breath, Liam turned the handle and pushed the door open.

The boys entered room 212 to a scene of relative mayhem, as thirty plus children tried to decide where they wanted to sit before the form teacher arrived. Liam smiled at the look of pleasant surprise on Sean's face the moment he saw that Louise Duffy was in their class. He saw the spark reignite as the two of them made eye contact with each other, smiling.

What he didn't see, was the person watching him from the back of the room, also smiling.

###

Chapter 12

The moderate sized hangar set in a disused army training base just north of Brighton, had been an excellent yet ironic choice of venue. Located in a clearing in the middle of a wood, the base was only accessible by one road that was little more than an oversized dirt track. All the buildings within the complex were painted in a camouflage green that made detection from the air near on impossible and its new, yet temporary occupants, were sardonically grateful for the British Army's sense of anonymity.

The site itself had been closed for two years with the services of a private security company being employed in the first year to deter any would be thieves from entering and looking for a bounty of copper piping and other scrap metal to steal and *'weigh in'*. However, since the M.O.D's decision to dispel the services of *Securicor*, the only remaining deterrents were faded signs hanging intermittently on the wired boundary fence that displayed an artist's impression of a German Shepherd and carried the warning *'24hr Dog Patrol in Force'*. The reality was that no patrol, dog or otherwise, had set foot on the site for some time.

For the last three months, a team of highly trained specialists had taken residence on the site. A different army with different objectives to that of their British counterparts. Theirs was not the protection of Queen and country from attack, but the challengers of it and within a couple of months, they would strike at the very heart of the nation.

A black car drove slowly through the entrance of the site watched closely by two *guards* hidden in the undergrowth. One of the guards spoke into his radio informing the listener of its arrival, whilst the other trained his rifle on the vehicle itself. A short but precise reply on the two-way and the guards relaxed, resuming their original positions.

"That's the big man himself then!" one of the guards exclaimed to the other.

"Aye, sure enough," came the reply.

"Lucky you didn't fuckin' shoot then," the first guard added. "Or we would have been out of a job for sure!"

Both men chuckled for a moment before continuing their watch. The conversation was over.

Michael and Joseph Connor stood waiting to greet the occupants of the car way before it had pulled up outside the hangar. The impromptu visit seem to unnerve Joseph though Michael remained calm, secretly hoping that the campaign would be called off. Although exceptional progress had been made, he still believed that time was not on their side and costly mistakes could be made at a risk to him and his comrades. Nevertheless, his skills of organisation and delegation coupled with the excellent team he found himself privileged to be working with, had produced results beyond his expectations and his optimism had flourished slightly as each day passed ... *still.*

The rear door of the car opened and whilst there were two passengers in the back seat, only a tall well built man in his mid forties stepped out and glanced around the site. He was dressed in a way that was neither extravagant nor befitting his status as a leader but, as he had often stated to his closest colleagues who had dared suggest a replacement for his ancient tweed jacket and brown slacks ... "It's war we're at, not a fuckin' fashion show!"

71

His square, silver rimmed spectacles and bushy hair and beard, gave him a look mostly reserved for geography teachers, doctors or arty playwrights and had on many occasions, led people into a false sense of security, much to their cost. When he spoke, his course Irish tone attracted both respect and fear from its listener, depending on whom he was speaking to at the time and for what purpose. His reputation was far reaching and whilst his public persona was that of a fair yet passionate man who would only challenge the British Government politically and legally, the people closest to him knew different. This was a not a man to be crossed.

The passenger who remained in the car was also known. Not for his political acumen or public speaking abilities, but for his skills in close protection and particular penchant for arranging the *retirements* of party members who had become less than loyal. He watched closely as his superior exited the car, stared briefly at Michael and Joseph through the open door and then turned his attention back to the dossier perched on his knee.

Having taken in his immediate surroundings, the first man turned to the driver, also out of the car and nodded before turning his back on both and strolling away, seemingly surveying the woodland beyond the base. The driver, acknowledging the non verbal request, went to the rear of the vehicle, opened the boot and removed a brown attaché case from within. He then walked over to Michael and handed him the case before returning to the car, starting it up and driving to the side of the hangar out of sight of the three men. Michael looked at the case, confused and then to Joseph who frowned and shrugged, equally confused. As if given his cue, the man turned back around, walked over to the brothers, smiling and shook their hands. "Michael, Joseph," he said nodding to each of them. "It's good t'see you both again."

"And you Sir," replied Joseph, though at this moment in time, he thought, it seemed less than good.

"What's in the briefcase?" Michael asked, immediately making Joseph wince slightly at such a direct question, wondering how their Commander would react. The man looked at Michael for a while, glanced briefly at a perspiring Joseph and then back to Michael. He took off his glasses, removed the handkerchief from his breast pocket and started to clean the lenses. There was a significant pause before he replied.

"I had the honour," he started, holding his glasses up to the light in between rubs, "of meeting your father many years ago." He put his glasses back on, returned the handkerchief to his pocket and looked up at the brothers. With an eerily warm smile, he continued. "A great man. An inspiring man. A man with vision and dexterity but above all else ..." he paused, looking directly at Michael. "A man with faith and belief. Not just in himself, but in those he led." Michael wanted to say that he knew all that, but what had it to do with the case? As if sensing his thoughts, the man glanced briefly at the attaché case and then back to Michael. "You're so like your father Michael," he added. "Your drive, your spirit ... it doesn't go unnoticed my friend and the party's gratitude is immeasurable, believe me." Michael listened, still wondering what it had to do with the case. "What upsets me Michael," the man continued, frowning slightly. "Is that you appear to have lost a little ..." he paused as if searching for the right word, then added. "Shall we say ... faith!"

Michael felt a sudden wave of contempt for the man standing before him. Who was he to challenge his faith, his loyalty. He opened his mouth to say his piece that, had he been allowed to continue, would have surely made Joseph pass out. But the man smiled and raised his hand quickly, signalling that there was no need to say anything. He knew Michael spoke his mind and knew what he would have said. Although his respect for Michael would have allowed for a few minutes' rant, any other 'soldier' of a lesser standing willing to air their views in such a way, would have been referred directly to his colleague still sitting in the car.

Certain that Michael was, for now, willing to hold his tongue, the man lowered his hand and spoke softly, a look of genuine concern on his face. "When I hear that one of my most trusted officers is unhappy, it makes me unhappy. Knowing that there are concerns with an operation, makes me want to know why and what, if anything, I can do to help." He placed a hand on Michael's shoulder. "I make it my business to help in any way that I can Michael. That is my pledge in this struggle for freedom and I will stop at nothing to deliver!"

'Spoken like a true fuckin' Politician!' Michael thought, calming slightly.

"That," the man said, pointing to the case, "is something that I believe will interest you greatly my friend and hopefully, if my instincts are correct, give you back that temporary loss of faith." The man smiled again and gestured towards the doorway of the hangar. "Shall we?" he said and the three of them headed into what had become their operations room.

Inside the hangar, makeshift workstations had been erected over half the floor space, all manned by individuals working on their contribution to the mission. Every piece of the operational jigsaw, from false documentation to the monitoring of Police radio channels, from plans and diagrams to firearms maintenance, was being covered at these stations. On the orders of Michael, every person working within the hangar wore white coveralls, a safeguard against their own clothing fibres being left and discovered at a later stage by forensic busybodies should the hangar's *redeployment* become linked to an undoubted police investigation post October 12th.

At the far end of the hangar, a large space had been set aside for one man to painstakingly prepare his lethal donation to the cause. Awash with wiring, various timers, soldering irons and dismantled VHS video recorders, the station could have been mistaken for a TV repair shop, had it not been for the large amount of plastic explosive next to it. Patrick McGinley looked up from his work, saw the three men enter the hangar and immediately recognised the man with Michael and Joseph. He put down his tools and went to join them, curious to know why their Commander had turned up at such short notice.

"How are you Patrick?" the man asked, holding out his hand as Patrick joined them.

"Grand Sir," replied Patrick, as the two men shook hands. "Is there a problem?"

The man laughed and shook his head. "Why do I get the impression that everybody assumes something is wrong?" He glanced at the three men before him and continued. "No, no. Nothing's wrong Patrick. Quite the opposite in fact!" He turned to Michael and motioned to the case he was still holding. "If you would be so kind Mike?"

Michael put the attaché case on a table, opened it and removed the contents. Up until this moment, Michael had grave doubts about the mission and had often voiced his opinions with no regard as to who might have been listening. He felt aggrieved that he had had no valuable intelligence from his covert operatives at the proposed location and even less intelligence from his superiors. And, up to this point, he had no idea of how they were expected to deliver and detonate a device in the Grand Hotel with full effect. Other than the date and location of the conference, they had no information about where the Prime Minister and her cabinet members would be at any given time during their stay at the hotel in Brighton and it looked like they would have to be going in *blind*, a situation that Michael had seen happen before, a situation that had resulted in either prison or death of his colleagues; a situation that he begrudged being a part of again.

However, as he sifted through the papers, skim reading the details on each page, he frowned a little, glanced up at the three men standing round him and then returned his attention to the files, studying them more closely. A few minutes later, and for the first time in many weeks, a genuine smile appeared on Michael's face. Joseph and Patrick watched him closely, eager to know the importance of the find. The Commander also watched him, sure that a little *faith* had been restored. Michael passed the documents to Joseph and Patrick, documents that contained highly classified information about seating plans, schedules and precise times of activities at the Conservative Party Conference. There was correspondence regarding the role of the Security Services and an itinerary of what security measures they proposed to put in place and at what point, during the event. But what Michael thought to be the most important information of all, was the detailed list denoting the exact hotel suite each member of the attending Cabinet had been allocated to, including the Right Honourable Mrs. Thatcher.

Before Joseph and Patrick had even taken in the relevance of the documents, Michael had begun to formulate a new plan in his mind. A plan that would not only speed up their current process, but would result in maximum destruction of the British Government. He felt a new surge of enthusiasm, not just because of this unexpected delivery of information, but because now, at last, he would be able to avenge the unnecessary death of a close friend and comrade. A death he spoke little about but a death that all members of the party knew had affected Michael greatly. Soon, he thought, it would finally be time for Prime Minister Thatcher to regret her stance on *Political Prisoners,* a stance that had seen a great man of only twenty seven years of age, die. A man who stood by his beliefs, constantly fighting for his rights and the rights of his comrades also imprisoned within the walls of the Maze prison. A man, who for sixty six days, refused to take food so that the Government might listen and change. They hadn't and they didn't and on 5th May 1981, Michael was informed how his friend, Robert 'Bobby' Sands, had passed away.

His initial thoughts and doubts about this campaign had now all but vanished and he felt a little embarrassed that he had not put more trust in his Superiors. The man watching him sensed this quiet remorse.

"Right," the Commander said, looking at Joseph. "How about you give me the grand tour of this place Joe and show me how our money's being spent?" Joseph looked a little disappointed that he was to be dragged away from the main event of the day, but obliged their guest nonetheless.

As he and the man walked through the hangar, Joseph introduced his comrades at the various workstations and explained what each was doing. However, after about fifteen minutes, Joseph stopped in his tracks and turned to the Commander, a quizzical look on his face.

"Is there a problem Joe?" the man said, frowning a little. Seeing the hesitance in Joseph, he added, "Spit it out man, whatever it is!"

"With respect Sir," Joseph started, wishing he hadn't, "I get the impression that a tour of this shite hole is not what you pulled me away for ... am I wrong?"

The man stared at Joseph for what seemed like an eternity. Joe felt beads of sweat running down his back and wondered if he had crossed the line. He could never read the man's face, which unnerved him no end. Eventually and surprisingly, the man laughed out loud wagging his finger at Joseph. "You're an astute man Joseph Connor, there's no denying that ... does anything get past you?!"

Joseph also laughed, though it was through nerves and not because he found anything particularly funny. The man's laughter died down as quickly as it had started and Joe quickly followed suit. "But you're right of course," the man continued sombrely and added. "Come, walk outside with me Joe ... as they say, 'walls have ears'!" He glanced over at one of the workstations where its occupant was staring at them intensely. "Have y'work to be doing Comrade?!" the man barked, making the onlooker jump, apologise profusely and put his head down quickly, feigning activity.

Once outside the hangar, the man took a cigarette case from his inside pocket, opened it and offered a *Treasurer Black* to Joseph before taking one for himself. He then produced a gold lighter from another pocket and lit both cigarettes. The two men stood in silence for a few moments inhaling and exhaling the smoke, enjoying the rush of expensive nicotine.

"Is everything Ok with Michael, Joseph?" the man suddenly asked through a plume of smoke, making Joseph feel both defensive and uncomfortable. He was not one to discuss the feelings of his family with anyone other than his family and he wondered where the question was leading. He himself knew that everything with his brother was far from ok of late, but he wasn't about to tell this to a man who he knew liked to dispense with anybody showing signs of weakness faster than he could smoke one of his fancy cigarettes. *"Loose cogs in a tight machine!"* the man had often been heard to say which, in laymen's terms, was as good as the death knell itself.

"Of course he's ok," Joseph replied with a little more enthusiasm than was necessary. "Why shouldn't he be? ... Has something been said? 'Cause if it has, I can tell you now that it's a bag of ..."

"Joe, Joe relax!" the man interrupted, giving Joseph time to drag hard on the last of his cigarette. "Nobody has said anything. But I'm not a stupid man Joseph, I notice things, differences. Changes that affect the way a man thinks, the way he works. And I have to look at those changes and ask myself why? ... why has he changed? What's on his mind and can it be resolved?" He took a last drag of his cigarette and threw it to the ground extinguishing it under his foot. "Over the last couple of years Joseph, I have seen a change in Michael and it concerns me. Not just because he is an important member of our party but because I see him as a friend. And what sort of person would I be if I wasn't concerned that such a friend might be ... well ... losing his passion shall we say?"

"What, Michael?" Joseph replied and began to chuckle. The man looked at him quizzically though Joseph saw this as a look of impatience and continued, quickly. "Jesus above. Michael is one of the most passionate men I know for sure and, with respect Sir, I'm including the two of us in that summary!" The man looked at Joseph as if needing to be convinced. Joseph obliged and continued. "Look," he said. "Bobby's death affected Mike more than most and probably more than we'll ever know. But if anything, it has spurred him on, given him *more* passion, if that was humanly possible!" Joseph glanced around as if checking to make sure nobody was within ear shot and lowered his voice. "When the campaign against the Government got postponed last year in place of the Harrods Job, well, let's just say that he wasn't best pleased ... Christ, he's a grumpy bastard at the best of times!" The man smiled and nodded silently, acknowledging the sentiment as Joseph continued. "But did you not see his face when he read those documents? The excitement in his eyes? He looked like a fekkin' dog wi' two dicks ... and you ask me if he's ok?" Joseph paused for effect. "Aye Sir, I would say he's just grand, wouldn't you?"

The man nodded again. "I had to ask Joe," he said. "You must understand that I only have his best interests at heart and I would be failing in my duties if I didn't act on the concerns voiced by others ... if I can help with a problem, then I will, you know that."

Joseph frowned as the man's words registered in his brain. *'Concerns voiced by others'* he thought. *'So some bastard has said something after all!'* He felt an anger rise inside him. Not only as he thought of the spineless shite who dared to talk behind Michael's back, spinning yarns to the Big Man and his lackey, but of the man who was standing before him now. The man who had assured him only a few minutes ago, that this was not the case. Assured him that it was a genuine and personal concern with no outside influence. *'Fuck you!'* he thought. He took a step closer to the man and spoke in a voice that didn't hide his disgust.

"Michael speaks his mind more than he should. We all know that and we live with it ... but he's also a man whose loyalty and passion are as strong now as the day he first held the *Patriots* flag all those years ago. The pledge he made to serve that flag and what it stands for, will be honoured with the same pride, the same hopes and the same commitment until he breathes his last breath on this Earth ... So, if some gutless arse hole tryin' t'make a name for himself has approached you, tellin' you schoolboy tales of disloyalty and dwindling faith, I implore you to consider this question ... Who is more loyal? A man who regales your strength and authority, or a man who seeks to exploit them? ... If it is the former, then I ask you to look no further than the man inside that hangar, a man whose respect for you Sir, would certainly not allow him to succumb to the guile of the latter!"

The man remained silent, staring hard at Joseph and gently stroking his beard as if in deep thought. Joe wondered if he could see him shaking from the sudden rush of adrenaline but was determined to hold his stare, looking for the slightest emotion. *'What are you thinking ya bastard?'* he thought as the sound of his heart, pounding like a battering ram, rang in his ears. Finally, with a faint smile, the man spoke.

"You're a good man Joseph and I appreciate your comments, truly." He lowered his voice slightly and added. "But I would also appreciate this conversation being kept to ourselves ... if you have no objections that is?"

Joseph shook his head. "None at all Sir," he replied. "As they say, 'loose lips sink ships'!".

The commander quietly mused at the irony of the reply. "Right," he began, changing the subject and ending the previous conversation as quickly as it had started. "Let's go and have a wee word with your men at the gate. I don't believe they've quite grasped the concept of being covert ... not unless their idea is to be seen nearly five hundred yards away!"

As they walked away, Joseph still had no idea of the man's true intentions. He had seen through this unannounced and transparent field trip by the Commander, knowing full well that any minion could have delivered that briefcase on his behalf. But what worried him, made him sick to the stomach, was that he had also worked out what had been planned for Michael. And now, other than grabbing the man by the lapels and shaking the truth out of him, he had absolutely no way of knowing if his little speech had afforded his brother redemption or effectively signed his death warrant. All he could do was wait and pray that it wasn't the latter.

###

A little over one hour later, the two men returned to the hangar to discover that Michael and Patrick had already developed and finely tweaked a strategy to exact their revenge on *'an arrogant and complacent Conservative regime'*

Michael told the Commander and Joseph that Patrick, as the explosives expert, would check into the hotel in Brighton and take a suite on the sixth floor. The reason for this, Michael explained, was that it was way above the bedrooms that would be occupied by the Cabinet members come October and therefore not be subjected to such rigorous security checks. It was also, Patrick pointed out, central enough to inflict greater damage to the hotel's structure. "If the device doesn't kill them," he said. "Then the collapsing building should!"

"What date are you thinking of checking in?" Joseph asked. "Surely the hotel will be fully booked around October time?"

81

"Mid September at the latest," interjected Michael.

For the second time that day, the Commander looked quizzical. "Mid September?" he enquired, frowning. "But how do you intend to detonate it? ... Surely timers are only good for a few days, a week at most!"

Both Michael and Patrick smiled before Michael said, "I think this is your cue to take the floor Paddy!"

Patrick obliged, cleared his throat and went on to explain his plan. He proposed to use a thirty pound device which would be wrapped in cellophane to mask the vapours of the plastic explosive, thus negating its discovery by any bomb squad 'sniffer' dogs allowed to roam on that floor. From looking at the layout of the rooms and the schematic plans of the hotel, he would need to request a suite where the bathroom was adjacent to a supporting wall. "Any room from 620 through to 635 would be ideal," he explained. "Which shouldn't pose a problem 'cause, looking at their reservation lists, almost all of those rooms are free around the fifteenth!" He went on to tell the group how he planned to attend the hotel with false identification posing as a business man on a sales convention and would stay no more than three days. During that time, he would fix the device behind a bath panel, so that it wouldn't be found by cleaning staff or subsequent residents of the room, prime it and set the timer on the day of checking out.

"And this gentlemen," he said, picking up a small black plastic panel with various wires spewing from its back. "Is a small yet highly important component, courtesy of the electronic genius that is Ferguson's!"

"What the fuck is it?" asked Joseph.

"Ah," replied Patrick. "This little beauty, is an led timer unit taken from one of the video recorders you may have seen at my workstation. Not only does it require a very small power source to run it, but it's also capable of being pre-set with dates and times of events up to *thirty* days in advance and ..." he looked round smiling, "is the reason why our device will be detonated nearly a month after I have left the hotel!"

Both Michael and Patrick watched as the two other men mentally digested the information and then smiled, nodding approvingly. The Commander looked at Michael for a few moments, stood up from his chair and offered his hand. As the two men shook, Joseph saw a look in the man's eyes that injected a rush of relief into his body. It was a look of quiet admiration, of respect, but more importantly, a look that confirmed to Joe that the Commander's initial agenda had now changed. Whether it had been the earlier conversation that had helped this decision or a realisation by the man that his information was indeed heavily jaded, Joseph didn't know and frankly, didn't care. All that mattered now, was that common sense and justice had prevailed ... Amen!

"Right," the man said glancing at his watch. "As time and tide waits for no man, I shall leave you gentlemen to carry on with what you do best!"

Michael walked the man to the door where his vehicle was already waiting. He turned to his boss with a look of curiosity on his face. "Those documents," he began. "Where the hell did they come from?"

The man smiled and raised an eyebrow. "Let's just put it down to some divine intervention Michael," he replied. "The Good Lord moves in mysterious ways and seems to have his Angels of mercy in all sorts of places ... even MI6!" He winked mischievously and both men shared a moment of laughter.

"Ok Michael," the man said as the two shook hands again. "Anything you need, just ask, yes?" Michael nodded as the man continued. "You do your country proud Michael, of that I have no doubt and I want to thank you sincerely. I only hope that my coming here today has been of some use?" He studied Michael for a few moments before quietly adding. "I know this campaign is of a great significance to you and I apologise if you felt that we were letting you down, but make no mistake, we too feel the loss of our comrade ... Our time has now come Michael, *your* time, to avenge that loss and ensure that the British Government will be left in no doubt as to the capabilities and passion of the Independent Republic Army ... we fight in the name of the Lord!"

"Amen," was all Michael said as he watched the Commander walk away and get into his vehicle.

As the black vehicle pulled slowly away, the man looked out of the window and watched as Michael turned around and walked back into the hangar. He let out a heavy sigh and turned to the person sitting next to him in the rear of the car.

"Well?" was all the passenger said to the Commander, who in turn, shook his head firmly. He then removed his glasses so that he could rub his eyes. He felt a headache coming on. The second male produced a two way radio and spoke briefly into it.

"Why is nothing straightforward anymore?" the Commander said to his companion. "Too many hurdles, too much animosity, too many people wanting to pull against the order of things instead of pulling together!" He turned and pointed at the dossier on his colleague's knee. "And make sure that is destroyed. Christ knows the damage it could cause should it ever be discovered!"

The second man slipped the dossier into a briefcase and locked it. Turning to the commander, he asked, "So what now?"

"Now," the Commander replied. "We need to revisit our source for a little *tete a tete* and find out the true motives behind his input ... 'cause if there was ever a benchmark for supplying information that was both inaccurate and potentially embarrassing to this party, then our friend Mr. Robert O'Neil has surpassed that beyond all measure!"

84

As the vehicle pulled out of the gate and disappeared from view, a man, hidden in the woodland that surrounded the base, was dismantling a high powered sniper rifle. He had been in situ some hours before he saw his boss arrive, stand by the boundary fence and give him the initial signal to prepare. Although he now felt hungry and a little tired, he bore no malice when he had received a brief radio message to stand down and move out with immediate effect, without completing his task. Once he had packed his equipment away, he pulled a photograph from his pocket, studied it for a while and then, using a match, set it alight. As the flames caught hold, he dropped it to the floor and knelt down to watch it burn. Mesmerised by the small fire of blue and orange, he wondered how many *targets* had been so blessed to evade the usual result of his work. He stood up and kicked soil over the burning embers, just as the final piece of Michael Connor's image turned to ash.

###

Chapter 13

September 1984

Jeanette Cho Lin was nervous, very nervous. Today was the first day of High School and though the academic side didn't faze her in the slightest, it worried her that she would know practically nobody at the new school. She had moved into the Manchester area only four months ago with her parents and whilst she had made a few friends, she still felt very much the outsider. It didn't help that there were no other girls, or boys for that matter, of Chinese origin in the area where she lived, which was great for her Mum and Dad's takeaway business, but not that great if you didn't care for *standing out* in the crowd. But in the years to come, as she developed into a young adult, it would be her stunning looks, not her ethnicity, that would make her stand out from any crowd. As she left her house to start the ten minute walk to St. Monica's, she was slightly relieved when she saw a girl she knew walking past, also on her way to the school.

"Hiya Jen!" the girl said chirpily. "Big day today hey? Are you excited?"

"A bit nervous really," Jeanette admitted. "I don't really know anybody and ..."

"You know me," the girl interrupted. "So that's one ... and most of the others going are from round here anyway and you've met a few of them before, haven't you?" Jeanette thought about this for a moment and smiled a little before nodding her head in agreement. "What ya smilin' at?" the girl asked.

"What? ... Oh, nothing!" Jeanette replied, a little embarrassed at being caught out.

"Come on, what?" the girl pressed. "And don't say nothing, I can see it on your face ... pleeease!"

Jeanette looked at the girl and pondered for a moment, wondering if she should tell. Within five seconds, she had reached her decision. "Well ... !"

Jeanette had initially met the girl she was now walking to school with, when she had come into the takeaway and ordered a bag of chips during the first week of opening. Jen had wandered into the serving area and noticed the girl of about the same age waiting for her order to be completed and decided to say hello.

"Hi," the girl responded, before adding. "You're new here, aren't you?"

"Yeah," Jeanette replied. "We've only been here for four days ... where do you live?"

"Just on the next road along, so not far really," the girl responded.

"Oh right," said Jeanette and there followed what seemed to be an endless pause whilst the girl was being served her chips.

Once she had been given the food wrapped in the familiar white paper, she looked at Jeanette, smiled and said, "Well, See ya!"

"Yeah, see ya," Jeanette replied, feeling a little low that the only person of her age she had spoken to since arriving in the area, was now going. But as the girl was about to leave the shop, she suddenly stopped and turned round to Jeanette.

"Hey," she said brightly. "We're just off to Joey's field, do you want to come? Only for an hour or so?"

"What's Joey's field?" Jeanette replied.

"Oh yeah," the girl said, realising her mistake. "I forgot you were new ... it's just a park about five minutes away and everyone goes."

Jeanette looked towards her Dad who appeared preoccupied with putting battered fish into the hot oil fryer. She waited a while until her father, without even looking at his daughter, nodded, once. "Thanks Dad!" she said smiling and left quickly, heading off to Joey's with her new friend.

###

That sunny May afternoon in 1984 was one that Jen would not forget for a long time. Not just because she felt immediately accepted by the few girls that were there with her new friend, but because she had seen something, or rather someone, who took her breath away.

At first, Jeanette didn't want to sit and watch some boys kicking a ball about and was considering going home. It was only because of her friend's plea to stay and see the boy she really liked, that Jen had finally, but reluctantly, agreed.

She was glad she did and could see why her friend liked the boy in question. He was very handsome and sporty looking and obviously good at football. In fact, Jeanette found herself liking him too ... a lot ... although she wasn't about to share this feeling for fear of upsetting her friend, who was obviously besotted with him. When it got to a point in the game that looked liked it was all about deciding a winner, Jen happened to mention that the other boy, who was about to kick the ball, was quite 'chubby' and didn't look suited to football at all. Her friend shot her a look of disapproval, pointing out that he wasn't *that* chubby and actually, he was very good at football, just before she turned back around and shouted, "Go on Sean!!"

Jeanette suddenly realised which of the two boys her friend liked and was immediately overcome by two emotions. The first was regret. Regret that she had obviously gotten the wrong end of the stick and upset her new friend Louise. The

88

second was joy. Joy that she had gotten the wrong end of the stick meaning that the other, better looking boy might just be free.

When he walked over to the group and started talking to Louise about how to kick a ball, Jen couldn't take her eyes off him. She hoped that he would talk to her, even if it was only to say hello. But he didn't and as he walked away with Louise, she couldn't help but feel a little hurt that he didn't even glance her way. *'Stupid,'* she thought to herself. *'Why would he speak to me, he doesn't even know me?!'* Despite mentally chastising herself, she still felt a strange sense of anguish and whilst her friend Louise was busy taking her place behind the ball, she decided to make her excuses to the other girls in the group and leave; a decision that she hated herself for as she didn't even find out the boy's name.

Over the next two weeks, she only went back to Joey's field on one occasion but didn't dare mention to her friend that it was in the hope of seeing that boy again. When he wasn't there, she again felt a little disappointed and decided that future visits to Joey's would be off her agenda. By the end of the third week, she had put the boy to the back of her mind. That was, of course, until he entered her shop one afternoon whilst she was helping her dad stack food trays. She looked up as the door opened and stood open mouthed as he and his friend Sean walked in and up to the counter. "Two lots of chips please," the boy said to her dad before glancing towards her, smiling. She stared back, still open mouthed, as if frozen to the spot, unable to return that lovely smile. "You'll catch flies," the boy said, making her snap back into reality and close her mouth, ready to reply to his little quip with graceful female venom.

"Maybe I want to!" she retorted but immediately thought, *'Maybe I want to? What the hell does that mean?!'*

"Oh. Right then," the boy replied, looking puzzled, before turning around to quickly gather up and pay for his chips.

Seeing her opportunity to talk to the boy slipping away with her stupid comment, she quickly regained her composure and, looking at the boy's friend, blurted out "You're Sean aren't you?"

The other boy looked at his friend and then to Jeanette before replying. "Yeah, why?"

"Oh nothing ... it's just that I saw you playing football with your friend here on the field not long ago when I was with your girlfriend Louise!"

Sean's face reddened slightly, not helped by his friend's sudden outburst of laughter. "She's not my girlfriend!" he denied loudly. "She's ... well, she's just ... she's not my girlfriend ok!"

"Oh, Ok, sorry," Jeanette said. "I just thought with her liking you so much, you were, y'know, going out with each other."

"Well we're not!" Sean strongly confirmed before looking towards his friend. "Are we going now or what?" But his friend was now looking at Jeanette as if deep in thought. "Er, hello!" Sean urged, but his friend ignored him for a few moments longer.

"I know you now," the boy said to Jeanette. "You were with Louise and her friends on Joey's when she scored that penalty against Sean?" Sean raised his eyes to the ceiling and shook his head.

"Yes," replied Jeanette. "I didn't think you would remember ... I'm Jeanette but everyone calls me Jen."

"And I'm Liam," the boy said. "And I see you know Sean ... the loser!" Liam laughed and looked at Sean who wasn't amused in the slightest.

"At least I'm not gay Connor!" he snapped. "Now are we going or what?"

Liam turned back to Jeanette and said. "Well, see you again ... Jen," holding her gaze for a few moments longer than was necessary. He then turned around and headed out of the shop with his still grumbling friend.

As she watched him leave she smiled and thought. *'I really hope I do Liam Connor!'*

Turning around, she was surprised to see her dad looking at her, also smiling. "What?" she asked defensively, as if nothing had happened. But her father merely shook his head and turned his attention back to the hot oil, still smiling.

###

"So," said Louise as they neared the school gate. "That's why you left Joey's without saying anything that day ... didn't know you fancied Liam!"

Jen stopped, holding Louise's arm to prevent her walking on. "Please don't say anything to him if you see him will you. It's just that ... well, I would feel a little stupid and he probably doesn't like me anyway and I probably won't see him for ages anyway so there's no point!"

"Well, I won't say anything but ..." Louise started.

"But what?" Jen enquired. Louise looked at her for a moment and started smiling.

"You don't know do you?"

"Know what?" Jen replied, a little anxious that her friend might say that he already had a girlfriend.

"When you said you might not see him for ages!"

"Well I won't ... so what is it?" Jen urged, still puzzled by Louise's remarks.

"Well, you will," Louise continued. "'cause he's going to our school and you'll probably see him every day!"

As the words sunk in, Jen's heart leapt and she wanted to shout out *'yes!'* But she decided to play it cool and simply replied. "Oh well, whatever ... but still, promise not to say anything!"

Louise made the promise as the two girls went and joined the masses of first year children heading into the school. Once inside the building, they were both a bit overwhelmed by the size of the place and the amount of people rushing around trying to find their allocated classes. But, with each other's help, they managed to fight their way through the chaos and eventually find their new form room. As they entered the class, Jen was pleased to see that there were only a few students already in there and whilst Louise went to speak to someone she knew, she found herself a seat at the back of the room and sat down. After only five minutes had passed, the school bell rang in the corridor and the classroom filled up considerably to about thirty children, each scrambling around, trying to find the best place to sit. Jen felt a little sad that nobody appeared to want to sit next to her as they opted to sit next to somebody they already knew instead. It made her realise just how much an outsider she was and wondered if she would actually last the morning let alone the day. A couple of minutes later, she looked up towards the classroom door as it opened and two further students entered the room. Her initial feelings of loneliness quickly faded and she began to smile, recognising the two new additions to the class, in particularly, Liam Connor.

###

Chapter 14

The first day at St. Monica's had not been as bad as either Liam or Sean had expected. It was mostly spent familiarising themselves with the different classrooms and meeting the teachers that presided over them and generally finding their way around the new school. Homework, for what it was worth, was merely to *back* the exercise books they were given in time for the lesson that they referred to. Their form teacher, Mr. Murphy, or *'Spud'* as the older students called him, gave the impression that he really didn't like or have time for first years and kept harping on about how he wouldn't tolerate lateness to registration, lateness to his English lesson, insolence, talking in class, chewing in class or, so it seemed, breathing in class. He also went on to explain that, due to the number of people in their form and the range of individual ability, they may not necessarily share the same teacher for other lessons. This depressed Sean a little, as he knew he was not as smart as Liam and would therefore probably never be in the same class as him. After seeing the timetable however, he was more than pleased that they would only be separated for lessons in maths (not his strongest subject) but not only that, he would be sharing *all* his lessons with Louise. For the latter part of the information however, he kept his excitement quiet ... it's not like they were going out with each other or anything.

Jeanette Cho Lin was also very pleased. Not just because she discovered that she was to share all her lessons with Liam, but, due to the fact that pupils were seated in class alphabetically, she would be sitting right next to him. The only downside to this was that Sean, having the surname

Bevan, was directly in front of them and was forever turning round asking her to swap places or talking to Liam, giving her little chance to build up a rapport. *'Small price to pay,'* she thought, especially as she had worked out that they would be together in maths, without Sean.

For Liam, the day had also turned out pretty well. Partly because that *'arse hole'* Walker wasn't in their form room nor was he in any other of their lessons apart from games (and Liam could handle that as he knew he was better than him at sports anyway) but mainly, because the power of the alphabet system used in the class seating plan, meant that Jen would be seated right next to him. The only slight downside to that, was that Sean had been seated in front of them and was forever turning round asking Jen to swap places leaving little chance for him to say more than *'hi'* to her and start a conversation. *'Never mind,'* he thought. *'At least we will be in maths together without Mr. Bevan going on.'*

However, despite the seating arrangements and shared lessons, it was not until three weeks into the first term that Liam and Jeanette finally had a *proper* conversation. A conversation that was ironically brought about by the actions of one boy ... Matthew Walker.

It was the end of the school day and Liam was by the gate waiting for Sean, who had landed himself a detention by chewing gum in class. To be fair to Spud Murphy, he had already warned Sean about chewing but Sean, with the memory of a fish, had entered the form room after lunch not only chewing gum, but merrily blowing a bubble with it. What else could Spud do, when the bubble burst with a loud bang and covered Sean's lips and nose with a sticky pink residue? "Right Bevan!" he said firmly. "Obviously a warning wasn't good enough for you, so may I suggest half an hour's detention after school!"

Sean had wanted to say something but decided against it, realising it would have only taken his detention up to an hour.

As he sat at his desk, he looked sheepishly at Liam and apologised, knowing that they had made plans to go to Joey's after school.

"S'pose I'll just have to wait for you then?" Liam sighed. "But don't go getting any more y' mong!"

Sean smiled as sweetly as he could manage before sitting down. Jeanette saw a possible opportunity to get Liam on his own for a while.

When the school bell sounded at the end of the day, it took a mere fifteen minutes for the building to be more or less void of any students and only a few stragglers were now passing Liam as he kicked a football against the railings. Jeanette was one of the last to leave, a situation she had planned knowing that Liam would be waiting for Sean. As she went through the main doors of the school out onto the front, she saw Liam by the gate and her mind began to race thinking of what she could say to him. As the door closed behind her, she heard a loud bang and somebody shout that made her jump and turn around quickly. "Shit! ... Didn't you see me coming you stupid cow?!" Matthew Walker said angrily whilst holding his head.

"Oh God no!" replied Jen truly shocked. "I'm so sorry. I didn't see ...!"

"Maybe if you didn't have such slitty eyes you would've!" interrupted Walker who was now standing right up to her. "Or are they full of chip fat?"

"There's nothing wrong with my eyes," Jen said defensively. "And why would they be full of chip fat?"

Walker gave her a look of incredulity, wondering why she couldn't understand his question. "Because you work in a Chinky chippy, don't you?" he said sneering, before looking towards his ever present sycophant, Simon Boland, for appreciation; he wasn't disappointed as Boland chuckled on cue.

"And what do you think I do idiot, wash in it?" Jen replied sarcastically, starting to feel a little annoyed.

"Ooo ... hit a nerve did I?" Walker replied, holding his hands to his face in pretend shock.

"Just get lost Walker!" Jen snapped. She turned away from the pair and tried to walk off only to be stopped in her tracks as Walker stood in front of her blocking her path.

"Aw, is the little Chinky girl getting upset? ... Pwease don' cwy!" Walker mocked in a stereotypically false Chinese accent.

"Get out of the way you idiot!" Jen shouted, now feeling that the abuse wasn't going to end anytime soon.

"And what if I don't?" asked Walker. "You gonna karate chop me ... Ay yah!" He made a chopping gesture with his hand towards Jen that made her flinch and Boland laugh even louder.

"Leave her alone Walker!" a voice from behind the bully commanded, making Walker swing round quickly. He was more than surprised to see Liam Connor standing there, holding a football in his hands, clearly interfering in something that didn't concern him, and couldn't help but burst out laughing.

"Well well. If it isn't Paddy Connor the Irish puff!" he said, once his laughter had stopped. "And without his girlfriend Bevan too ... What do you want Connor, apart from a panning that is?"

Without answering, Liam looked at Jen and said. "You ok?" She smiled slightly and nodded, pleased that somebody had stepped in to help but more pleased that it was Liam. Walker looked from Liam to Jen and back to Liam again before glancing towards his friend.

"Look Si," he said. "I think they're in love. Whatever will fat boy Bevan say?" Boland laughed as Walker turned and glared at Liam. "Now piss off Connor, it's got nothing to do with you ... unless of course you like little yellow girls?"

"You need to shut your mouth Walker," warned Liam. "It will get you into a lot of trouble one day ... or is bullying girls all you're good for?"

"Who's gonna shut me up paddy boy, you? Or are you gonna get your IRA friends to blow me up?"

"You're such a dick Walker!" Liam replied, shaking his head.

"Yeah," said Walker taking a step towards Liam, fists clenched. "A dick who's now gonna smack your 'ed in!"

As Walker advanced, Liam threw the ball he was holding towards him but he managed to bat it away causing it to thud loudly on the school door. "C'mon then!" Liam shouted, but felt himself shaking from the rush of adrenalin as his body entered the mode of fight or flight. He figured it was too late for flight so readied himself for the attack. As Walker grabbed his jumper and pulled back his arm to deliver a punch, Liam himself also drew back an arm, waiting to return a blow, should he get the chance. Before either boy managed to release their offensives, a voice boomed from somewhere above making all four jump.

"You boys ... what are you doing?!" Walker immediately released Liam as all four looked up to see Mr. McSweeny glaring down at them from a first floor window.

"Nothing Sir," he answered in a positively sweet and innocent voice. "Just messing about Sir!"

"Then *mess* about in your own homes please and not on my school premises ... now get yourselves off!" Mr. McSweeny instructed.

"Yes Sir," Walker replied before turning back to Liam, murmuring. "Luck of the Irish Paddy, but don't worry, there'll be other days!" He looked at Jeanette and in the same ridiculous oriental accent said. "Tawar me ol China!" and puckered his lips to feign a kiss.

"Now!!" the voice from above boomed again and Walker, together with Boland, walked off down the school path and out of the gate. Jen pretended to be checking her bag giving her and Liam a couple of minutes grace before they themselves set off under the watchful eye of the Headmaster.

As they approached the school gate, it was Jen that broke the prolonged silence. "Thanks for that," she said. "Nobody's ever stuck up for me before. It was ... well, thanks."

"That's ok," replied Liam softly and after a short pause added. "Are you going home now?"

"Well," she replied, looking around as if checking the area. "I was, but I hope Walker's not still around"

Liam noticed the anxiety in her voice and wanted to say, '*I'll walk you home*', but worried that she might take it as a chat up line and walk off leaving him standing there feeling foolish. Thing was, he really wanted to be with her for a little while longer and had to come up with a plan that would give him that chance. '*What if she doesn't even like me?*' he thought. '*And she really wants to get off on her own but is too polite and is waiting for me to leave and...!*' His body language reflected how his mind was racing which was immediately noticed by Jeanette.

"Are you ok?" she asked frowning.

"What? ... Yeah, fine. And you?" Liam replied trying desperately to keep his cool. He wasn't winning on that score.

"Me? ... I'm fine. Probably just get off home now anyway ... Don't think Walker's still about, thankfully!" Jeanette looked at Liam with as much intensity as she could manage, willing him into action. '*Say you'll walk with me, say you'll walk with me,*' she thought as if trying to hypnotise him with her mind. But it didn't seem to be working.

"No ... think he's well gone now," Liam replied looking around. "I'm just gonna wait for Sean ... we're going to Joey's for a bit, once he's finished his detention that is!"

"Oh, right," Jen replied, sounding truly disappointed. "Well, I'll get off then ... ok, see ya ... oh and thanks again." She smiled at Liam, turned around and started to walk off.

'*Can't believe I'm walking away ... God!*' she thought, annoyed that she had blown an opportunity.

"Yeah, see ya," Liam replied, mentally beating himself up. '*What you doing? she's walking away,*' he thought. '*Say something before it's too late. What've you got to lose? Ask her to stay? Better still ask her to come to...*' "Joey's!!" he shouted out loud as his thoughts finally made the transition to speech. Jen stopped and turned round, a puzzled look on her face, her heart suddenly racing.

"What d'ya say?" she asked. Although she had heard the word, she didn't understand what he meant by it.

"Erm ... Joey's," Liam repeated feeling himself blush. As Jen stared at him in silence he thought. '*Right, just say it how it is Liam!*' and with all the confidence he could muster, blurted out. "I just wondered if you wanted to come to Joey's, with me I mean, 'cause me and Sean were going anyway but he's not out yet and he'll know where I'll be if I leave now anyway and I just thought that ..."

"Yeah, ok," Jeanette interrupted trying not to sound too eager but secretly thinking '*finally!*'

"What?" Liam responded, slightly shocked, wondering if he had heard correctly. As Jeanette started walking back towards him, he realised that he had heard correctly and smiled. "Ok ... right, let's go," he added, now also trying not to sound too eager. It was a ploy that didn't work for either of them and as they headed off to Joey's, they suddenly found their voices and talked like they had known each other for years. It seemed that they both had a thousand tales to tell and the earlier incident with Walker disappeared from their minds completely. Had either of them been asked, both would have smiled and agreed that today had been a good day.

###

Chapter 15

12th October 1984

Liam woke up with a start and felt his heart beating heavily in his chest. His body dripped in a cold sweat and his breathing was temporarily laboured as it took him a few moments to realise that the nightmare he had just had, wasn't in fact real. He sat up and blinked at the early morning sun shining brightly through the gap of his bedroom curtains. He sighed heavily, rubbed his face and looked at the clock by his bed. The big red digital numbers told him it was seven fifteen, a good three quarters of an hour before he was due to get up. *'Shit!'* he thought and slumped heavily back onto his pillow. Looking up at the ceiling, he tried to recount the details of his dream but could remember nothing other than being chased by a black car. As the car mounted the pavement and was just about to mow him down, he woke up. He had had the same nightmare on a few occasions and though he could only ever remember the ending, he had no idea what any of it meant. Sean had said that it meant that he had been a spy in his former life and there was an outstanding mission and the KGB of the past were trying to catch up with him to finish it off. Sean, however, had convinced nobody other than himself with this diagnosis and Liam had decided to keep any future dreams firmly to himself.

No matter how he tried, he was unable to force himself back to sleep and with the noise of his mum and sister now up and moving around the house, he decided to get up.

As he went downstairs and into the lounge, he was surprised, not only because the television was on, a piece of the furniture rarely used till the early evening, but because his mum was watching it intensely, an event that only occurred during episodes of '*Coronation Street*' and never first thing in the morning. "What y' watchin' Mum?" he asked curiously, but was only answered with a loud '*shush*'. Liam shook his head and walked into the kitchen to get himself a bowl of Rice Krispies. His sister was sitting at the kitchen table huddled over a small mirror applying make up to her eyes, the rest of her cosmetics lay strewn across the table, leaving little room for Liam to put his bowl down. "Sure you've got enough room Mags?" he asked sarcastically, which served only to receive an equally sarcastic smile from his sister. Seeing that Margaret wasn't about to move her stuff and Liam daren't touch it for fear of her wrath, he sighed heavily to make his point and took himself and his breakfast back into the lounge to eat there.

He sat down in the armchair and started shovelling spoonfuls of cereal into his mouth as he stared uninterested at the programme on TV. Some man in a suit was stood talking to the camera with a load of busy looking people and rubble in the background. '*Not exactly Top of the Pops is it?*' he thought, wondering why his mum was taking such an interest. The noise of his munching and the constant snap, crackle and pop of his breakfast made his Mum glare at him, '*tut*' loudly and head over to the television to turn it up. Liam momentarily thought about sucking rather than chewing on the contents of his mouth, but decided against it especially as the now elevated volume on the TV was drowning out any evidence of him eating.

As the man on the television finished what he was saying, the scene changed to a newsreader sitting behind a desk looking quite morose. Liam guessed that the first man he saw must have been a reporter ...'*Our man first at the scene,*' he thought. '*Bit like Klark Kent!*'

"And there it is," the newsreader said. "The carnage at the Grand Hotel in Brighton that has claimed the lives of five people and injured many more. The Conservative conference that was to be led by the Prime Minister Margaret Thatcher this day, the twelfth of October, has ..."

Liam stopped eating and stared at the TV thinking, *'Twelfth of October, why do I know that date?'* He listened more closely, racking his brain as to why the date was familiar, as the Newsreader continued,

"... Minister, who was herself unhurt, vowed to bring the people responsible for the bombing to justice and in a strong display of defiance, has stated that the conference will still go ahead ..."

Bridie Connor stood up and went to turn the TV off but was stopped, and surprised, by Liam's request. "No Mum, leave it on, please," he said. "I just want to watch it for a while." Bridie looked slightly bemused but left the television on nonetheless.

"Well make sure you get yourself ready for school soon Liam," she said. "And turn it off when you've finished."

As he nodded his understanding, she looked at him for a moment and frowned a little before heading off into the kitchen.

Liam's mind was racing. He had heard that date mentioned before for some reason but just couldn't remember where or when. Was it in his dream? Had he heard it at school? Did Sean mention it for some reason? Somebody's birthday perhaps? *'No,'* he thought, *'none of the above.'* So what then? As he dug deep into his memory bank, the recollection of past events came flooding back, hitting him like a freight train and causing him to drop his spoon into his breakfast bowl, splashing milk onto his pyjamas. "Shit!" he exclaimed, brushing off the droplets of milk in a half hearted manner as he recounted the words he had overheard back in May whilst outside this very room.

102

'The bastards will have no choice but to listen!' and *'It'll be Irelands voice they'll be hearing come the twelfth of October!!'*

He tried to work out what it all meant. Who will have to listen? What or who is Ireland's voice and who will be listening today? He looked back at the television now displaying more scenes of the devastation at the hotel in Brighton and listened in horror as the newsreader enlightened the viewing nation.

"The IRA has confirmed that they are responsible for the bombing at the Grand Hotel, stating that *'Today is the time for Ireland's voice to be heard*!'"

Liam slumped back into his chair feeling sick to his stomach. Is this what his Uncle Joe was talking about? Could it possibly be that he was responsible for what had happened at that Hotel? Worse still, was his Dad involved? Liam's head spun and he felt a wave of nausea wash over him. He jumped up from his seat causing his bowl of breakfast to fall onto the floor. Hearing the noise, Bridie started walking back towards the lounge only to see a sallow looking Liam rush out and up the stairs.

"Liam?" she called after him, wondering what was wrong, but got no reply as the bathroom door slammed shut. Frowning, she looked into the lounge and saw the spilt cereal and bowl on the carpet. She went up the stairs and knocked on the bathroom door. "Are you ok Liam?" she enquired with concern.

"Yeah, fine," Liam replied. "I just needed to go ... sorry!"

"Are you sick sweetheart?" Bridie pressed.

"No, no ... I'm fine Mum, honestly," Liam lied as he sat behind the bathroom door trying to gather his thoughts, willing his Mum to leave him alone.

"Well, Ok!" she conceded, unconvinced. "But call me if you need anything won't you?"

"Yeah. Thanks mum, but I'm ok," Liam answered, trying to sound as 'okay' as possible.

Bridie stood by the door for a while before she headed back down the stairs and into the lounge. As she started to clean up the mess, she couldn't help but listen again to the television as the newsreader reported.

"... in the wake of this atrocity, which happened just five hours ago, the IRA have released a further statement to the press saying that, *'Mrs. Thatcher will now realise that Britain cannot occupy our country and torture our prisoners and shoot our people in their own streets and get away with it'* and with the news that Mrs. Thatcher was relatively unscathed in the attack, added. *'Today we were unlucky but remember, we only have to be lucky once, you will have to be lucky always. Give Ireland peace and there will be no more war!'* ... Shadow Cabinet Ministers have today pledged their support and ..."

Despite the immediate concern for her son, a faint smile appeared on Bridie's face as she turned off the television and thought of her husband's contribution to the day's National News.

###

Sean listened intently to his friend's story without interruption or wisecracking. He could tell from the look on Liam's face and the tone of his voice, that this was a serious matter and there was no room for joviality. When Liam had finished, Sean looked at him for a while, wide eyed and silent, partly in disbelief at the tale he had just been told and partly because he was wanting to consider all the facts before answering. Liam had presented a good case why he thought his dad and Uncle Joseph may have been responsible for the bombing in Brighton earlier that morning, but Sean just couldn't, or wouldn't, accept it. "Nah, no way ... your dad? ... Nah ... You probably heard it wrong!" he said hoping that Liam would agree and leave it at what it most probably was, a coincidence.

"I know what I heard Sean," Liam retorted. "And why shouldn't my dad be involved? After all, he's Irish, he's away all the time doing God knows what and I know my Uncle Joe hates the English. It all makes sense!"

"No, it doesn't Liam," Sean insisted. "It makes no sense at all ... Your dad in the IRA?... think about it. It sounds stupid"

"Stupid?!" Liam said angrily. "Then what about the stuff I found in ...?" He stopped abruptly as if realising that too much had been already been said.

"What stuff?" Sean asked with a puzzled look.

"Nothing, it doesn't matter ... let's get into school," Liam added quietly and began to walk off.

"Whoa hang on!" Sean said and took hold of Liam's arm. "C'mon, what stuff?"

Liam looked at Sean and sighed. He then glanced around his surroundings awkwardly as if trying to find the right words or perhaps wondering if he should say anything at all. Finally, he looked back at Sean and began, "Promise you will keep this to yourself!" Sean gave him a look of mild shock, as if that comment should have gone without saying. "Yeah, sorry," Liam said and pressed on. "Well," he started, "A couple of months ago, just before we were going on holiday, my mum asked me to get a suitcase out of her wardrobe. Thing is, when I looked, it wasn't there so I checked my dad's and saw one in there. I pulled it out, but it felt like it had something in it so I decided to take a look, you know, to empty it out really?" Sean nodded as Liam continued. "When I opened it, there were a load of old newspaper cuttings inside and some sort of green book, like an instruction book."

"Mate," Sean interjected. "What's all this got t'do with your dad being in the IRA ... I collect football cards but it doesn't make me the centre forward of United!"

"Sean!" Liam said firmly, raising his tone a little. He looked around again but lowered his voice as he continued. "The cuttings were all about different bombings that have happened in England, going back ages and the green book looked like some sort of army manual, though I didn't get a good look 'cause my mum started coming upstairs so I had to put them back pretty quick!"

Sean looked a little taken aback by this revelation, but initially refrained from speaking as he pondered for a moment on the additional facts presented. He then frowned as he looked at Liam and finally said, "Why didn't you tell me about this before or whilst we were away?"

"Because," Liam replied, "I didn't think anything of it until today, it didn't seem important"

"Exactly!" Sean said. "It's not important. It's just coincidence and it will take a lot more to convince me that your dad is an IRA bomber bloke, as it should you!" He put a hand on Liam's shoulders before continuing. "Mate, think about it yeah. Your dad is well sound, and your mum is too of course, but I just don't think it makes any sense that he would blow shit up, do you, really?" Liam shrugged and began to wonder if he had in fact over reacted to the morning's news bulletin. "Plus," Sean said. "The cops would have been round your house pretty quick if your dad was part of it wouldn't they?" He smiled at Liam before adding. "C'mon. Let's get going. The first five minutes in Saint *Moan*-ica's will take your mind off it!"

The pair set off towards the school with Sean rambling on about Louise Bevan ... again. Liam listened and nodded and added his bit where necessary but in the back of his mind, despite agreeing with Sean's speech logically vindicating his dad of any IRA involvement, he couldn't help but feel some small doubt, harbour some slight suspicion. As they entered the gates of St. Monica's, Liam stood open mouthed and scowled at a presence that was standing by the foyer of the school. A presence that caused an immense rush of stark realisation to hit home, a presence that was to beg a very poignant question. *'What if his taunts and speculations turned*

106

out to be right after all?' Thankfully, Matthew Walker hadn't seen the news that morning.

To the surprise of Sean, and Louise, now with them, Liam strode off quickly and disappeared around the side of the building. Once out of sight of everyone, he sat down against a wall breathing heavily, wondering if he was having some sort of panic attack. He actually felt like crying. Trying desperately to control himself, he thought. *'Shit Liam c'mon, calm down man ... Sean's right, he has to be ... there's no real proof, not really ... and it's your dad you're thinking of here ... as if!'*

After what seemed an age, but was in fact a few minutes, Liam had calmed down enough that his breathing was steady and his highly emotive state had returned to the status quo. He shook his head and stood up, thinking *'Walker is a dick anyway!'* Feeling slightly better, he headed back round to the front of the school building and rejoined a concerned Sean and Louise. A couple of paraphrased sentences between the two boys confirmed to Sean that Liam was ok and had put the morning's events deep into his memory bank. Despite this, it would be years later that an unexpected event would unlock that memory bank and convert Liam's suspicions into fact.

###

Chapter 16

December 1984

The man felt uneasy. And with good reason. After all, it was he who, in the past, had been responsible for putting other men in the position that he now found himself in. The difference being, he mused, was that most of those other men had deserved it. Traitors, grasses, men not fit to fight alongside him or class themselves as worthy to the cause. On many occasions, his services had been called upon to deliver those men to a *Court Martial*, a hearing to determine and decide the fate of military personal accused of breaking rules and regulations. But in contrast to the rules and regulations of the British Army, a finding of guilt at these proceedings would not result in a dishonourable discharge or imprisonment, it would result in death.

He had witnessed so called *hard* men crumble and literally soil their pants when the decision of Judge and Jury had offered them no reprieve and he had smiled mockingly as the scum had been led away to be *dealt with* accordingly. There was no place in his heart for mourning the weak. *'But why am I here?'* the man thought, trying to come up with a logical explanation, though his efforts to find that logic were in vain.

He guessed that a couple of hours or so had now passed since he was driven from his home to an unknown location by an unknown driver and led into the room where he now sat alone, waiting. Other than relaying a message from the hierarchy, the driver had said nothing to him and gave no clues as to the reason behind his superior's invitation to present himself for a *little chat,* an invitation he knew was not open to refusal.

He tried to look around the room but was unable to see past the bright light shining directly into his face. He knew that it was cold and from the musty odour of damp, imagined that it hadn't benefited from heating in a long time. From the inky black darkness beyond the glare of the spotlight, he knew that there were no windows, a feature designed to discourage any thoughts of escape. *'But why would I want to escape?'* he thought. *'That's for the guilty and I've done nothing wrong!'* He shuffled nervously in his seat, realising that the strategy of leaving somebody alone in the cold and dark to *loosen their minds*, was being applied to him, a strategy that, ironically, he had applied to others on many occasions. He shivered slightly, though not entirely due to the cold.

"Focus man!" he said to himself before getting up from his seat to pace the room. As he racked his brains for the reason behind the summons, he became aware of a drum sound far off in the distance. He stopped and cocked his head, trying to establish the direction it was coming from and how far it was away. As if woken from a trance, he snapped back into the reality of the room and mentally cursed. *'What the fuck are you doing listening out for fucking marching bands?'* he thought. *'C'mon ... Concentrate ... why are you here? ... why?'* "Why?!" he suddenly shouted out into the darkness of the room. Nobody replied.

He sat back down on the chair and put his head in his hands trying to think, but found it impossible to gather his thoughts. How could he, with the sound of that fucking drum getting louder? His hands felt cold and clammy against the unshaven skin of his face and as he pulled them slowly away, he saw, to his surprise, that they were trembling. He clapped them together and stood up again quickly, knocking the chair over as he did so.

"Hello!!" he called out. "Is anybody home?!" But again, nobody replied. He shook his head, trying not to listen to the drum sound that now seemed to be all around him. "What do you want from me?!" he shouted again, though he knew he wouldn't be finding out just yet. After a few moments, he picked up his chair and sat back down again. "Fuck yus all then," he said quietly but loudly added. "And stop that fuckin' drummin'!!" He leant back into his chair and closed his eyes, feeling his temples throb. As he listened in his own darkness, a smile appeared on his face. A smile that soon developed into a cackle as he suddenly realised that the drum he could hear, was in fact the sound of his own heart beating heavily in his chest and resounding in his inner ears.

He quickly sat upright, blinking, as a door beyond the table opened. Shielding his eyes from the glare of the spotlight, he tried to focus on a large silhouetted frame that entered the room, but as the door was closed, the new arrival was quickly encased in the darkness, retaining anonymity. "Why am I here?" the man asked the figure, now sat opposite him, remaining in the shadows. "What have I done?"

The figure stayed silent for a while before pushing a pack of cigarettes and a lighter across the table, revealing a large, powerful looking hand. "Smoke?" was all he asked, before retracting his hand back into the darkness. The man quickly removed a cigarette from the pack, lit it and inhaled deeply. As he exhaled, the smoke hung in the beam of light like a wall of thick smog trapped within a yellow prism.

"So?" he asked, before dragging on the cigarette again. "What kind of shit am I in?"

Both of the dark figure's hands appeared in the light as he clasped them together and rested them on the table. "It seems that the Commander is a little displeased with you son," a voice said in a deep course tone. "It appears that you have given him incorrect information and he would like to know why?"

"What?" the man replied frowning. "The Commander? What information? I don't understand!"

"Come now. Surely you can remember? Or do you need some help with your memory?" the figure asked menacingly. The man swallowed hard. He knew the sort of help that was on offer, as he was usually the one offering it. But it was not the sort of assistance you would willingly subscribe to. The thing was, he genuinely didn't have a clue, but was all too aware that a reply of that nature wouldn't have been good enough in this situation. He thought hard but could only remember speaking to the Commander on one occasion, in confidence and that was only to air his concerns about ...

'Shit!' he thought as the recollection of the meeting came back. *'Surely they didn't think!'* "Jesus!" he said sharply. "Could he not see that it was genuine concern ... there was no malice intended, not towards *him*. Jesus!" The man didn't see the figure smile from under his cloak of darkness, satisfied that they were now both reading from the same chapter. He watched as the man lit another cigarette from the burning end of the first one and waited a while before speaking again.

"A good man nearly died because of your *genuine concern*, a concern you should have maybe taken up with him directly, don't you think?"

"I couldn't," the man replied. "I mean, he wouldn't have listened to me, that's why I ..."

"Went telling tales?" the figure interrupted.

"That's shite and you know it," the man responded angrily. "It's not my fault the Boss reacted the wrong way!"

"Or maybe he reacted exactly as you thought he would," said the figure. "After all, *retiring* the man in question would have gotten you a step further up the ladder, no?"

"Fuck you!" the man shouted, standing up quickly.

"Sit down!" the figure barked back. "Now!!"

The man hesitated for a few moments, before retaking his seat. Things were not going well and he realised that there needed to be a lot of convincing, if not pleading, before this was over. "Look," he said, "I had no idea it would go that far

... it was just ... it needed to be said and I thought I was doing the right thing!"

"Aye, I'm sure you were son," the figure replied softly. "I'm sure you were ... so be it."

The man looked up towards the dark figure surprised yet wary. Was that it? Was it over? He couldn't tell for sure, but that last comment sounded like it. There was a long pause before either of them spoke again, but it was the voice in the shadows that broke the silence with a question that was far removed from anything they had just been speaking about. "D'you know that Paddy McGinley's been arrested for the Brighton operation?"

"What?" the man replied confused. "Paddy arrested? No ... when?"

"Aye," the figure said. "Yesterday. They found his fingerprints apparently. Looks like he's in a heap load o' shite to me!" He paused and studied the man opposite him lighting yet another cigarette, before adding. "You wouldn't know anything about that now would ya?"

"Why would I?" the man replied, frowning.

"No reason," the figure said. "It's just that, in my line of work, I get to hear lots of rumours. You know how it is?"

The man looked nervous, wondering where this particular line of questioning was leading. "Well, whatever rumours you have heard on this occasion are obviously bollocks ... I had no idea!"

"Maybe," the figure replied. "But perhaps you can answer me something else?"

"What?" the man said quizzically.

For the first time since being in the room, the dark figure leant into the light revealing a large, bulldog looking face sat upon a thick neck. His nose looked like it had been broken several times, no doubt the result from years of street fighting and a three inch scar ran up his left cheek, the legacy of an inaccurate gunman. His dark piercing eyes shone in the bright glow and remained unblinking as he stared at the man across the table. When he spoke this time, the tone of his voice was like a low growl, demanding an answer to his question. "Have y'bin turned?"

The man stared open mouthed, as the colour drained from his complexion. He knew all too well what the questioner meant and it was a question that no member of the party would ask without strong reason. He could feel himself shake slightly as he prepared to answer the question of whether or not he had become an informant for the Police or the British Government.

A simple 'no' would not suffice in this situation as he knew that even the wrong tone of voice or misinterpreted body language could see a man condemned, regardless of his innocence. He could feel panic setting in. Despite knowing how serious the question was, his mind wouldn't allow his body to react accordingly and from a rush of nervous adrenaline, he began to giggle.

"Did I say something funny?!" the figure demanded angrily, which only seemed to fuel the man's laughter more. And then, as suddenly as it had started, the man's laughter stopped as he regained some composure. He ran his fingers through his hair and sighed heavily. With his face dripping heavily in sweat, he leaned across the table and looked directly into the figures eyes.

"I'm no fucking grass!" he said angrily. "So fuck you and your rumours and go rot in hell!" The man slumped back into his chair waiting for the figure to speak. It was some time before the voice in the darkness asked.

"When did they approach you son? Was it money they offered or immunity perhaps?" The man shook his head unable to believe that the bulldog opposite was still fishing for an admission. "C'mon son, give me something," he added. "Show me that I'm wrong so we can all go home and forget about this nasty little episode!"

The man snorted in defiance. "Fuck you!"

The dark figure sighed, realising that this might be harder than he thought. "Your lack of cooperation disappoints me," he said calmly.

"I told you!" the man spat. "I'm no fuckin' grass!"

"Yes, but I'm sure that Paddy won't see it that way, sitting in the Maze, do you?"

The man glared at the interrogator, clenched his fists and brought them down heavily onto the table. "Look!" he began, angrily. "Paddy's fuck up has nothing to do with me ... he got careless and that's all there is to it. So whatever fuck-wit has spun you a yarn of shite, I suggest you speak to them and leave me about my business!"

The interrogator removed the cigarettes and lighter from the table, stood up and started to walk towards the door. The man looked on with a small feeling of relief. "And if you're off to speak to the Commander," he called, "tell him from me that it's probably just as well that that drunken eejit is in the Maze, for all our sakes! ... If he's stupid enough to leave his fingerprints all over a fuckin' swipe card, who knows what shite his incompetence could bring for the rest of us!"

The interrogator stopped and stood with his back to the man for a few moments. He then turned around and returned to the table, leaning back into the light. "That's funny Son," he said, looking at the man with a slight smile on his face. "I don't remember ever mentioning a swipe card, do you?!"

As he felt the world around him collapse in a moment's breath, the man remembered little of the subsequent events. He vaguely remembered two further men entering the room once the interrogator had spoken into a two way radio and vaguely remembered how he came about his now swollen and bruised face and body. He didn't remember how he came to be in the rear of a car with two men sitting either side of him, but knew beyond all doubt, what his fate now was.

As he looked down through slatted and tearful eyes, Robbie O'Neil could definitely not remember at what point he had wet himself.

###

Chapter 17

June 1986

Nearly two years had passed since Liam, together with the majority of the local children, had become a pupil of St. Monica's High school and for him, it seemed to have flown by. He had settled in far more quickly than he had anticipated and noticed that even Sean seemed to be enjoying school life, probably helped by the fact that he and Louise Duffy were now going steady. What also amazed Liam, was that Sean was now only getting one detention a month as opposed to one a week which, again, he put down to the influence of Louise.

Despite there being no official line on his own relationship status, Liam was only too happy to spend time with Jeanette Cho-Lin and it was taken as read by any onlooker, that they were an item, a situation that Liam neither confirmed nor denied. The truth was that Liam found a certain solace in Jeanette, a comfort that he sought eighteen months previously when his Uncle Robbie had very suddenly passed away. Not that Liam was close to his Uncle, but witnessing the subsequent grief of his mum was enough to affect him to the point of withdrawal. Jeanette had been there for him from the start of that episode, listening patiently as Liam told her how his mum had become a different person since Robbie's death. Jen had found it prudent to speak only when she felt he needed her support, showing maturity beyond her years and her help and advice was, without doubt, the saving grace of Liam's mental state.

In the weeks that followed her brother's passing, Bridie Connor appeared to become more and more irritable to the point where Liam would find himself not wanting to speak to her, even for the smallest of things. The initial explanation of Uncle Robbie's death, was put down to a heart attack though Liam, for some reason, suspected that this was not the truth. What he did know, is that the loss of his mum's brother in that December of '84, not only put paid to any form of a happy Christmas that year, but from the many heated arguments between his mum and dad that followed, changed the usual smooth running of things in the Connor household, indefinitely.

Sean had also proved his worth as a friend over that difficult period and for a while, irony played its twisted part in that Liam spent most of his time at Sean's house. Liam truly appreciated his friend's empathy, but wished, after a couple of weeks of going back for tea, that there had been more on the menu than cheese or peanut butter sandwiches.

Though, as the great healer that is time went by, Bridie's mourning period gently subsided and she eventually became a close picture of her former self. Normality, in a sense, returned to the home and it pleased Liam (and Sean) no end that Irish stew and good home cooking was back on the menu. Despite the return of the status quo, Liam still felt that a piece of his mum was missing, that something just wasn't there. Granted, she was no longer irritable and had in fact found some laughter again, but Liam sensed that a part of the Mum he knew pre-December 1984, was noticeable in its absence. Sadly, it didn't take him long to recognise that it was the once bright sparkle in her Irish eyes, which had now gone.

###

June 22 1986

After watching Argentina beat England 2-1 in the World Cup earlier that evening, Liam lay in his bed unable to sleep. He felt that he had been tossing and turning for what seemed like hours, but when he looked at his clock, he was amazed to see that it was only ten thirty. He got up and headed for the bathroom, deciding that a toilet break and a drink of water was probably what he needed before he could sleep. As he came out from his room onto the darkness of the landing, he heard the raised voices of his mum and dad from downstairs, seemingly arguing, again. He was about to ignore it but stopped and listened as he heard his mum mention his name. "And where would Liam be then?" she asked in a sad tone.

"Bridie," he heard his dad say. "Everything will be fine ... what happened to Robbie was..."

"What happened to Robbie was a disgrace!" she cut in angrily. "But what happens if you lose their favour too? What then Michael? Will that be for the sake of the fucking cause as well?!"

Liam's eyes widened and his jaw dropped open. He had never heard his mum swear, ever, and realised that whatever it was they were talking about, must have been very serious. So serious in fact, that now probably wasn't the best time to eavesdrop. He also remembered what had happened the last time he'd listened into a conversation whilst outside the lounge door. He shook his head to dismiss any thoughts about sticking around and quickly retreated back into his bedroom. Had he stayed and listened, he might have heard his dad telling his mum that there was no choice but to continue with the campaigns of the IRA to make sure he *didn't* lose favour. He may too have heard him agree that Robbie's death was a disgrace but also, heard him ask Bridie if she would rather her brother lived whilst, as a result of his conscience, she became a widow.

Back in his bed, Liam's mind raced with multiple versions of what the conversation between his parents might have been about but this only served to bring on a slight headache. Convincing himself that he would rather not know, he decided to focus on the earlier football match and how England had lost a war in front of millions of viewers. Unbeknown to Liam, his youthful innocence and naive loyalty to the three lions would, in the future, be sharply transformed by a cruel twist of fate. With his assistance, England would continue to lose battles. But of a kind far removed from that of football.

###

Chapter 18

14th May 1990

Sean walked slowly across Joey's field, half heartedly kicking a football along as he made his way towards his friends sitting on the grass near the entrance to the woods. He had not had a very good day at school and it didn't help that Louise had had a go at him for receiving yet another detention, a detention, incidentally, he thought was completely unjustified. After all, it wasn't his fault the chair had broken. *'Surely,'* he thought, (and had argued earlier) *'if school chairs aren't designed to be leant back on, then they shouldn't be supplied to schools!'* Et voila, a detention was imposed.

Not that he cared much anymore. In a few weeks, he would be out of that school and out of the education system forever, starting his new job as a trainee car mechanic at Ken's garage, making a mint. Fifty five pounds a week to be exact. Result. He couldn't understand why Liam, Louise and Jeanette had opted to go on to college, thus expanding their *prison* sentences, willingly. It just didn't make any sense to Sean whatsoever. *'Bet they'll wanna sponge off me though,'* he thought, then smiled as he silently mused. *'Well sorry hombres, no can do!'* As he reached his three friends, he smiled and nodded at Liam and then looked at Louise who merely shot him a disconcerted look, shook her head and then looked away. "What?" Sean asked innocently.

"You know *what* Sean," she answered sharply. "Getting yet another DT, that's what!"

Sean sighed heavily, threw his school bag off his shoulder and sat down atop his football. He stared across the field for a moment before turning to Liam. "Fancy a kick about Condor?" he asked, which resulted in a loud tut from Louise.

"Three and you're in?" suggested Liam as he stood up and removed his blazer.

"Yeah," replied Sean. "But you're in net first ok?"

"Yeah, whatever," Liam agreed as the two of them made their way to set up makeshift goal posts.

Louise and Jeanette sat in silence for a while as they watched the boys play. After a few minutes, Louise turned to her friend and asked. "So, have you kissed him yet?"

Jeanette laughed, partly through her friend's directness and partly through embarrassment that the answer was in fact, no. "It never seems to be the right moment," she said sullenly. "Either that or he doesn't fancy me."

"Oh my God!" Louise said slightly shocked. "How can you say that? He well fancies you. And as for that *not the right moment* excuse, well..."

"Well what?" Jen asked defensively. "It never seems the right time, that's all!"

"Jen," Louise began. "You two have been together for years, how have you never found the right time? That's just a cop out!"

"Firstly Miss Duffy," Jeanette offered, "me and Liam are not officially together in case you forgot, even though we do see a lot of each other and secondly, it is not a cop out, I'm just ..." She stopped short, sighed and looked to the ground.

"Just what?" Louise pressed. "Shy? Scared? A lesbo? What?"

Jeanette laughed again. "Well I'm definitely not a lesbian ... but, I am a bit scared maybe."

"Scared of what? Liam?" Louise asked incredulously.

"No," Jeanette replied. "Not of Liam, of me. Well, not of me exactly, but of what I am ... oh, I don't know!" Seeing the look of confusion now on Louise's face, she took a deep breath and continued. "Look, I'm Chinese yeah?"

"Really?" Louise interjected with a smile and fake look of surprise. "Chinese eh? I hadn't even noticed!"

"Yeah yeah ok," said Jeanette. "But Liam is Irish Catholic or something and I'm not sure if he's allowed to, you know, go with anybody that isn't, Irish. So I don't want to scare him off by forcing myself on him 'cause I like him being around. Do you know what I mean?"

Louise looked at Jeanette and genuinely felt a little sorrow. Here was a girl that obviously fancied the pants off Liam, but would rather do nothing about it than run the risk of losing him as a friend. But as much as Louise thought it was quite endearing, she also thought that Jen needed educating, not to mention a little push in the right direction. "Jen," she began. "It's the twentieth century not the dark ages. Liam isn't like that. Firstly, he's not really that Irish and secondly, when does he ever go to church?" She paused for a moment before adding. "And thirdly, Sean told me that Liam told him that he would love to snog you!" Louise saw that she now had the full attention of Jen, a girl who was obviously seeking persuasion and encouragement to make the necessary step. Ok, so the *thirdly* bit was a little white lie, but what the hell. Nobody said that playing Cupid didn't allow for a slight bend in the truth now did they?

"What? He said that?" Jen asked with a smile. "When exactly?"

"Ages ago," Louise lied. "But like you, he doesn't think you'd be interested!"

"Oh," was all Jeanette offered, before turning to look at Liam, now wrestling with Sean on the ground. As Liam got up from the floor, leaving a grass stained, chuckling Sean in his wake, he glanced at Jen and gave her a smile that made her tummy fill with an army of butterflies. She smiled back coyly and, sensing somebody else watching her, turned to see a smiling Louise looking back at her.

"Talk about being smitten," Louise began. "You two really have got it bad. Such a shame that neither of you want to make the first move, eh Jen?" She raised her eyebrows indicating that her point had been made.

Jen smiled back with a look of understanding that the issue had to be resolved, sooner rather than later. *'Watch this space Lou,'* she thought as she turned again to look at Liam, now pinned to the ground under the bulk of Sean.

###

Later, as they were all heading home, Sean and Louise, with their earlier quarrel forgot, walked arm in arm, trailing behind Liam and Jeanette. Louise whispered something to Sean, who then stared at her with a puzzled look on his face. "Why?" he asked in a low tone so as not to be overheard by his friends.

Louise glowered at him and said, "Just do it!"

Confused as to where this was going, Sean complied and called out to Liam. "Oh, by the way Li," he started. "I can't come to yours tonight mate. I have to ... er ... go to the library ... ow!" He winced as Louise gave him a quick dig to the ribs with her elbow, clearly not impressed with his feeble attempt at an excuse.

Liam stopped and turned to his friend, a look of astonishment on his face. "You?" he asked. "Going to the library? Why? Have they got free food on?" The girls chuckled though Sean didn't see the funny side.

"Ha ha, very funny Connor!" he replied.

"Ok then, why?" Liam asked, feeling a little suspicious.

"What?" Sean replied, slightly flummoxed. He wasn't expecting to give a reason and a little panic began to set in. "Oh ... Why?" he repeated Liam's question, now playing for time. "Right ... well I, erm ..." he spluttered hopelessly and quickly glanced at Louise, desperate for support.

"Oh, he's helping me," Louise intervened calmly. "I need to get a couple of books out which are a bit heavy and Sean offered to help me carry them." She turned to Sean and continued. "It's nothing to be embarrassed about Sean. It doesn't make you any less of a 'man' helping your girlfriend out you know?" Sean guffawed pathetically and felt himself turning red as his nerve began to falter, wishing the ground would open up and swallow him whole.

Liam frowned and studied the pair for a moment waiting for the punch line to be delivered. Sean felt a bead of sweat trickle down his armpit whilst Louise stood there smiling as innocently as her face would allow. Realising that they appeared to be serious, Liam raised his eyebrows and simply said, "Ok, no worries. My mum's not home till late anyway, so it would only have been a sandwich for tea." He turned back around unaware of Sean letting out a long silent breath as the four of them continued walking.

Sean looked at Louise. "What did I have to lie for?" he whispered, searching for an explanation, but she was far too busy plotting her next move to worry about him.

"Hey Liam," she called. "What sort of sandwiches are they?"

Sean raised his eyes to the heavens and thought, *'Oh God, now what?'* Liam stopped for a second time and turned around again, now completely puzzled. Even Jeanette looked confused.

"What?" they asked in unison.

"Sandwiches?" Louise repeated. "At yours. What's on them?" Seeing the vacant expression on Liam's face, she continued. "Liam, it's not rocket science. What will you put on your sandwiches? Y'know, for tea?" Liam shook his head feeling slightly confused, searching for an answer to a very bizarre question.

"I don't know," he replied honestly before adding, "Cheese? Peanut butter? Whatever we have in. I don't really know. Why?"

"Jen likes peanut butter, don't you Jen?" Louise said, ignoring Liam's question, and looked at her friend. Liam also looked at Jeanette as if her reply might make some sense of the whole conversation.

"Do I?" was all she offered, totally bewildered.

"Course you do. Everybody likes peanut butter, don't they Sean?" Louise turned to a now distressed and gormless looking Sean who stared back at her blankly.

'Why are you bringing me into it again?' he thought as he turned to Jeanette, smiled painfully and merely nodded, the power of speech temporarily gone.

In the few moments of silence that followed, all eyes were back on Louise. "Hey, I know!" she said in a false *eureka moment* way. "Why don't you ask Jen for tea Liam? That way you won't be bored 'cause Sean's not there and she can try peanut butter at the same time!" Jen smiled and looked to the ground, now realising Louise's plan. Liam looked a bit flustered and went slightly pink, that didn't go unnoticed by Sean.

"Maybe he doesn't want to, *Lou!*" he said, quickly finding his voice and emphasising her name to indicate that the subject should be dropped.

"Shut up, *Sean!*" she replied and scowled, indicating that *she* wasn't about to. "Course he does, why wouldn't he?" She turned back to Liam and added. "What do you think Li?"

"Well," Liam replied, "I suppose I could." He turned to Jeanette and added. "If you fancy it that is?"

'Hell yes!' Jeanette thought, but merely smiled at Liam and said. "That would be nice. If you don't mind that is?"

'Hell no!' Liam thought, but casually replied. "Course not!"

"That's settled then," said Louise merrily. "But let's get moving 'cause I felt rain then!" She looked up at the greying sky and then back at Jen, giving her a quick wink and a smile before they all set off again.

"What the hell was all that about?" Sean asked Louise quietly as they walked. "All that '*Sean's carrying my books and loves peanut butter*' crap ... I felt a right twat!"

Without looking at Sean, Louise smiled and simply replied. "Female prowess Seanster, female prowess!"

By the time they had gotten to the exit of Joey's field, the heavens had opened and the rain fell with a relentless ferocity. The four friends began to run, shouting their goodbyes to each other as they split up in pairs. Sean and Louise headed off in the direction of the library (though Sean had no idea why) whilst Liam and Jeanette continued the short journey to the Connor household. As they quickly approached his house, Liam tried to get the door key out of his pocket but in his haste and because of the wet, it slipped from his hand, falling to the ground. "Shit!" he exclaimed and stopped to pick it up, causing a lagging Jeanette to run into the back of him and knock him unceremoniously to the floor. Sitting in the bouncing rain with a look of utter shock on his face, Liam could only watch as Jeanette tried unsuccessfully not to laugh.

"Oh God!" she said through the giggling. "I'm so sorry. Are you ok?"

He wasn't really, but as laughter can be infectious, it wasn't long before Liam was also seeing the funny side and joining in with a highly amused Jeanette. He picked himself up but decided to walk the remaining few yards to his front door. After all, what was the point in running now?

Liam entered the hallway of his home first and attempted to shake the water from his hair, cursing the weather as he did. "Hello!" he called out, but then remembered that his mum and sister had gone to some makeup party somewhere and wouldn't be home till much later. When Jeanette entered and closed the door behind her, Liam turned around and physically felt his jaw drop open. He saw that the rain had soaked through Jen's blouse causing it to cling to her body and reveal a profile of ample breasts, breasts that Liam didn't even realise she had. The cold wetness of the cloth against her skin had caused her nipples to become erect and protrude through her bra, causing Liam to feel a stir between his loins. He wanted to look away, but remained fixated on the vision before him. "Liam!" Jeanette softly scolded before crossing her arms over her chest. Liam snapped back into reality and felt himself quickly redden, not only at being caught staring, but because he was now one hundred percent sure that his erection was totally visible to Jeanette.

"Oh, I, er ... sorry ... I didn't mean ... I just," he blurted out and looked down as he feebly attempted to hide his manhood by brushing sodden dirt off the knees of his trousers.

"Have you got a towel then?" Jeanette interrupted, smiling.

"A towel? ... Yeah, a towel, right, hang on," Liam replied, keeping his head down. He raced off up the stairs to find one, thankful for the *get out* clause that Jen had just presented to him. Searching through the airing cupboard for the nicest towel he could find, he started to mentally chastise himself. *'God Connor you dick, what were you playin' at! ... She well caught you lookin' at her tits! ... Shit, she's gonna think I'm a perv or something now!'* As he pulled out a towel, he looked down to his crotch and quietly added. "And you better disappear as well you sneaky bastard ... like now!" When he finally went back downstairs, he was surprised to see that Jeanette was no longer in the hallway. "Where are ya Jen?" he called.

"I'm in here," she replied from the lounge. "Can I put your fire on, it's freezing?"

"Yeah, course you can," he replied. Before he entered the lounge, he checked himself in the hall mirror to make sure that his redness, and his growth, had subsided enough to be no longer visible. Feeling a little nervous, he took a deep breath and walked into the room. "Oh Shit, sorry! ... Shit!" he gasped as he found Jeanette kneeling in front of gas fire, blouse removed. He turned away and was starting back out of the room until Jeanette stopped him.

"It's ok Liam, you can come in you know, it's only a bra!" she started. "But I had to take my top off 'cause it's soaking. Now please can I have that towel?"

Liam hesitated for a moment. *'Only a bra?'* he thought. *'Yeah, that helps ... not!'* He eventually turned back round and walked over to Jeanette, his arm outstretched offering the towel.

"Thanks," she said as she took it from him and started to dry her hair. Liam supposed that he ought to have left the room, but just couldn't bring himself to do it. As he stood there, watching, Jeanette looked up and smiled. "What?" was all she said.

Totally unscripted and with no pre-planned agenda on his mind, Liam simply, but honestly answered. "You're beautiful!" Now it was Jen's turn to blush, though she was truly flattered, and surprised, by the impromptu comment. She gazed at him for a second and then held out her hand which Liam took hold of instantly. He knelt down in front of her and, as if it was the obvious next step, leant in to kiss her. Jen responded without hesitation but, after a few moments, pulled quickly away. Liam looked a little disappointed then panicked slightly wondering if he had overstepped the mark. "Are you ok?" he asked genuinely, but thinking that she might slap him for taking advantage.

"Yeah," she replied. "But your wet shirt is freezing!" She smiled slightly and gently pulled on the bottom of his shirt before resting an encouraging hand on his arm. Liam frowned, looked down and started to feel his shirt.

"It's just a little damp," he pointed out. "It'll dry soon, 'specially in front of the fire!"

Seeing that he hadn't quite grasped the nettle, Jen sighed and decided to take control. "Liam, take your shirt off!" she instructed sharply and after a brief delay, the penny dropped and Liam finally complied.

Jeanette wrapped the towel around his shoulders and pulled him in close, meeting his lips with hers. It wasn't long before their hands were caressing and exploring each other's bodies, only stopping momentarily to allow Jen, assist a fumbling Liam to remove her bra. The inevitable intercourse that followed, was gentle and tender, a pleasure that neither had experienced before but took to as if they were well versed in the act of love making. Once they had finished, they lay entwined, silent but content, gently stroking each other. Liam started to chuckle causing Jeanette to lift her head and look at him, confused. "What you giggling at?" she asked softly.

"I was just thinking," Liam replied. "This certainly beats a peanut butter sandwich!"

"Oh, I don't know," Jeanette responded playfully. "I've not tried peanut butter yet!" The two of them laughed and then, in their embrace, kissed passionately again, the prequel to a second act of love making.

For the next hour, Liam and Jeanette lay in front of the fire enjoying their time together. They talked about anything and everything, revealing their hopes and dreams and some of their most intimate secrets. With each new topic of conversation, they felt a strong bond developing, a closeness that seemed to be pre-ordained by fate. This was their moment and for a short while at least, it seemed that there was no better place on earth than in the lounge of Liam Connor's home.

Later that night, after walking Jeanette home, Liam lay in bed thinking. He couldn't remember when he had felt so content and smiled when he thought of his now *official* girlfriend. As he closed his eyes, he assumed that sleep would be continuous, only broken, as usual, by his alarm clock the following morning. It was an assumption that would prove to be far from correct.

###

Chapter 19

0200hrs 15TH May 1990

Briefing room, Greater Manchester Police .

Detective Superintendent Peter Gale sat on the edge of his desk, waiting impatiently as numerous colleagues from varying ranks, filed into the large, fluorescent lit briefing room. He had been on duty for nearly fourteen hours, putting the final touches to an operation he and his team of Special Branch officers had been developing for the last six months and he felt surprisingly charged. This was to be the final input before operation *Daybreak* went live in less than three hours time and it was now that any ambiguities, any misunderstandings or any questions relating to the task, must be raised and addressed accordingly but swiftly. He wanted, no, *insisted*, that the outcome of this job would result in key arrests, good intelligence and heavy disruption to the network of *scum* they were targeting. Mistakes were not an option and he needed to be sure that everybody in that room, knew their role to the letter.

As the remainder of the officers entered the room, chatting amongst themselves and looking for places to sit or stand, Gale suddenly stood up. "Quick as you can please!" he gestured to the end of the line. "And can the last person in close the door behind them?"

Peter Gale had been in the Greater Manchester Police for twenty six years, the last four of which had been spent, on promotion to Superintendent, at Special Branch, working specifically with the anti terror unit. He had joined the regular Police force in February 1964, at a mere eighteen years of age, after acquiring a taste for it during two previous years as a cadet. After seven years of 'plodding' the beat, he felt that he had learnt his trade sufficiently enough to take (and subsequently pass) his Sergeants' exam, launching him into a whole new realm of responsibility that he thrived on. After a further two years in uniform, he yearned for new challenges and feeling that he had to change direction to enhance his skills and deal with *real* crime, he applied for a new posting in CID. His natural flair for detecting and arresting criminals and his no nonsense approach to the interviewing of suspects, yielded excellent results and earned him the endearing label of *The Copper's Cop*. However, once he had attained the rank of Detective Inspector in 1979, his dress sense, or more importantly his choice of Colombo style raincoat, replaced this initial title with that of *Mac*.

Working out of Bootle Street Police station in Manchester City centre, Mac and his team of Detectives worked tirelessly to bring many hardened criminals to justice and it was only a mere three years later, and at the relatively young age of 36, that his efforts were recognised and rewarded by his superiors, earning him the promotion to Detective Chief Inspector for the A Division of the Greater Manchester Police.

1984 saw the introduction of the Police and Criminals Evidence Act, or PACE as it was known and introduced various practices and procedures covering, to name but a few, the identification, detention, interviewing practices and basic treatment of any suspect or offender before, during and after arrest. Chief Inspector Gale, together with a great number of serving officers of that time, saw this act as pure interference from the Government, giving *scrotes* and defence solicitors, more ammunition to launch successful pleas of '*not guilty Your Honour!*' It wasn't that ninety nine percent of the criminals hadn't committed the crime in question, but with the new act in its infancy, many barristers were finding ways to challenge the processes and procedures of the judicial system and get their clients off on technicalities. Needless to say, Gale had aired his feelings many times during heated exchanges with the Crown Prosecution Service.

"Why is it that scum are walking away free men from these Courts?!" he had once angrily questioned a senior prosecuting barrister, after seeing a case he had been highly instrumental in, collapse on a mere technicality. "Does anybody actually possess any competence in this office?!"

"Chief Inspector," the barrister had rebuked in a calm tone. "If your officers were, shall we say, a little more diligent in their work practices, then this kind of thing would be relegated to the exception rather than the norm. Wouldn't you agree?"

Gale's anger rose. "I'm sure the family of the deceased will be greatly comforted knowing that some pompous fool had allowed his killer to walk free. Not because the murdering bastard was innocent, but because he wasn't given a fucking caution on tape. Wouldn't *you* agree?!" With that, Mac had stormed out of the CPS office to find the nearest pub. Less than two days later, he was receiving empathetic, yet slightly more than informal, words of advice from the Chief Constable regarding his unprofessional conduct. From that day on, the DCI vowed to himself never to have a case thrown out of court based on something his officers had failed or forgotten to do.

Gale's philosophy of detective ethics was simple; Work hard, play hard but hit the criminals harder. Though his legendary methods in obtaining *the truth* from suspects was frowned upon by some higher ranking officers, especially given the advent of current legislation, their opinions and lips remained tightly sealed. Partly because Gale's efforts had become publicly revered by the Chief Constable and partly because it was common knowledge that they shared the same Masonic Lodge. It was therefore no surprise, that in 1986, Mac was promoted again to the rank of Detective Superintendent and gratefully offered the prestigious position that he now held. This came with an added double bonus. The first was that Gale was able to take up residence in the resource rich headquarters that was Chester House and the second, he would only be three floors down from the man whose personal friendship would allow him carte blanche to run the department free from the interference of self obsessed, unenthused and bureaucratic senior officers who seemed intent on wrapping his operations up in red tape.

"Right, listen in please!" he instructed the gathered officers as the last one entered the room and closed the door. "Good morning Ladies and Gentlemen," he continued, pausing for the reciprocal greeting. "Now, I assume that you all know the purpose of our little operation this morning, though I have been reliably informed by members of my team that to *assume* anything, would only serve to make an *Ass* out of *u* and *me!*" There was a small murmur of laughter around the room before he went on. "Right, the task, in itself, is quite straightforward and self explanatory. At zero five hundred hours this morning, the three addresses, as listed in your briefing pack ..." There was a noticeable rustle of paper as every officer in the room turned the pages of their handout, " ...will be forcibly entered, secured and searched. And when I say forcibly, ladies and gentlemen, I mean forcibly. These are not addresses where we want to be ringing the door bell like Avon ladies or Jehovah's witnesses!" Again, there was a ripple of laughter throughout the room. "Each address will be attended by a team of eight, made up of four tactical firearms officers and four uniformed. I apologise in advance for the numbers, but even our overtime budget comes with constraints!" Gale quickly checked his watch before continuing. "Ok. Team one will be headed by Inspector Jones, team two by Inspector Stiles and for those lucky people in the room, team three will be headed by myself!" he paused to allow the subsequent mirth to pass. "The objectives of this operation are to arrest the targets shown in your packs, and any other person present who tries to hinder

134

you in your duties, and to seize any property that might relate to their activities. The intelligence we have received to date, would suggest a seventy five per cent chance that those targets will be at those addresses this morning and believe me, seventy five percent in this scenario, is extremely high. However, I want each and every one of you to assume, one hundred percent, that they *are* in those addresses. That way, we will not fall foul to complacency and will be prepared for every eventuality." The Superintendent paused for a moment and glanced around the room, making sure all eyes were on him. "Make no mistake," he said in a very sombre tone, "these people do not want to get caught and will use every possible option at that their disposal to evade arrest ... and you *can* assume, that the use of violence with weapons, including firearms, may well be one of those options!" He could see that the group hung on his last statement and he was pleased. Pleased because they now realised the gravity of this morning's activity and that would keep them sharp and hopefully, safe. What he didn't want, was to return for a debrief later that day with a fewer number of officers than he had now. "The firearms officers will enter and secure the properties first," he went on. "And under no circumstances does anybody else enter until they give the all clear, is that understood?" There was a resounding acknowledgment throughout the room just as the briefing room door opened. "All stand please!" Gale instructed as a man entered the room.

Each and every person in the room stood to attention recognising the thick set man with the distinguishable black hair and bushy beard. What they hadn't seen before was his mode of dress. Casual trousers, shirt and a well worn brown sports jacket made up his attire, an ensemble that was a far cry from the usual pristine black uniform donning insignias of a wreath and a crown of the realm on his shoulders.

"Good morning everyone," the Chief Constable said before adding. "Please, be seated." He looked over to Superintendent Gale and asked, "Everything ok Peter?"

"Yes Sir, just finishing off now," Gale replied. "Unless there's something you wanted to add Sir?"

"No no," the Chief said and looked around the room. "By the look on everyone's face, I think my presence has shocked them into submission anyway!" He smiled as the occupants of the room laughed dutifully and waited a few moments before adding. "What I will say to you all is this. Today's operation will not only be challenging for everyone here, but potentially hazardous and my only request is that you are professional and above all, diligent at all times. Look after yourselves and look after each other and let us pray that the day is one of victory and not of sorrow!" He paused for a moment before looking again at Gale. "Ok Peter, I'll see you in a little while."

Mac nodded respectfully and again gave the instruction to stand as the Chief Constable left the room. When the officers resumed their seats, he continued. "Ok, are there any questions?" When he could see there were none, he concluded. "Good. Well in that case, can I ask you all to now make your way into the canteen where, courtesy of Special Branch, you should find bacon butties and mugs of tea waiting for you!" There was a grateful cheer from the room. "Be back in the car park ready to go no later than zero four hundred hours and can the Inspectors and Sergeants stay behind for just a couple more minutes? Ok, thank you all!"

Peter Gale watched with some pride, and a little sadness, as his officers filed out of the room laughing and joking amongst themselves. Although he enjoyed his current position, it was at times like this, that he missed the banter and camaraderie of being a uniformed Bobby, on the streets, at the sharp end of business. To them, he was just another suit putting together another operation and signing another overtime sheet.

'Whatever happened,' he thought glumly, *'to once being the 'Copper's Cop'?'*

###

Chapter 20

Liam walked slowly along the road, studying the small cluster of shops on the opposite side. He had passed the same shops a million times before but on this occasion, they appeared to be different. Everything was there. The newsagents, the launderette, the off-licence and of course, Jen's dad's take away, but for some reason, something was out of place. He stopped to ponder for a moment but as much as he tried, he just couldn't put his finger on what had changed. What he did notice, however, was just how hot the weather had become and he wondered why he had chosen to wear such a big winter coat on a day like this *and* have it zipped right up to the top. He went to unfasten the coat but the zip got caught on the lining part way down and jammed. "Shit!" he cursed as he tried to release it but the more he tried, the more it became impossible to move and the hotter he became. It was useless. There was no way it was going to budge and he eventually decided that the best way to remove the coat would be to pull it over his head.

As he started to do this, a car sounded its horn, making Liam jump slightly. "Dick 'ed!" he muttered angrily as the offending vehicle passed but was immediately surprised to see that his best friend, Sean, was sitting in the back seat looking out of the window, smiling and casually flicking two fingers at him. What Liam found even stranger, was that Sean, for some bizarre reason, appeared to be wearing his pyjamas. "Sean?" he said in quiet disbelief as the car continued along without stopping, leaving Liam, waving half heartedly in its wake.

Liam shook his head and glanced back across the road which caused his stomach to flip. He couldn't believe his eyes when he saw Jeanette, his supposed girlfriend, outside the takeaway, talking to and laughing with, Matthew Walker. "What the fuck?" he said sharply, feeling emotions of confusion and jealousy rise within him. "Jen, hey Jen!!" he called out and held up his arm to get her attention. Neither Jeanette nor Walker looked up, oblivious to the shout as Liam's voice became lost beneath the hum of the traffic. Liam watched as Walker leant in towards Jeanette and said something to her that made them both laugh, resulting in Jen playfully smacking Walker's arm. It was like a freight train had smashed into Liam. He felt his heart beating so hard that he thought it might explode out of his chest and could feel himself wanting to be sick over this staggering discovery. He needed to get across the road but its width suddenly seemed to have increased tenfold and now had the appearance of a motorway, carrying an equally relative amount of traffic on it. 'Shit,' he thought as he looked from left to right, not being able to see a safe gap to cross. He looked across the road again and could see that Walker was now moving off, slowly, whilst Jeanette was heading back into her shop, stopping briefly to glance back at Walker and wave. Liam needed to know what was going on as the uncertainty rushing around his mind was becoming unbearable. "Wait!!" he shouted pleadingly and though Jen appeared not to hear him again, he was sure that Walker shot him a mocking smile before he rounded the corner and went out of sight. "Argh, you bastard!" Liam spat and felt his eyes begin to well with tears of frustration and anger as he appeared powerless to cross a simple road and confront the two of them. "Come on, come on for fuck's sake!" he hissed as he waited desperately for an opening in the run of vehicles. Thinking he had seen an opportunity, he stepped out into the carriageway only for a black car to suddenly appear and screech to a halt narrowly missing him.

The driver of the vehicle opened his door and leant out, calling to Liam. "Get in quickly!" he instructed casually.

Liam looked at the man with overwhelming shock. He was unable to move a single muscle yet somehow managed to call on all his bodily reserves to help him assemble a response. "Uncle Robbie?" he asked quietly, doubting his own senses. "But I thought you were dead?"

"Why would I be dead when I'm teaching over there?" the man replied, pointing across the road. As Liam looked, he realised why the local shops looked so different. For sitting on top of them, as if in a natural and obvious location, was none other than St. Monica's High school.

"But how do you get in there?" Liam asked, seemingly unperturbed by the strange addition to the shops' roofs. Before Uncle Robbie could answer, there was a loud bang that made Liam jump. "What the hell was that?" he shouted.

"That's the new school bell," Robbie replied. "We need to get in, now!"

As the second loud bang sounded, Liam closed his eyes and covered his ears and the scene around him quickly faded.

When he opened his eyes again, he found himself lying in total darkness. Momentarily disorientated, he sat up quickly feeling hot sweat roll down his body. Within seconds, he thankfully realised, that he was in his own bedroom; a gratitude that was short lived.

The third bang was not only unexpected, but a great deal louder than the previous two, mingled with the sound of splintering wood and shattering glass. *That came from downstairs!'* thought a startled Liam and heard the sound of heavy footsteps on the stairs. *'Shit, somebody's breakin' in!'* More out of panic than bravery, Liam shot out of his bed and headed towards his door, freezing part way as he heard somebody call out.

"Police, Police, stay where you are!" then, "Clear!" followed by another, "Clear!"

He frowned, now totally confused as to what was going on in his house. '*Police,*' he thought. *'Why are the Police here?'* He then heard a thud and a high pitched scream from his sister's room that made him jump yet urged him to move himself forward and go to her aid. Suddenly, his bedroom door flew open and Liam was blinded by a very bright light shining into his eyes. He held his hand up, trying to shield his face from the brilliant white glare.

"On the floor, now!" a man's voice boomed from behind the light, causing Liam, in his fright, to automatically raise his arms to the ceiling.

"Mum!" he shouted with a terrified screech as the person behind the torch advanced.

"I said get on the floor you little twat!" the voice demanded and Liam immediately complied; not of his own volition, but because he was subjected to what felt like a battering ram being smashed into his stomach, causing him to lose his wind and drop to the floor like a sack of lead.

"Leave him alone!" he heard his mum shout from somewhere outside his room, panic in her voice. "What the hell is going on? What do you want? What right have you got to force your way into my house? Have you got...!"

"Shut it you gypsy slag!" a different man shouted, cutting Bridie short.

Bridie ignored the instruction. "Who the hell are you talking to? You've no right ... I'm going to report you for this. Who's ...!"

In one quick movement, she was pinned against the wall, a hand around her throat as a menacing voice growled at her. "I said, shut the fuck up, now!" This time, Bridie decided to obey the command.

With tears rolling down his cheeks and still very much in pain, Liam managed to look towards the landing. With the overhead light now switched on, he could see his mum and his sister standing outside their rooms both visibly shaking with fear. There were also three other people close by. All of them were dressed in black overalls, commando style black boots, helmets and what appeared to be gas masks. From their physical build, Liam assumed that they were men. What scared him the most, was the fact that they were all carrying sub machine guns and only the presence of the word *Police* emblazoned on their body armour, distinguished them from any usual paramilitary organisation.

Two of the three stepped aside as a fourth male appeared on the landing. In contrast, he was dressed quite normally in a shirt, trousers and a raincoat, which, adding to the current surreal circumstances, reminded Liam of an American detective he had seen on TV. Liam also noticed that he too was wearing a bullet proof vest.

The fourth man glanced towards Liam, sighed a little and then looked towards Bridie, smiling slightly. "Good Morning Mrs. Connor" he said in a low, falsely pleasant tone.

"It's hardly good!" Bridie snapped. "What is going on and why are ..."

"Ssssh," the man interjected, putting a finger to his lips patronisingly. When
he was sure that Bridie was going to remain silent, he continued in the same low tone. "Where is he Mrs. Connor?" he asked almost casually.

Bridie frowned a little. "Where's who?" she replied. "There's only us three here, you can see that!"

The man gave another little sigh and repeated the same question. "Where is he?"

"I don't know who you mean," Bridie replied.

"You know damn well who I mean!" the fourth man suddenly barked at Bridie, making her flinch. "Michael, where the fuck is Michael?"

Bridie composed herself as best she could and looked at the man with utter contempt. *'Somewhere you won't find him y'bastard!'* she thought about saying, but merely shrugged before quietly answering, "I don't know any *Michael!*"

The man shook his head, smiled momentarily and then snorted an impatient laugh. "I thought you might say that Bridie, so here's a little deal for you." He turned and gestured towards Bridie's daughter Margaret who was standing by her bedroom door whimpering and shaking in her nightdress. "How's about we arrest pretty girl here and take her to the station for some questioning? Maybe she can tell us a bit more than her loving mother, eh boys?" He looked around at the other three men who immediately grunted their approval.

Margaret looked at her mum with despair on her face, mentally pleading for help.

"You've no right, she's only a child!" Bridie exclaimed, anxiety now showing on her face and in her voice.

"No right!" the man responded angrily. "No fuckin' right? ... Under the Prevention of Terrorism Act I've got every fuckin' right ... Under the Prevention of Terrorism Act, I am a fuckin' God ... Take the little bitch away!" he nodded to one of the men stood next to him.

"No!" Bridie screamed and stood in front of Margaret, trying to stop the advancing Police officer from getting hold of her.

"Leave her alone y' bastard!" Liam shouted attempting to get back on his feet but the weight of an officer's foot pushed him easily back down to the floor again. "He's not here ... he's gone!"

"Ah, from the mouths of babes!" the casually dressed man exclaimed, looking at Liam and clapping his hands together. "Now we're getting somewhere!" He signalled to the officer who let go of Margaret's arm and stepped back. He turned towards Bridie again, smiling again. "Now Bridie," he started, "I will ask you once more. Where is your husband, Michael Connor?"

Bridie looked at Liam with defeated and sorrowful eyes and then back towards the man. "I don't know where he is," she answered. "He hasn't been here for weeks and that's the truth!"

"You're lying!" the man hissed, moving his face to within inches of Bridie.

"I'm not, I swear. He left about a month ago and ..."

"Where did he go?" the man interrupted impatiently.

"What? ... I don't know, just away!" Bridie muttered, not even sounding convincing to herself.

The man sighed and shook his head, stepping slightly away from Bridie. He remained silent for a few moments as if thinking and then looked towards one of the officers. "Fuck this shit," he said wearily. "Let's try the first idea and take the girl in, see what she can tell us!" He nodded again towards Margaret and the armed Police officer moved in.

"No, no!" Bridie pleaded and again tried to shield her daughter. The Police officer effortlessly pushed Bridie to one side and grabbed hold of a screaming Margaret, dragging her towards the stairs.

"Mum! Stop them, please, stop them!" Margaret howled with fright, trying to resist.

"Get off her y'prick! Leave her alone!" Liam shouted from the bedroom floor, powerless to move.

Bridie grabbed hold of the officer, trying to release his grip on Margaret's arm. "Get off her y'pig bastard!" she shouted and in her anger, spat at, then kicked the officer in the leg.

"Fuckin' slag!" the officer snarled and swung out at Bridie with his free hand, connecting with the side of her face, sending her reeling to the floor.

Liam was both stunned and furious that somebody had just struck his mum and the red mist of enragement fell into his eyes. Aware that the officer stood next to him had moved slightly away, his incensed mind gave him the strength to get to his feet quickly and run towards the officer who had dared to hit his mum.

"Aargh ... You're fuckin' dead y'bastard!" he screamed as he advanced towards the aggressor, desperate to seek retribution. Like an Olympic runner hearing the starter pistol, Liam felt his body draw on hidden energy reserves as his heart pounded hard, driving blood to his muscles in readiness for the task ahead. It was as if everything had been switched to slow motion and though focused on his objective, his peripheral vision became obscured by haze, only allowing him sight of the antagonist pulling Margaret away, a target that he now felt no fear of, only anger towards. In the blur of his tunnelled vista, Liam's mind partly registered the actions of the casually dressed man turning towards him but on this bizarre stage, the movement of his raincoat was translated into a comically accentuated swirl as if it was a superhero's cape playing catch up with the twist of the wearer's body. From somewhere in the distance, he heard his mum shouting *'No Liam!'* temporarily distracting him from his goal as he glanced towards her. Had he remained fixated on his intended mark, he may have seen Mr. Casual remove an object from his pocket. As it was, he would only register a sharp pain just before darkness closed in around him.

###

Chapter 21

Liam tried desperately to open his eyes, fighting against the unnatural heaviness that seemed to be pushing down on his lids. Somewhere in the distance, he could hear his mum's voice calling him and wondered why there was the sound of despair in her tone. For the shortest of moments, he saw fractures of dull light through his half open and blurred vision but the overwhelming sense of tiredness and an immeasurable sharpness of pain across his forehead, drove him back into the darkness and comfort of sleep.

When he later roused, it took a little time before he actually realised that he was in his own room, a comprehension only confirmed as he eventually focused on the familiar ceiling above his bed. He lifted his hand to his head as it throbbed with a dull ache and was surprised to feel a moist and cold flannel resting across his brow. Confused, he probed beneath the dampened cloth and immediately winced when he touched an egg sized lump just under his hairline. *'Where the hell did that come from?'* he thought, but had neither the energy nor the inclination to investigate it further, especially as the lure of sleep lay in wait to take him for a third time.

In his uneasy slumber, Liam heard the ghostly resonance of a ship's horn, distant yet stifled, as if engulfed in a malevolent tomb of dense and static sea fog eager to silence its counsel to other vessels. It wasn't until the third timbre, that his conscience deciphered the sound into the calling of his own name. "Liam!"

The recognisable voice, soft and warm, brought Liam slowly back from his dark world, a world where he had drifted to and from many times within the last hour, a world of dreams *and* a world of nightmares.

As he opened his eyes, he saw his mum sat beside him, gently stroking his head and he smiled. Though the smile was returned, Liam saw that it was marred by the tracks of recent tears on his mum's face and he frowned with concern. Looking beyond his mum, he noticed something different about his room. Not in shape, size or colour, but somehow, different. Turning his head slowly to take in his surroundings, he saw that his drawers and wall cupboards had been left open, alarmingly exposing ransacked interiors where usually, order and tidiness were the norm. Items of clothing, books and other personal belongings appeared to have been strewn all over his desktop and floor as if it were a legacy left by an impatient burglar searching unceremoniously for the family jewels. Unable to comprehend why this was so, he tried to prop himself up on his elbows for a clearer look but a wave of pain that surged through his head, caused him to fall back on to his pillow with a distressed moan.

"It's ok Liam," his mum whispered, putting her hand to his head. "Just lie still for a while darling!"

Liam turned again to his mum, a look of anguish on his face. "What's going on Mum?" he asked, bewildered. "My room? I don't ...!" he continued, but was stopped mid sentence.

"Sshh!" Bridie interjected softly. "Don't worry about that now. Try to rest. It'll be ok!"

He saw angst through the warmth of his mum's smile and wanted to ask why. Why was she so obviously upset? Why was his room, or what he could see of it, in such a mess? And why did he now have a lump on his head that was throbbing like a bitch? He turned away from his mum and closed his eyes tightly as if searching for recollection. Liam jumped slightly and quickly opened his eyes as the door to his room was opened hastily and a familiar figure entered. As if the flood gates of his memory bank had been opened to allow instant and total recall, Liam was suddenly awash with emotions of fear, anger and confusion, as he focused on the man who was dressed like a character from a Mickey Spillane novel.

"Ah good!" the man said, looking at Liam with no trace of emotion. "Little Big man's awake is he?" Liam held his stare with bitterness in his eyes, praying that the adage, *if looks could kill,* would actually come true. It was the man who looked away first, but only in reaction to the voice of Bridie.

"What the hell do you care?" she replied angrily. "You're just a bully hiding behind your Police badge!"

The man merely murmured a disinterested hum before turning his gaze to the other side of the room. "Anything?" he suddenly asked, speaking to somebody whom Liam, up until that point, had been totally oblivious to. He turned his head to see where the man was directing the question and was both surprised and shocked to see an armed Police officer silent and motionless in the corner.

"Nothing Sir," was all the officer replied. Looking a little disappointed, the man made a small gesture with his head signalling that the officer should leave the room.

Liam watched aghast as he moved towards the door realising that it must have been he who had trashed his belongings. "What about my room you idiot?" Liam hissed without thinking.

"Shush little boy!" the officer replied threateningly whilst glaring at Liam. "Or I will shush you myself!"

The man in the raincoat saw that Liam was about to react angrily and so, not particularly wanting a repeat of the incident that had occurred an hour earlier, quickly stepped in to avoid another confrontational clash. "Ok ok," he said in a tone of false joviality. "Let's not fall out again shall we?" and hastily ushered the armed officer out of the room.

Once the three of them were alone, the man leant down on his haunches, inches away from a vexed looking Liam, glanced at his face and then looked up towards the lump on his head, studying it for a few moments. Sighing heavily and shaking his own head, the man returned his gaze to Liam's face, staring intensely into his eyes. "You need to watch that temper of yours son," he advised quietly. "It could cause a lot of trouble one day!"

"Maybe," Liam replied bitterly. "But that might be the day you don't have your bodyguards with you!"

The man let out a contemptuous laugh as he stood back up and pointed to Liam's head. "I see that little knock to your bonce didn't fill it with any sense lad ... ha ... Typical Irish, thick as fuck!"

Suddenly, Bridie shot up from her seat with rage in her eyes, glaring at the man whose only virtues seemed to be those of arrogance and ignorance entwined. "I'll report you for all of this you nasty bastard, you see if I don't. And then you won't be so cocky!"

The man held up the palms of his hands towards Bridie in mock defence, leaning back slightly. "Whoa, don't shoot the messenger Mrs. Connor," he pleaded sarcastically. "I'm just doing my job. Surely you can understand that?"

"And nearly killing a child with your brutal ways is doing your job is it?" Bridie questioned angrily.

"Well," the man replied in a condescending tone. "If he hadn't been foolish enough to come at me and my officers with a weapon, then maybe there wouldn't have been any need for such unpleasantness!"

"Weapon? What weapon?" Bridie snapped. "He had no such thing and you know it!"

"Maybe," the man replied without concern. "But I have myself and at least three officers outside of this room that will testify beyond all doubt that he did have. So please, go ahead and make your complaint. Be my guest!" He stepped forward leaning in towards Bridie, his face suddenly contorted with menace. "But know this," he growled. "The moment you do, I will be back to arrest that little shit!" he pointed at Liam. "And that pretty daughter of yours, faster than you can say Leprechaun!!" He paused for a moment, allowing his words to register with Bridie before stepping back slightly. He then looked towards Liam and smirked. "I really don't think that either of them could cope with even just *one* day of cell life, do you Mrs. Connor?" he continued, still staring at Liam. "Unless your maternal instincts tell you different that is?" He turned slowly back to Bridie with his eyebrows raised, inviting a response but feeling sure that none would come. As expected, Bridie remained speechless. Although shocked and angry, she knew that it was pointless to challenge any of this man's lies and deceit and that her word, should she wish to complain, would carry no weight in an obviously corrupt world of Policing. She felt tears of frustration well in her eyes and looked to the floor defeated. "Thought as much," the man added smugly. "You see Bridie," he continued, "maybe it isn't the Police that you should be aggrieved with here. Maybe you should look at the man whose cowardly activities have actually brought us here in the first place, yes?"

"He's more man than you and all those eejits out there will ever be!" Bridie replied resentfully, though any trace of raised volume had long since left her tone.

The man chuckled and raised his eyes to the ceiling. "Oh, how love doth taint the eyes and blind thee to the devil's work," he said as if quoting from some obscure missal. Bridie frowned, confused. "You see Mrs. Connor," he continued more sombrely, "I do what I do because of, well, because of disillusioned men like your husband searching for some false recognition of grandeur. You would no doubt call them Patriots, Heroes perhaps, *'Soldiers of the People'* fighting for the rights of their country folk!" The man snorted a sarcastic hoot. "Soldiers!" he spat coldly and shook his head disapprovingly. "Soldiers are honourable men Mrs. Connor, men who conduct themselves with nobility and fairness in battle. Men who do not stoop to the gutter level occupied by your husband and his genus of thugs who believe that battles are won by causing the deaths of innocent people with their cowardly acts of terrorism!"

"What!" Liam shouted, suddenly sitting up, a look of desperate confusion on his face. "Mum, what does he mean?"

Bridie looked quickly at Liam and then immediately back to the man who clearly saw a look of horror and anguish on her face. The man also looked at Liam and saw that he too had a look of horror and anguish on his face, but, he surmised, for a very different reason. He gave an evil cackle before turning back to Bridie. "Oh my," he scoffed. "Don't tell me that little big man here doesn't know about his daddy's career?"

"You bastard!" Bridie snarled.

"Mum, what?" Liam demanded, choking on his words. "What's he saying about Dad!"

"How noble that you have kept him in the dark Mrs. Connor" the man mocked.

"Get out y'bastard!" Bridie said insistently. "Get out of my home and take your scum wit' ya!"

"Tell me what you mean, tell me what you mean!" Liam screamed at the man pleadingly, tears flooding down his cheeks.

The man merely turned to Liam, gave a slight grin and looked back at Bridie. Looking casually at his watch, he calmly announced. "I think we're done here now anyway," though intentionally wanting to add fuel to the fire, added. "And I think there are things you need to discuss with your son Mrs. Connor, don't you?" He gave her a conceited smile of victory before concluding. "Don't worry yourself, we'll see ourselves out." As he left the room, he could feel the hatred and enragement of Bridie burning through his body and into his very soul before the bedroom door was finally slammed behind him. He listened to the raised and sobbing voices of Liam and his mum for a short while and chuckled silently to himself, pleased with the outcome of an otherwise bad morning. *'Have a nice fucking day Mrs. Connor!'* he thought indignantly as he adjusted his raincoat and headed out of the front door, back into his own world.

###

Bridie listened as the Police left her home, noisily and with the occasional sound of rasping laughter as if the whole episode, to them, had been nothing more than one big joke. Although they had been present for just over an hour, it had felt like an eternity to Bridie, who had not only seen her house turned upside down and her daughter Margaret traumatised to the point where she was a trembling wreck, but had also witnessed, helplessly, the unnecessary assault of her son Liam, an assault that had rendered him unconscious as a result of the heavy handed methods of one unfathomably brutish man.

As she heard the last of the police vehicles pull away from her house, she remained silent, head bowed and tearful, only too aware that Liam was looking at her intensely, wanting answers. When he spoke, she flinched a little but remained silent for a while, wondering how best to reply.

"Mum, did you hear me? What ..." he asked.

"Yes I heard you Liam," she answered, immediately regretting the slight snap in her tone as Liam had started to repeat his question of *'what did they mean about Dad?'* She looked at her son who was now sitting up in his bed, his eyes red from the sting of many tears, the lump on his head seemingly growing bigger by the minute. The expression on his face only served to melt the heart of Bridie, encouraging more tears to roll gently down her own cheeks. It was a look of pleading, of innocent desperation, marred, she felt, by a sense of betrayal and hurt. How could she explain all of this to someone so young? How was he expected to understand the plight of his own father, his own flesh and blood?

Taking a deep breath, she took hold of Liam's hand and began to explain, the best way she could, the reasons behind the Police visit. She gave a small yet concise synopsis of her husband's *work* and though many of the details were either omitted or understated, Liam was left in no doubt as to what it was his dad was involved in. He listened intensely to his mum and was bombarded with feelings of shock, anger, sorrow and bitterness that rendered him speechless throughout his mum's enlightening tale. When she had finished, Liam remained silent feeling mentally and physically drained. It was like his world had just caved in around him as his mind spun with a million unanswered questions. He thought back to the conversation he had overheard whilst outside the lounge, thought about the newspaper clippings he had found in his dad's wardrobe and despite his friend Sean convincing him otherwise at the time, realised that his suspicions, however obscure and unsubstantiated back then, had suddenly and violently been confirmed as correct. Back then it wasn't real and with his friend's help, he had easily put it to the back of his mind, convinced that an over active imagination was to blame for his misgivings. But that was then and this was now and even with the most fantastical imagination, he would never, in his wildest dreams, have envisaged the sheer scale of what his mum had just told him. It wasn't long before the thought process brought to Liam's mind the one thing that was to cause him the most frustration. A thought that would neither change nor have any significant effect on the current situation, but a thought that Liam saw to be the most poignant in amongst all the proverbial stuff that had just hit the fan. "Shit ... Walker was right after all!" he spat bitterly, making his mum frown in confusion.

"Who's Walker?" she asked softly, initially thankful that her son had at least said something. Her question however, only resulted in Liam glaring at her.

"Who's Walker?" he repeated angrily. "Oh, he's no one important, y'know, a nobody? ... Just somebody at school who seems to know more about my fucking dad than I do!"

"Liam!" Bridie chastised. "There's no need for that language!"

"No need for ..." Liam stopped and began to laugh. "So," he continued incredulously. "Let's get this right. The coppers have just smashed their way into our house, treated us all like shit, twatted me on the head and then you tell me that my dad's got a secret life as a terrorist, but oh, '*don't swear Liam*'... ha!" He shook his head and pulled his hand from his mum's. "Y'know what mum?" he said, "the whole thing's wrong. This is not how I should be spending my day. I should be at school living the life of a normal teenager, getting ready for my exams and enjoying time with my friends!"

"I know darling," Bridie agreed. "And you still can do all those things. Just because ..."

"What?" Liam snapped. "How exactly? My life is now well and truly fucked up thanks to my dad!"

"Your father ..." Bridie started defensively, "does what he does for a belief, a belief that has been running in his family and the families of many Irish people for generations. But despite his convictions Liam, he would never ... *never* ... do anything to intentionally involve any of us. He's a good man Liam and today's episode will destroy him, believe me!"

"Oh yeah," replied Liam sarcastically. "I bet he will be well pissed off that he's not been caught ... but what about me? What am I supposed to do now knowing he is what he is?"

Bridie stood up over Liam. "It's not all about you Liam!" she said, angry with frustration. "What about your sister? And me? How do you think we feel in all of this? We have suffered too Liam and then there's your dad!"

"What about my dad?" Liam asked.

"Don't you think he'll suffer more than any of us, despite what you think now?" Bridie replied.

Liam looked at his mum with a pained grimace. "What I think," he began angrily, "is that he brought this on himself and he deserves to suffer ... he's a fuckin' joke!"

Liam didn't see the swift movement of his mum's hand, but more than felt the sting as it made contact with his cheek taking him by total surprise. "Don't you ever disrespect your Father again, do you hear me!" Bridie shouted fiercely. "You would have nothing if it wasn't for him. Do you really think he wanted any of this? He would lay down his life for you and despite his beliefs, he would fight tooth and nail not to have you or your sister involved in that world in any way!"

"But now we are involved!" Liam shot back through the addition of new tears brimming in his eyes. "And it's not fair mum, it's not fair!"

He broke down and began to sob, holding his head in his hands. Bridie's anger immediately diffused as she took a hold of her son tightly in her arms. "I know son, I know," she said tenderly. "It'll be alright, you'll see ... don't cry darling!" As she soothingly rocked Liam, she couldn't help but think that the situation they now found themselves in, would be far from alright.

A few hours later, Liam lay in his bed staring blankly at the ceiling. His mind was jammed with thoughts of the morning's incident and every now and then, new tears would form in his eyes, testament to the hurt and confusion he felt. His mum had looked in on him a few times but he had always closed his eyes and pretended to be asleep thus avoiding any form of conversation. He didn't feel like holding court with somebody who he felt had turned his life into a mockery with their lies and deceit. He glanced at his clock, which showed him that the time had seemingly fast forwarded to three in the afternoon and decided that he needed to get up, go out and try and clear the gridlocked traffic of deliberation in his head. He also needed to speak with someone, desperately. Someone who wasn't related and therefore wouldn't twist explanations and details to make it sound better than it really was. He needed to speak to somebody who could help him try and make sense of the whole revelation without judging, without prejudice. He knew, without doubt, that Sean was his man.

After putting on his clothes, he made his way, as silently as he could, down the stairs. Once he had gotten to the hallway, he cursed as the option to slip out of the front door was negated by the presence of temporary boarding, used to cover the damage made by the Police's forced entry.

Making his way to the rear of the house, he noticed that the lounge door was open and could hear the sound of his mum as she spoke on the telephone. This time, he wanted to listen.

"We'll have to, for the children's sake," he heard his mum say. "But where?" She went silent, obviously listening to the person on the other end of the phone and then added. "I agree. But I'm just worried about them, especially Liam!" More silence, followed by. "Not too good. Maybe you should speak to him and tell ..." More silence followed as his mum was cut short mid sentence. "Yeah, I heard him get up a few minutes ago," she continued. "Ok, hold on. Oh, but don't mention the move just yet ... wait till it's arranged ... ok, hang on!"

'Move? What move?' Liam thought angrily. 'I'm not moving anywhere!' He decided that now was the time to leave the house and started to walk towards the back door. As he passed the lounge, he set his gaze directly ahead intending to avoid glancing into that room at all costs. His mind was working on the false premise that if he didn't see his mum, then she wouldn't see him. He was wrong.

"Oh, Liam, there you are," she said as he passed the open doorway without stopping. "Your dad is on the phone and ..."

"I don't care!" he interjected bitterly. "I'm going out!"

"Liam, Liam!" she shouted after him but was answered only by the noisy slam of the rear door. She bowed her head for a moment as if in quiet reflection before putting the telephone back to her ear. "I think the move should be sooner rather than later," she informed the listener. "Maybe Ireland will help put this family back together!"

Liam arrived at the gates of St. Monica's just as the home time bell was sounding and felt a sudden rush of anxiety. Not because he was planning to speak to Sean, but because, in amongst all of this, he had totally forgotten that he would inevitably see Jen coming out of school and would have to offer up a reason for his absence that day. What could he possibly tell her that would make any part of this situation acceptable and how would he explain the sudden appearance of a non too subtle lump on his head. Oh, he could lie and say that he had cracked it on a cupboard door or something and then felt sick, but in the long term, she would eventually find out the truth and no doubt hate him for the rest of time. As hard as it was, he decided that he would have no choice but to spare the girl's embarrassment and break up with her. *'Let her find somebody whose family doesn't go around planting bombs,'* he thought bitterly, subconsciously clenching his fists.

As the first of the pupils started to exit the school, Liam noticed that some of them appeared to be staring at him longer than necessary before hurrying past. Initially, he put it down to the fact that he was standing there looking like shit and probably looked a little suspicious. But, as the prolonged staring turned into obvious pointing and whisperings, paranoia kicked in with all the subtlety of a car crash and he found himself backing away from his position at the gates. *'They all know,'* he thought, horrified that his family business was now very much the topic of conversation and conjecture at the school. *'But how?'* he continued to muse, checking his own logic. *'It's not even been on the news, so they couldn't know!'*

With great effort, he blanked out this fear and tried to ignore the migrating pupils, instead focusing on trying to locate Sean in the now growing crowd. As time passed, he became concerned that he couldn't see his friend and hoped that he hadn't managed to acquire himself another detention. *'Come on Sean,'* he thought impatiently. *'Where the fuck are you?'* A few minutes later, he saw Sean exiting the school building but was immediately dispirited when he noticed that both Louise and Jen were also walking out with him. "Shit," he said under his breath. "Now what?" After a moment's consideration, he decided that he would walk away and catch up with Sean later. He couldn't handle having to speak to the two girls as well, not now.

As he turned around, hoping to quickly head off, he was stopped almost immediately by the sound of Sean's voice calling out to him. "Liam, Liam!" he shouted, causing Liam to grimace and turn back around. As he watched Sean jogging towards him, he was thankful, at least, that Louise and Jeanette didn't appear to be quite as keen to get to him as quickly, instead, merely sauntering to where he now stood. "How are you mate?" Sean asked once he had gotten up to Liam.

"Not good mate," Liam answered, as he glanced over Sean's shoulder, estimating how long he had to speak before the girls caught up. "Listen," he continued, "I need to talk to you about ..."

"Mate," Sean cut in, a look of despair on his face. "I know about the police at yours this morning!"

"What? How?" Liam replied, stunned.

"Walker," Sean said. "It's all over school!" Sean saw the look of disbelief on Liam's face and continued. "He said his dad knows someone high up in the cops and he told him all about it, so he's been spreading shit to anyone who will listen!" Sean appeared hesitant, looking at Liam with both sadness and foreboding.

"What?" Liam asked, knowing there was more to be told.

"He said your dad's wanted for terrorism and that's why they were there. I told him to keep his big mouth shut and that he doesn't know jack but ..." He paused and looked around as if checking that nobody could hear, before continuing quietly. "I kept remembering when you told me about what you found in your dad's wardrobe and it kind of ... well ... it kind of all fits!"

"What fits!" Liam said angrily. "The fact that the cops have been to mine and Walker says it's because we're terrorists ... and so now it fits?"

"Sorry mate," Sean responded immediately. "I was thinking about what you said, not what that dick Walker said!" Liam was about to say something to Sean, but was stopped by the arrival of Jeanette and Louise who both greeted him in unison.

"You ok?" asked a genuinely concerned looking Jen who then tried to hold Liam's hand.

"Why shouldn't I be?" snapped Liam, pulling his hand away. "I mean, who wouldn't want everybody in school talking about them and thinking their family are crims!"

"Nobody's thinking that Liam," Jen replied, a little hurt that he was taking it out on her. "Especially us!"

"Yeah," said Louise. "And it's not Jen's fault Li!"

"I know, I know," replied Liam. "It's just ..." He stopped mid sentence as he happened to glance over Jen's shoulder and saw the familiar frame of Walker heading towards them, a sickly grin on his face. "Shit," he continued. "That's all I need!"

"C'mon mate," urged Sean as he too saw Walker. "Let's piss off before he gives us more grief!"

As the four of them started to walk away, Walker, not wanting to miss an opportunity, called out, "Paddy ... hey paddy wait up!"

"Just ignore him," Louise said calmly. "He's not worth the breath!"

As much as they tried, Walker refused to be ignored and had soon caught up with them, walking just behind the group with his ever faithful companion, Boland, in tow. "Whoa, what's the rush Paddy boy," Walker incited. "Off to plant a bomb somewhere?" Both Walker and Boland sniggered mockingly, though the sound was quickly replaced by a loud nauseating crack as an incensed Liam turned around and promptly drove his fist into Walker's face, breaking his nose. If the first punch was unforeseen, the subsequent torrent of blows that rained about his head certainly weren't, yet Walker appeared powerless to react to the swift and painful hands of Liam. He held up his arms in a cowering and defensive stance until he was finally knocked to the ground, shocked and blooded. Boland stood open mouthed, the colour driven from his face as he looked on, unable (or rather not willing) to step in and assist his friend. Louise and Jeanette watched with mixed emotions of admiration and horror. Admiration that Liam had at last put Walker in his place, horror at the scale on which he had done it. Sean smiled at the beating that was long overdue.

Liam stood over the defeated boy, furious. "Don't you ever call me, my family or my friends again you piece of shit. Do you hear me dick 'ed!!"

Walker sat holding his battered face in his hands, blood oozing from his nose. He knew he had been defeated and wasn't prepared to try and play the hero with a lad who seemed to have replaced his placid manner with that of a street fighter. He looked up to Liam with tearful eyes, not once anticipating a sequel to this event. He would have assumed that that was that. Connor had beaten him and would walk away triumphant. Neither Walker nor anyone with the same frame of mind, would have envisaged the further actions of this particular victor, actions that saw Liam swing his foot towards Walker's head, catching it full on with a heart stopping thud before he straddled his victim and continued to shower him with a seemingly unstoppable barrage of punches. Walker, unable to fend off the sustained assault, became delirious in a prequel to unconsciousness. The two girls screamed at Liam to stop and at Sean to do something. Sean, who had since lost his smile, stepped in to try and pacify an enraged Liam.

"Ok ok Liam," said Sean worriedly, taking hold of one of Liam's arms. "I think he's had enough mate!"

"Get the fuck off me!" Liam responded with a rasp that was normally reserved for possessed souls in horror movies and as he snapped his arm from Sean's grasp, added. "This is for all those years of shit you little bastard!"

As Liam tried to land another blow, he was prevented from doing so by the bulk of Sean bear hugging him from behind and forcefully dragging him off Walker. Like a snared animal bidding for freedom, Liam began to thrash about as Sean pulled him away from the battered mess that was Walker, lying on the ground. "Get off me, get off me!!" Liam screamed as he was unceremoniously manoeuvred away from his prey.

"Leave it Liam!" Sean instructed sternly. "He's had enough man, it's over!" As Sean grappled with Liam, Jeanette and Louise watched with dumb struck anxiety, neither knowing how, if at all, they could help. Jen was aghast that the boy she had known all these years, the boy with whom she had quickly and willingly fallen in love with, was now unrecognisable in this current livid state. Worse, she thought, was the saddening fact that he appeared not to recognise anyone around him as his eyes, burning with ferocity, remained fixed on the now disabled Walker. As if a natural and obvious next step, she moved towards a restrained Liam, hoping that her voice might bring him back from his dark place and calm him down.

"Liam please," she implored softly. "It's me, Jen. Please stop Liam. Please, For me!"

Whether Liam had heard but ignored her, or just didn't register the sound of her voice was irrelevant. What was relevant, was that Liam, in a seemingly last ditched attempt to free himself from the clutches of Sean, pulled his feet off the ground and started thrashing his legs about. As he kicked out, he caught an unsuspecting Jeanette directly in her stomach, causing her to cry out and drop heavily to her knees. Almost immediately, as though somebody had flicked an invisible switch, Liam stopped flailing and looked horrified towards his injured girlfriend. "Shit, Jen!" he shouted. "No, no. Jen ... Sean, let me go, let me go please. I've hurt her. Shit!" Reluctantly, though equally concerned, Sean released his grip and watched as Liam threw himself at Jeanette's side. "Jen, I'm so sorry," he began through fresh tears. "Are you ok?" Jeanette sobbed as she held her stomach, temporarily winded and unable to answer.

"You went too far Liam!" scolded Louise as she knelt on the opposite side of Jen and put an arm around her. "What's wrong with you? You could see that he was finished!" She gestured to Walker now groaning as Boland attempted to help him up.

"I know," replied Liam. "But I never wanted this to happen. Jen, I'm so sorry. What can I do?"

Jeanette looked up from the comforting embrace of Louise towards Liam, tears mixed with mascara, running down her cheeks. "Sorry's not enough Liam," she whimpered. "You really hurt me. Just leave me alone!"

"Yeah, just go Liam!" Louise endorsed. "I think you've done enough!"

Liam was speechless. He couldn't understand why they failed to see his remorse for what was basically an accident. Disheartened, he looked towards Sean for support who merely shrugged his shoulders unable to help. Liam looked back to Jeanette and gently touched her hand. "I'm sorry," he repeated softly, before standing up and facing Sean again.

"Mate. You need to go, now!" Sean instructed sternly.

"Ok Sean," Liam replied, slightly taken aback with Sean's tone. "I know ... though I didn't expect you ..."

"No Liam," Sean cut in hastily. "You really need to leave ... now!" He nodded in the direction of the school where the figures of the headmaster, Terence McSweeny and 'Spud' the English teacher, were now hurriedly making their way to the

162

scene after having being informed of the incident by a concerned younger pupil.

"Connor!" the headmaster called. "Wait right there boy!"

"Shit!" Liam exclaimed.

"Go Liam, quick!" encouraged Sean. "I'll talk to them but you need to go now!"

"But what about ..." Liam started, looking at Jen, but was quickly cut off as Sean started to push him away.

"She'll be ok mate ... now piss off!"

Liam hesitated for a moment, wanting to stay and make things good between him and Jeanette again, but he knew it was pointless, a seemingly lost cause. He also knew that if he stayed, he would be hauled into the headmaster's office and made out to be the aggressor. It was always the case if, despite the antagonistic reasons for the fight, one of the pugilists came out on top relatively unscathed, making him, in the eyes of school law and logic, the bully. Liam gave Jen a final look, feeling his heart aching with sorrow. Turning to Sean he said. "Look after her mate!" Sean nodded his agreement as Liam turned and ran off in the opposite direction from the advancing masters.

Sean watched as Liam raced off, wondering if his best friend would be ok. He saw him hesitate at the entrance to Joey's field, look back and then continue on into the park, becoming lost in its boundary of dense foliage.

What neither Sean nor Liam knew, was that they would not see each other again for the next six years.

###

Chapter 22

Friday 18th May 1990

Superintendent Gale sat at his desk, despondently gazing at the near blank report form that lay before him. Most of the paperwork relating to the early morning operation that had occurred a few days before had all but been completed, yet his inspiration to compose anything on this particular form was as nonexistent now as it had been seventy two hours ago.

The press release on that day had deemed the job *'A significant success'*, focusing on a couple of arrests (albeit for relatively minor offences which, incidentally, had been kept from the media) and the seizure of many items *'believed to have been used for terrorist activity'*. Gale knew that this was a load of bollocks, Press Office spin to convince the general public that their taxes were being spent successfully fighting the war against terrorism. In truth, The Police had acted on, what now appeared to be, half baked intelligence resulting in a big fat nothing. The overwhelming sense of personal defeat that his quarry had managed to elude him on that day, was compounded further when, less than twenty four hours later, on 16th May 1990, the IRA detonated a bomb under a military minibus in London causing the death of one soldier and injury to four others.

In retrospect, he remembered feeling at the time that the job had appeared a little too straightforward, a little too easy considering the importance of the potential catch. And now, with that luxury of hindsight, Gale wondered if in fact there was a power beyond the realms of GMP's Special Branch that already knew Michael Connor was not going to be there in the first place. Was there some hierarchy using his department as mere pawns in the hope that this highly trained IRA member would be tempted to emerge from his true hiding place, flushed out by a sense of loyalty and concern for his family? *'He's not that stupid,'* the Superintendent thought bitterly. *'But if someone did know about the imminent attack, then why the fuck weren't we told?'*

He sighed heavily as, not for the first time that week, he ran a million *what ifs* through his mind, dwelling on the negatives, considering conspiracies. Had the team been manipulated for the sake of some greater good, or had they genuinely just been unlucky? Did everyone think that the operation had been a washout or was it indeed *'a significant success'* as the papers would have its readers believe?

Suddenly, as if beckoned by the dulcet tones of a hypnotist bringing him back into reality, Gale sat upright and rubbed his eyes. "No," he mused out loud, shaking his head. "In the grand scheme of things, our operation was little more than crap!"

It didn't help that some little shit had decided to play hero on the day, causing him to take positive pre-emptive action, action for which he was now required to write and submit a sizeable report justifying his reasons for the use of force. He had started his report on the day of the incident but only got as far as writing *Sir* on the form before thinking, *'Fuck it, there are more important things to worry about!'* With that, the report had taken the proverbial backseat; until now.

He sighed as he picked up his pen, no longer able to put off what needed to be done. *'It won't write itself,'* he thought and began the odious task of composing a *'Why he deserved it so don't discipline me,'* tale of events, events that would naturally show Gale in a good light. His one consolation was that the Chief Constable had asked for it to be forwarded directly to himself thus negating any influential pushes in the wrong direction by certain parties determined to see him fall.

"Peter," his friend and boss had said on hearing the circumstances. "Operations like this, as we all know, are fraught with many dangers and often, not without casualties. I'm only pleased that on this occasion, the casualty wasn't one of ours. Make your report but submit it directly to me and if somebody wants to make a song and dance about it, then they better have good cause to come and bother me!"

The Superintendent knew that the incident would *disappear* appropriately, but it didn't stop him feeling that it was all just a waste of precious time, time that could be spent doing effective Police work instead of justifying his methods and covering his back. *'Politics gone mad,'* he thought cynically. *'And I thought we were a Police Force not a Police Service!'*

Before he began to write, he replayed the scenario in his mind time and time again, second by second, adapting the facts accordingly so that when he would eventually project his thoughts and commit them to paper, nobody would be left in any doubt that his actions were not only justified but bordering on heroic. As far as Gale was concerned, the facts were thus:

He and his team had entered a property where there had been intelligence to suggest that a known, wanted member of the IRA was not only present, but potentially armed. His team had made an authorised forced entry into the property, putting aside any possible risks to their own safety in order to locate and arrest a person who posed a real and serious threat to the well being of Great Britain and its citizens. They had been met with hostility immediately upon entering the property, not from the initial target himself, (who, it later transpired, was in fact not present at the address) but from other members of his family and in particularly, Bridie Connor, the wife of the intended target and a known sympathiser of the IRA.

This hostility manifested itself in Liam Connor, the sixteen year old son of Bridie, who, on seeing Police officers in his house, had, without hesitance, advanced towards them in a frenzied state and an obvious mindset of assault. Fortunately, due to the quick thinking of Firearms Officer Mullen, Connor was quickly controlled and instructed to lie on the floor. At this time, it was not apparent that Connor's actions were only a prequel to a further attempt at an unprovoked assault later that morning.

The Connor family were relentless in their abuse and aggression towards the Officers attempting to execute their duties. Furthermore, it should be noted, that at one point, Margaret Connor, the eighteen year old daughter, (no doubt encouraged by her mother as a decoy tactic) had hinted at sexual favours to one of the Officers, if a house search was avoided. To his credit, Police Constable Thomas (to whom the suggestion was made) recognised this as a ploy to undermine our presence at the location and exhibited both professionalism and integrity in that he not only reported it directly to me immediately, but also rightly suggested that discretion be used with Miss Connor as opposed to arrest. This was because he knew that to arrest her, would only fuel the fire of hate towards us and hinder the progress of our objectives even further. At this point, though I agreed with the officer's assessment, I gave the instruction for her to be removed to the downstairs area and to be watched constantly by the one female officer present amongst us.

It would appear that this direction did not bode well with any of the Connors as they immediately upped their level of aggression, resulting in Bridie and Margaret kicking at and spitting towards officers. It was at this point, that I noticed Liam Connor get up from the floor, physically shove a momentarily distracted officer to one side, before advancing towards PC Thomas whom, under my command, was escorting Miss Connor downstairs.

Sir, to say that Liam Connor was like a possessed animal would be an understatement and coupled with the fact that he now appeared to be wielding some form of weapon, I had no option other than to take positive and decisive action to protect both myself and my officers. Despite me shouting at Connor telling him to stop, he continued on his course towards us and it is for this reason and the reasons stated above that I used my truncheon as a means to subdue him. Had I not felt in fear for the safety of myself and the other officers present, I would not have resorted to such means, but, given the circumstances and the fact that Connor appeared intent on causing harm, I believe that my decision to use such force was truly warranted.

It should also be noted that Liam Connor did not sustain a life threatening injury and, once the situation within the target house had reached a calmer level, Officers (who should again be praised for their total unbiased professionalism) offered medical assistance and advice to Connor regardless of the family's continued hostility and resentment towards the Police.

In conclusion, I trust that this report fully outlines the circumstances surrounding the actions taken by myself and will evoke support in my belief that those actions were fully justified.

Respectfully.
Superintendent Peter Gale.

Gale allowed himself a slight grin of satisfaction as he cast an eye over the completed report and decided that he would take it immediately and directly to the boss to avoid any mishaps within the internal mail system. However, no sooner had he risen from his chair than the door to his office opened and the Chief Constable walked in. "Have you got a minute Peter?" he began. "I have some news that I believe will interest you greatly!"

"Of course Sir," Gale replied. "I was just coming to see you actually, with the report on that unfortunate incident with Liam Connor!" His sardonic tone was lost on his boss who seemed unusually excited.

"Forget about that for a while Peter," he said, waving his hand dismissively. "I have just received this from Special Branch at New Scotland Yard. You'll find it's quite self explanatory!" He passed Gale a copy of a telex and stood with his arms folded, waiting for a reaction.

Superintendent Gale read the text, frowned in disbelief and read it again, slowly. When he had finished, he sat (or rather slumped) back into his chair and looked up, open mouthed, at his boss. The Chief merely nodded in confirmation, a faint smile appearing on his lips, as Gale read it for a third time.

"I think that can be classed as *a result*, wouldn't you Peter? ... Have a good weekend," was all the boss said before turning around and leaving the office, satisfied that his colleague and friend would find the news cause for celebration.

###

Chapter 23

Friday 18th May 1990

The last three days of Liam's life had travelled forward at an almost unbearably slow snail's pace, with each and every second bringing back dire memories and renewed torment. He had wished, several times, that the maxim of *'turning back the clock'* was an option that was actually available to him in more than just words. If it was, he knew that he wouldn't have changed putting Walker on his arse, but knew more than anything else in the world, that he would have changed what he had done to Jen. He had wanted to see her and tell her how much he was sorry, how much he had missed her and, in an unusual first, how much he actually loved her. Each time he thought of her, his stomach would initially tingle from the playful flight of a thousand imaginary butterflies. But then came the ache, as the vice like grip of frustration and anxiety took hold and mercilessly twisted his innards. It hadn't helped when the Headmaster of St. Monica's had telephoned his mum and recounted all of what had occurred that Tuesday afternoon, finishing his conversation with the suggestion that it *'might be best for all concerned if Liam remained at home for the rest of the week!'*

That certainly wasn't what Liam had wanted nor was the ridiculous adage that came from his mother. "And don't think that you will be leaving this house or seeing your friends until the weekend!" she had said sharply, which made Liam snort in total disbelief.

"What?" he had quizzed disdainfully. "After everything that has happened in this dump and you're *grounding* me for sticking up for our so called *good name* ... what a joke!"

Despite his objections (and the blatant irony of it all), Liam knew that his mum was not going to budge on her decision and so he had been confined to barracks with only his troubled mind as a companion.

Sean had called round the evening after the fight, checking on Liam's welfare with great concern. Though Liam didn't get a chance to see his friend, he had heard him talking to Bridie at the front door and had been proud of the earnest explanation pitched to her in the hope of exoneration. Frustratingly for Liam (and Sean), vindication was not forthcoming as his mum, steadfast in her decision, refused to concede and allow her son to go out, sending a dejected and bitter Sean on his way.

And now, three days on, Liam could only wait as the clock ticked by with no sense of urgency, towards the time that he was permitted to leave solitary confinement and see his friend again. *'Another eight soddin' hours!'* he thought despondently as he saw that his bedside clock only registered 9.00am. With a sigh, he got off his bed and went to open his curtains feeling sure that the brightness of day cascading into his room would make him feel a little more upbeat. As he pulled back the material, he squinted and held up his hand in reaction to the sudden burst of blinding sunlight hitting his pupils. After a moment, Liam closed his eyes, lowered his hand and remained still for a while, happy to allow the warmth of the sun wash over his face through the window pane. As he slowly reopened his eyes, he blinked a little, and then quickly looked down into the street as his peripheral vision caught sight of a black car pulling up outside his house.

As the vehicle came to a stop, the passenger in the rear seat looked out of the car window towards the Connor house and sighed heavily. He then glanced around the immediate area, quickly but thoroughly, as if checking for something in particular, before eventually opening his door to step out. He paused before alighting from the vehicle and spoke to the driver without bothering to look at him. "I won't be too long," he said rather sullenly, receiving no more than a nod of the head in acknowledgement from the man at the wheel.

Once outside the car, the man instinctively looked up and then down the road making sure that there was nothing untoward occurring, nothing suspicious. It was a ritual that he had carried out for most of his adult life, a routine that becomes second nature in his particular line of work. In truth, the man knew that he shouldn't have even been at this address and was taking a big chance by coming here, especially as he was fully aware that certain factions of the law enforcement fraternity were looking to speak to him on one or two rather important matters. Nevertheless, this visit was considered extremely necessary given the circumstances and to this man, no risk was too great.

As he walked up to the gate, he paused and looked up at the house as his eye caught somebody staring down at him from a bedroom window. When he saw that it was Liam, he held up his hand in greeting, but the boy seemed to ignore him and turn away without returning the gesture. The man frowned in dismay and sighed again before opening the gate and heading up the path. As he reached the entrance of the house, he scowled and cursed under his breath when he saw the temporarily yet badly repaired front door and felt a sudden wave of guilt wash over him causing him to hesitate from pushing the door bell. He momentarily reflected on the reason why he was here and though he had gone over it a million times before, his plan of how he would approach speaking to Bridie on this occasion, was rapidly falling to pieces. Anxiety quickly started to rise from the pit of his stomach making him feel a little nauseous and though he took in a few large breaths of air to try and compose himself, it was a feeling he suspected was not going to leave him any time soon. In all honesty (despite his everyday persona as a man not to be reckoned with) he knew that he was actually losing his bottle and it was only through his strength of loyalty and love for this family, that he eventually managed to reach out and press the bell.

Bridie stood in the kitchen staring out into the rear garden, her thoughts a million miles away from the flowers and grass that filled her immediate line of sight. She too had replayed the recent events in her mind over and over again and still firmly believed that a move back to Ireland was the answer; it seemed the only logical option. For herself, she couldn't have been more eager to return to her birthplace and would have gone the same day as the Police had stormed her home had she been able to. Her only sorrow was for her children, Margaret and Liam, who would have to leave their friends and the life they had, behind. *'But what sort of a life would it be for them now?'* she thought. *'It's hard enough for them just having Irish parents!'*

In amongst her melancholic thoughts, she happened upon one that caused her to smile a little as she remembered Sean calling round for Liam three days earlier and explaining all about the fight between her son and that boy, Walker. Though she could not be seen to condone Liam's behaviour and had grounded him accordingly, she was secretly pleased that he had put this outwardly annoying little shit on the seat of his pants. *'Typical English bigot dragged up by a nobody. Good on ya Liam Connor!'* she had thought at the time, but had sent Sean away ignorant of her personal feelings on that particular subject.

She let out a heavy sigh and turned away from the window deciding to focus on the positives of the future rather than the negatives of the recent past. "Right," she said quietly whilst scanning the room. "Time to organise things."

She walked over to one of the kitchen drawers, opened it and removed a notepad and pen before sitting at the kitchen table, eager to start making a list in respect of the pending move. *'Once we're all back together as a family, the kid's will see that it was for the best,'* she thought, as she began writing bullet points on what needed to be done.

No sooner had she begun to write when the door bell sounded, making her jump a little. *'Who the hell is that?'* she thought warily. *'I'm not expecting anyone!'* She leant back on her chair and peered down the hallway thinking that she would be able to make out who it was through the glass panel in the top of the door. She cursed under her breath when she was visually reminded that the glass had been replaced by a board, courtesy of the Police and in order to reveal the visitors identity, she would now be required to get up and physically answer the door. She waited for a while surprised at her sudden anxiety and wondered if whoever it was would leave if the musical summons was ignored. The subsequent *'double'* press of the bell and an added knock proved that this was not to be the case and reluctantly, Bridie made her way slowly to the door. Another two loud knocks before she had even walked halfway down the hall, gave her the impression that the caller was either very impatient or just stupidly persistent. "Ok OK!" she shouted out, her anxiety quickly being replaced by irritation. "I can't come any faster!"

As she struggled to pull the makeshift, ill fitting door from its frame, the person on the other side gave it a sharp encouraging shove causing it to suddenly give and a startled Bridie to shout out. "Hey, what the hell are you doing?" she asked in a vexed panic, pushing the door back and keeping her hands on it in the vain hope of preventing it from being opened again. "Who is it? What do you want?" she demanded, alarm now evident in her voice as it began to tremble.

"Bridie, it's me!" a voice answered from the other side. "Will ya let me in, please?"

Bridie immediately recognised the male's tone but frowned as she tried to comprehend why he should possibly be outside her front door and not in Birmingham or wherever it was he was supposed to be. He very rarely called at the house and if he did, it was always to see Michael and surely he knew that Michael was still in Ireland. So why?

"Bridie c'mon will ya," the voice encouraged with a sense of urgency bringing Bridie out of her temporary daze.

"Joe?" she began quizzically. "What in God's name are ...?" Her voice trailed off as she yanked open the sticking door and came face to face with her brother-in-law. Studying the man before her, she immediately noticed how incredibly tired he looked and how his usually powerful stature had ostensibly been replaced by the emergence of a distraught and humble being. The suit that he wore, though no doubt expensive, had the appearance of having been slept in, a look compounded by his skew-whiff tie and his uncharacteristically tousled hair. His complexion had become markedly ashen accentuating his grey eyes which now stared, glazed and lifeless, at Bridie. The man was little more than a shadow of his former self. Whether it was the physical appearance of her brother-in-law, his unannounced visit or just an overwhelming surge of intuition, Bridie suddenly knew the reason why Joseph Connor was standing at her door. She slowly shook her head in wanton disbelief and held her trembling hands up to her face, praying that her growing fear was unjustified. When Joe broke his gaze and looked awkwardly to the floor, Bridie felt an instant torrent of silent tears cascade from her eyes as she realised that he wasn't about to contradict her instincts. The only question remaining now, was *how* her husband Michael had died.

###

175

Chapter 24

15TH June 1996

The noise of a car impatiently sounding its horn made Liam jump a little, bringing him back from a momentary trance and causing him to look around hastily and then check his watch. He had spent far too long with this man as it was and needed to make his excuses and leave quickly. Now was certainly not the time or the place for reminiscing with a childhood friend. Liam opened his mouth to speak but was cut to the chase by an ever talkative Sean.

"So what happened to you then?" he asked curiously.

"What?" Liam replied frowning. "When?"

Sean snorted in surprise. "When?" he repeated. "Six years ago, that's when. The day I came round to yours and found that you had all mysteriously disappeared to fuck knows where? I was well miffed mate I can tell you, not knowing where my ..."

"My dad died!" Liam cut in coldly, not wanting the conversation to progress any further, though Sean clearly had other ideas.

"Aw Mate, I'm sorry!" he said genuinely. "How did it happen?"

"Heart attack!" Liam lied sharply, yet immediately sensed that Sean knew he had not been honest. He saw the suspicious look on his former friend's face and quickly added. "And we had to go back to Ireland, you know, for the funeral 'n' all and we ... well, we just decided to stay!"

"Oh right," replied Sean, not wholly convinced with the tale, but then gave Liam a look that conveyed his understanding that the subject was not to be pursued.

Liam hated lying to Sean as it was something that he had never done in all the years he had known him. It was like he was breaking an unwritten law of trust, crossing that predetermined moral line so often established in close friendships. But how could he possibly tell him what had gone on over the last six years and where the hell would he start? It would be an impossible task and one that would merely bring an involuntary Sean into a totally new world. A world that he would otherwise only read about in the papers or hear about on the news, a world that was a far cry from any nine to five job or engagement to a childhood sweetheart. It was a cold world of darkness and vengeance, a world that Liam had needed little encouragement to enter, especially when his Uncle Joe had informed him of his father's untimely death.

Liam recalled how, on the eighteenth of May 1990, the youthful and carefree life that he knew, was dramatically taken away and discarded in place of a dark and resentful future. He remembered how he had felt when his mum and uncle had sat him down in the lounge of their home and told him about his dad. He remembered his mum crying and hugging him tightly and his uncle Joe saying over and over again how sorry he was before he himself broke down. He remembered feeling like somebody had physically ripped out his very soul and replaced it with a sadness that was beyond description but he also remembered an incomprehensible inability to cry or express any emotion related to his loss. Unbeknown to Liam, he had begun to build a psychological barrier that would not allow for sentiments of grief or remorse, only hate and retribution.

Within an hour, Joseph had suggested that they leave immediately for Ireland using the car waiting outside to take them to the ferry port. They would collect Margaret on the way. Bridie had agreed unreservedly and went to quickly pack the bare necessities required for the move, leaving Liam and his uncle alone in the lounge. A few minutes went by before Liam looked up and stared quizzically at Joe.

"How did he die?" he asked quietly. "I mean, you said he was dead, but you never said *how* he died!"

Joseph shifted uneasily in his seat. He had not really prepared for this question from a sixteen year old and wrongly assumed that he wouldn't have asked. "Erm, his heart," he replied quickly. "He had a heart attack ... there was nothing anybody could do, God bless him!" He looked down at his watch and suddenly shot up from his seat. "What's keeping your mother?"

Liam frowned then glared at his uncle. "You're lying!" he said sharply. "Why are you lying?"

"Whoa, hold on there Son!" Joe rebuked calmly. "Don't be calling me a liar now!"

"But you are. I can see it on your face!" Liam spat before standing up in front of his uncle.

"Liam," Joe began, placing a hand on Liam's shoulder. "You're naturally upset, but ..."

"Don't fuckin' patronise me!" Liam cut in angrily, shrugging off Joe's hand. "Tell me how he died!"

Joseph stepped in towards his nephew, his face reddening in annoyance. "There are things you will never understand Liam!" he growled, "and for that reason, when I say that you're father died from a heart attack, then that's the way it was and that's all you need to know!" He stepped away from Liam, calming a little. "Now, you're Michael's son and for that I will always love you and I truly understand the pain you are going through, as we all are. But don't ever question me again Liam or I might just forget that you are my nephew, is that understood?" Liam scowled at his uncle saying nothing as Joe added. "You need to show a little respect son!"

"Respect?" Liam repeated bitterly. "Why should I respect you? You're not even ..."

"Not me, you eejit!" Joe snapped. "Your father. Show some respect for him, his memory. And think about your mother Liam. D'ya not think she needs our support now instead of all this stupid bickering?" He sighed and shook his head. "Look Liam," he continued quietly. "Your dad was a good man, a man whose life ended much before his time y'know? But let's remember him that way, as a good man, who always wanted the best for his family. If you think I'm lying about his passing, then so be it. But what I do, I do for you and the sake of this family"

"Then tell me how he really died!" Liam demanded. "I want to know!"

"I told you," Joe replied. "It was a heart attack!"

"I don't believe you. Tell me the truth!"

"Liam, why can't you just accept what I'm saying?"

"'Cause he was stronger than that. It ... it can't have been his heart!"

"It wasn't his heart!" Bridie interjected nonchalantly, now standing at the lounge door. Both Joseph and Liam looked round in surprise at her unexpected appearance.

"Jesus, Bridie," Joseph started ashamedly. "I didn't know you were there. Are we ready to go or have ...?"

"Tell him," she cut in again, ignoring her brother-in-law's obvious attempts to change the subject.

"What?" Joseph asked, hoping that he had heard wrong.

"Tell him!" Bridie repeated, not faltering. Joseph glanced quickly at Liam and then back to Bridie.

"But he's only a child Bridie!" he exclaimed softly.

"He's older than you or Michael were Joe," Bridie pointed out quietly as she entered the room and sat on the arm of the settee. "And I think he has a right to know."

"But Bridie," Joe began to protest. "This is not what Michael would have wanted. He would have expected ..."

179

"Michael wasn't *expected* to die Joseph!" Bridie interrupted sharply. "But I'm damn sure that he wouldn't have wanted his life to have been in vain nor would he have wanted his family torn apart by lies and deceit. God knows, there'll be enough of that shite thrown about by people wanting to blacken his name as it is. Let's not give them a helping hand by lying amongst ourselves!" She paused as Joe gave a heavy sigh and looked to the floor. "I want him to know everything Joe," she continued as she turned and stared at Liam, smiling a little. "He's got a good head on his shoulders and he's strong enough to hear the truth." She turned back to Joe and added. "But it's *our* truth he should hear Joe and only ours. Let him make his judgements based on fact, not malicious rumour or fabricated hatred, but honest fact!" She stood up and walked slowly over to Liam, tenderly stroking his face as she reached him. She saw the pain in her son's eyes, a look of hurt and confusion, desperate to find comfort. And though his mouth quivered, she saw how he fought hard to hold back his tears, as if crying would show signs of weakness or confirm his status as a *child*. "Your dad loved you so very much you know?" she continued softly. "And you filled him with great pride!" She paused for a moment and then, as new tears rolled down her own face, she hugged Liam and kissed him on the cheek before whispering in his ear. "Don't let them win Liam!"

Liam returned his mum's hug but frowned at her quiet sentiment, wondering what it was she meant. As she pulled away, her gaze remained fixed on Liam as she pondered her son. "You're the head of this family now," she finally said before turning slowly to face Joe. "And you will be his guide," she instructed. Joe nodded slowly, surrendering to her will and acknowledging what needed to be done. As Bridie left the room, Joseph turned to Liam and gestured towards the chair, urging him to be seated. Liam complied as Joseph sat opposite him, a stern look on his face.

"What I tell you now Liam," he began after a few moments, "is for your ears and your ears only, is that understood?" Liam nodded his head in silence, suddenly anxious and unsure if now, he really wanted to know. Joe leaned forward and raised his finger as if to emphasise a point. "What is said in this room remains in this room," he continued. "But if you can't promise me that Liam, then this conversation is finished and we move on ... it's your call son!" Joseph glared at Liam as he waited for his decision. He felt grossly uneasy about what he might have to reveal to his nephew and was secretly pleading with the Great Man above to make Liam see sense and walk away none the wiser. Joe sighed heavily, feeling his heart sink a little, when Liam voiced his solemn promise.

Over the next hour, Liam listened intently as his uncle gave a detailed account of Michael Connor's life and the struggle that he and generations before him had faced whilst fighting against British rule. Whatever thoughts or preconceptions Liam had harboured about his dad were quickly erased and replaced by fantastical stories conjuring up graphic mental images that both shocked and amazed him. As time passed, the notion that Michael Connor was a *terrorist* was not only forgotten by Liam, but transformed spectacularly into that of a legendary soldier, a warrior striving to bring justice to his homeland by ridding the enemy within. In the closing stages of the detailed biography, Liam learned how his father had been killed, shot by the SAS just outside Portadown in County Armargh. He bowed his head in silent reflection, taking in the gravity of what he had just been told, trying to justify the loss. After a short while, he lifted his head and looked longingly at Joe. "Did he put up a good fight?" he asked quietly.

Joe opened his mouth to speak but just couldn't find the right words to say. He knew that Liam was looking for a hero's ending, wanting to be told that his dad went out in a blaze of glory, fighting for freedom till his last breath. Liam saw that his Uncle was faltering and he frowned suspiciously. "What?" he asked, but was only answered by a sigh and a slow shake of the head. "Uncle Joe, what is it?" Liam pressed, "What's wrong?"

"Liam," Joseph began hesitantly. "Your dad ... well, your dad ... he was unarmed son!" He saw the look of confusion on Liam's face, wondering why an unarmed man, his dad, would have been shot. "They just shot him on sight," Joe continued. "No warning, no judge or fuckin' jury, nothing!"

"But, but they can't do that can they?" Liam asked disbelievingly. "Don't they need a reason or something? ... Aren't there rules?"

"Rules! ... Those bastards make up their own rules!" Joe replied angrily. "And the whole tragedy will be swept under the carpet and lost, like it always is with those British bastards ... and they said a *shoot to kill* policy never existed ... fuckin' liars!"

Liam stood up sharply, his face enraged with anger. "So you're saying they murdered my dad, for nothing?" he questioned bitterly. "And we've got to live with that like it's the fuckin' norm!" He began to shift erratically on his feet as fury consumed his body. "I'll fuckin' kill them myself, I swear to God!" He looked at his uncle as he himself also stood up. "What can we do Uncle Joe? We need to do something!"

Joseph laid his powerful hands on Liam's shoulders and looked at him with earnest. "We can wait for our time Liam," he replied calmly. "And when that time comes, we will be prepared to do what we need to do!" Liam looked mystified and Joseph could see that he was about to explode as his anger fused with his impatience. He held up his hands in a calming gesture and asked. "Have you ever heard the expression, don't get mad, get even?" Liam nodded as Joe continued. "Well, that's what we do Liam ... And when I say *we*, I'm including you, if that's what you truly want?"

"More than anything!" Liam replied. "I want to ki ..."

"Then we prepare Liam," Joe cut in quickly, trying to quell his nephew's intolerance. "And for you, that means learning the craft, from the bottom!" He glared at Liam who now appeared to be controlling his emotive state and listening intently, which silently impressed Joe. He had only ever seen one man able to draw upon bodily resources as quickly as Liam had and use them to manage, and then hide, his true feelings and that was his own father, Tommy Connor. "I can tell you now Liam, that it won't be easy and there are no shortcuts. Time, patience and belief son, that's what turns a good man into a great soldier!"

"Together with this!" Bridie interjected as she suddenly re-entered the room. Both Liam and Joseph looked towards her hands, with only the latter immediately recognising what it was she was holding. "Thank God the Police were too stupid to find this during their visit!" she added, placing Michael Connor's copy of '*The Green Book*' into Liam Connor's hand.

###

PART TWO

Chapter 25

Life as a teenager is supposed to be simple. A time that is meant to follow a particular pattern. A pattern that, despite having to attend school or college, should be all about enjoying new experiences with close friends and sharing the laughter or tears that come with them. Whether it's about trying to sneak into the cinema to see an x rated film, wandering aimlessly around the city centre whilst girlfriends check out the latest fashions or heatedly debating which band churned out the best music as denoted by the NME, it should be about simplicity. It is a time of life that is seen as a learning curve to adulthood where mistakes can be made safely in the knowledge that there is always somebody close by to offer advice or a hug and tell you that everything will be ok. It was a time of life, that by a harsh twist of fate, had ended sharply for Liam. Whilst his childhood friend Sean had drifted through the last six years in relative ignorance of the bigger world outside his own, Liam had been subjected to an education that would never be included within any National Curriculum yet was an education that he not only excelled in, but was destined to become a master of.

###

Taken from the familiarity of home and friends in Manchester to an unconventional setting of a *safe house* just outside Ardboe in County Tyrone, Ireland, would have proved quite daunting for any normal sixteen year old. But Liam, who had developed a certain distaste for the glory of England the day he learnt about his dad's death, had found himself surprisingly eager to leave its shores. His only regret at the time was not being able to say goodbye to Sean or Jeanette, though he suspected the latter would have only been too pleased to see the back of him after what he had done; it was a thought that, unbeknown to him, couldn't have been further from the truth.

In this new and strange town, Liam was amazed at how many people he had never met before, actually knew all about him. In a surreal setting, it was like he had suddenly become an overnight celebrity with admirers of all ages wanting to see or speak to him. Even the local priest, Father Donoghue, had made it his business to make a special visit to the Connors' to offer his blessings and support. Liam later found out from his uncle Joe, that the overly warm, yet curious welcome he had received, was shown out of a mark of respect for his father, a man who had great influence in the town and whose dedication to the struggle was greatly revered, even in the highest of places.

Within a few months of arriving, the highly premature transformation of teenager into adult began, as Liam was relocated to Tralee in Kerry to begin his intensive training as one of a dozen new recruits in the Irish Republican Army. It was here that he would lose his ignorance about the IRA and be taught the truth about their continuing struggle, unhindered by the lies of media speculation. He would be schooled in the arts of weaponry, military tactics, security and interrogation techniques, yet be reminded on several occasions how these skills would be useless without one key element; comradeship. "You can have all the technology and expertise in the world," one of his trainers had exclaimed. "But without the support of your comrades' gentlemen, it is worthless. In this army, we ensure that no man will become an island, for if he does, then death is almost a certainty and we will have failed him in our duty!"

Liam was in awe of his mentors and thrived more and more on the information they passed on to him. For the first time, ever, he had developed a sense of belonging and purpose. This was a cause to believe in, to fight for and if God decreed, to die for. As time went by, he felt less hurt at the loss of his father and gained more pride, not only from the many revelations of his dad's achievements, but in his own, proving himself to be a most worthy and eager recruit. His dedication, flair and unrivalled willingness to learn his craft did not go unnoticed by his peers, an observation that was quickly disseminated to various members of the hierarchy. "He's like his Father," one high ranking official had pointed out with some warmth, only to be corrected and told that Liam was in fact better than his father ever was at this stage.

This praise, though never mentioned to Liam, would eventually find its way to his Uncle Joe who had specifically asked for regular updates on the progress of his nephew. When he in turn had passed the news onto Bridie, she simply smiled and said, "Of course, he's a Connor, isn't he?" There were not enough words to convey her own pride.

For the next year, Liam lived and breathed his new found love, becoming extremely proficient in every aspect of his education. From the basement of a disused house in Donegal, that had been converted into an efficient bomb making factory, he discovered the uses of Semtex and was taught how to make crude but effective nail bombs using only Nitrobenzene and fertiliser packed into an old baked bean can. At a remote farmhouse in Kerry, he was trained in the use of firearms and it wasn't long before he could strip and rebuild anything from a 9mm pistol or Colt 45 revolver to an AK47 or Barret Light 50 sniper rifle in record time. Above all else, he learned to have the greatest respect for the tools of his trade and the lengths that his comrades had gone to, to acquire them. Yet, even with the vast arsenal of weapons that were to hand, he knew that in a world obsessed with the use of chemical, biological and radiological weapons, it was in fact the simple methods used by the IRA, combined with the most complex, sophisticated planning and training, that would cause the most pandemonium in this particular war.

His display of discipline and obedience earned him the respect of other *volunteers* and, like his father before him, it wasn't long before he too began to rise in the ranks. At eighteen years of age, whilst his old friend Sean Bevan was contemplating which job to try after quitting his role as a car mechanic, Liam had been involved in several attacks on the British security forces and the Ulster Defence Regiment in Northern Ireland and had been instrumental in the death of a Special Branch Detective following a violent skirmish in the town of Ormagh. Liam's penchant for the planning and execution of jobs was seen as a gift, a gift that was to involve him in one of the IRA's most ambitious campaigns to date.

31st July 1994

The moderately sized church hall in Ardboe appeared to be literally bursting at the seams as men, women and children took up their invites to join the celebration that was Liam Connor's twenty first birthday party. A whole host of people, from neighbours and relatives to prominent figures of the IRA network, had turned up to give Liam their best wishes, present their gifts and enjoy the plentiful array of food and drink that was on offer. The late July weather had remained pleasantly warm throughout the day and well into the evening, allowing people to socialise in the grounds outside the venue as well as inside; a gift from the great man above that Father Donoghue would almost certainly give thanks for.

As with any other such gathering, this was seen as a time for the women to dress up and gossip, the men to drink ale and discuss Ireland's future and the children to bounce on a tired looking inflatable castle before sitting down, red faced with sandwiches and pop, to watch a Punch and Judy show. Any outsider watching the event would have been forgiven for thinking that this was a popular summer fete laid on by the

Church and not just the coming of age of one young man, such was the atmosphere of it all. Entertainment was plentiful, provided by a local comedian, an Irish folk band and a budding solo female singer, all of whom had given their services to this particular occasion for free; mainly as their gift to Liam, on this his milestone birthday, but secondly (and secretly more importantly) because all of them knew that there would be a sufficient number of impresarios in the crowd capable of lending them more than a helping hand to further their careers.

As the Irish band came to the end of their set, Father Donoghue stepped up to the microphone and, after thanking the '*Isle of Dreams*' for their musical input, brought the gathering of people to order.

"Ladies and gentlemen, if I could just have your attention for one wee moment!" he announced, immediately stepping away from the microphone with a grimace as the speakers whistled with feedback. After a minor adjustment to the sound system, he spoke into the mic once again. "Hello, is that any better?" he asked the attentive crowd who murmured their approval. "Can you hear me alright at the back there Martin?" he added, looking towards the rear of the room whilst shielding his eyes from the glare of the overhead spotlights. A man with thick grey hair and a glistening red face, stood by the bar area at the back of the hall, raised his half empty glass of Guinness towards Father Donoghue as confirmation that all was well. "Ok then, right," the priest continued, looking round the room and smiling with satisfaction that he had everyone's attention. "Well, I promise not to keep you for too long folks, especially as I know you'll all be waiting to hear the lovely voice of our very own Sian McCreedy!" He paused to allow the inevitable cheers and wolf whistles from the men in the crowd to quieten down. "But," he continued, "as it's my church hall that you're all in, then you're just going to have to bloody well listen to me for a while!" He paused again until the dutiful laughter faded to near silence. "Firstly, ladies and gentlemen, I would like to thank each and every one of you for coming here today to help celebrate this special occasion. I realise that for some, personal plans had to be put to one side in order to make this gathering and to those people I give you my warmest gratitude. Though in these our troubled times, it's not every day we can find something to rejoice about, so what better way to do it than here, amongst family and friends, with good food, great entertainment and enough of the black stuff to sink a British battleship!" The crowd voiced their *'here here's'* and raised their glasses before allowing Father Donoghue to continue. "And whilst I'm on the subject of food, I'm sure you will all join me in thanking Eileen Doherty and Mary O'Toole for the excellent spread they have laid on for us today ... isn't it grand?" There was an appreciative round of applause from the audience as they followed the priest's gaze towards the kitchen and focused on two embarrassed looking middle aged ladies stood by the doorway. As if pre-rehearsed, both of them giggled and curtseyed in unison before everyone turned their attention back to the main speaker. "Now," he continued. "Could I have young Liam up on the stage please?" Father Donoghue looked around the room but couldn't get a fix on Liam. He waited a few moments but saw nothing of him. "C'mon Liam, don't be shy ... has anybody seen Liam?" Everybody looked around the room trying to spot the birthday boy, but to no avail.

"I tink he's outside Father!" a small boy shouted from the crowd, causing the majority of people to look round at him, including the priest.

"Well then, will you go and get him young Kieran?" Fr. Donoghue asked. "And if you're back here with him in thirty seconds, there'll be a treat in it for you, ok? Go on now Son!" The young boy stood there, hesitant, biting his lip. "Is something wrong Kieran?" Father Donoghue enquired as the child seemed reluctant to move. Kieran slowly looked up at the Priest, his cheeks flushing as he noticed a hundred pair of eyes glaring back at him. An eerie silence fell on the room as everybody seemed to be waiting on the boy's response.

"I ... I tink he's wit a girl Father," he replied softly then jumped a little as thunderous cheers and laughter erupted from the priest and his flock. Suddenly, six or more children (mainly girls) had volunteered their services to go and find Liam and immediately raced out of the room in the hope of catching him in the act of kissing somebody. In less than a minute, a red faced Liam was being led into the hall by a small army of giggling ten year olds, greeted by rapturous applause from the waiting entourage.

"We didn't interrupt anything did we Mr.Connor?" Father Donoghue asked Liam via the microphone, which received another burst of laughter and cheers from the crowd.

"Nothing I can't continue with later on Father!" Liam responded with a wink and a smile as he went up onto the stage, which again, evoked cheers and applause from the crowd. Father Donoghue warmly shook Liam's hand and gave him a small embrace before turning back to the onlookers, bringing them to silence again by slowly raising then lowering his hands. He looked at Liam and smiled and then returned his gaze to the guests.

"I have had the privilege to know three generations of the Connor family," he began. "And the way things are going, maybe a fourth, eh son?" He turned and smirked at Liam as laughter rippled through the hall. Liam bowed his head in respectful acknowledgment of the priest's gentle quip. "Thomas, Liam's grandfather," he continued with a more sombre tone, "was not only a great patriot and soldier of this country, but also a devoted father. A father who, together with his dear wife Margaret, brought up two of the most caring, honourable and decent men I have ever known, Joe and Michael Connor!" Father Donoghue lowered his voice slightly as he continued. "I often recall with pride, how Michael entrusted me, a mere man of the cloth, with great responsibilities during our campaigns of the early seventies and for that chance to be involved, I will always be thankful. I only hope that I did him and my fellow countrymen, proud!"

"You've no worries there Father!" a voice shouted from the crowd, which received appreciative applause.

Father Donoghue smiled and gave a small, humble wave to his flock before continuing.

"Though it ails me to think about how Michael was brutally taken from us six years ago, I cannot help but give thanks to our Lord above for the deliverance of such a fine young man into our community," he gestured towards Liam, turned to him and smiled as the crowd voiced their agreement. "As Michael and Joseph were to your granddaddy, you are a fitting testament to the caring, loyal and selfless life of your father and to that Liam Connor, I raise my glass!" The onlookers once again added their '*here here's*' whilst holding up their tipples. "But as some fine philosopher once said ladies and gents," Father Donoghue continued, a little more light hearted, "behind every great man, and his son, is an undeniably greater woman."

"You got that right Father!" a woman shouted from the crowd, much to the enjoyment of the other females around her.

The priest also chuckled before continuing. "Then let us show our appreciation for the fine woman that she truly is. Bridie Connor!" The people applauded and looked towards a table in the corner of the hall where Bridie was sitting with her brother-in-law Joseph, her daughter Margaret (who was looking decidedly disinterested) and a few friends. "Will y'come up here Bridie?" Father Donoghue asked, beckoning her with his hand. A slightly embarrassed Bridie got up off her seat and walked onto the stage to a genuinely warm reception from the crowd.

She gave Liam a prolonged hug, whispering "I love you Son!" in his ear before turning to find that she was the recipient of a very large bouquet of flowers that Father

Donoghue had suddenly produced from behind the stage curtain.

"And these are because I love you too Mum!" Liam said, resulting in tears from Bridie and a noticeable '*aw*' from the fairer sex within the audience.

Father Donoghue, who had temporarily stepped back whilst the public show of affection between mother and son took place, walked back up to the microphone and again brought the people to order. Within a few moments, the hall was filled with the sound of voices singing the traditional '*Happy Birthday*' as the catering ladies, Eileen and Mary, walked carefully to the stage carrying a monstrous birthday cake, iced in a style to denote the flag of Ireland and finished with twenty one candles. As Liam extinguished the flames in one breath, three cheers were given followed by the resounding verse of '*For he's a jolly good fellow*', an ironic tribute given its reputation for being an English folk song.

In the corner of the room, Liam's sister, Margaret, watched and listened as her brother became King for a day. As the singing began, she shook her head and downed her newly replenished drink in one, before heading off, quietly and unnoticed, to the ladies room; using the facilities for what they were intended for wasn't on her list of priorities.

###

Chapter 26

From the day Liam Connor was born, his older sister Margaret would find herself destined to live in his shadow. Not that this had any immediate effect on her, as she had developed a strong trait of independence from a very early age, but in the events that were to unfold in later life, she would find herself desperate to be noticed and supported as she struggled to come to terms with the death of her father.

Despite being loved unconditionally by her family, Margaret soon realised that the most attention would be given to her younger brother, the son and heir in her dad's eyes, the apple of her mum's and she often secretly wondered if she had done something wrong that had caused her to lose favour with her parents. This, however, was a feeling that only lasted until her dad put her on his knee, kissed her gently on the forehead and asked. "Who's Daddy's favourite girl then?"

She would smile sweetly at him but, with a quizzical expression, reply, "Mummy?"

"Nope!" he would answer and start to twiddle his fingers in the air before adding. "And you know what's next if you get it wrong again, don't you Miss?"

"Oh no!" Margaret would reply through the onset of the giggles and her eyes would light up with a warmth reserved only for her dad and this, their moment. She knew what was coming next and could have easily avoided it, but where was the fun in that? As the giggles turned into staggered laughter, she would shift around on her dad's knee to find the comfiest position and look around the room as if pondering over the answer. "Erm," she would utter with a finger placed pensively on her chin, before she was reminded by her dad that time was running out. He would then move closer to her with his twiddling fingers making her yelp in playful anguish and laugh even more. She would hold up her own hands to her dad's in a feeble attempt to stop the advancement of the fingers and laughingly plead, "No, wait Daddy, I'm thinking!"

"Quickly, quickly," he would say. "I don't think I can stop them without the correct answer!"

Eventually, through uncontrollable mirth, Margaret would look at her dad and blurt out the reply. "It's Grandma!" she would incorrectly answer in time honoured tradition and though she would try, there would be nothing she could do to stop the inevitable tickling and tireless raspberry blowing on her tummy that would follow. Despite the game lasting no more than a few minutes, it was a time that Margaret cherished every second of and though the rules of engagement would change the older she got, she would always smile warmly whenever her dad asked who his favourite girl was before holding up his hands and twiddling his fingers. As she reached her teenage years, her initial stock answer to the question had changed to "Me of course!" Like her dad, she figured she was too old and too heavy to bounce on his knee anymore but also, like her dad, she missed it all the same.

Margaret had the looks that most girls would die for and numerous female celebrities would pay good money trying to achieve, but she never thought for one moment that this put her above anybody else. She had a humble quality that those around her found endearing and as such nobody, male or female, felt threatened by her natural beauty whilst in her presence. Her long, thick, black hair shone with a brightness that likened it to the plumage of a raven basking in the midday sun, seemingly shimmering with hues of deep greens, blues and silver, whilst her porcelain, unblemished complexion accentuated her deep blue eyes and full crimson lips. Make up had no purpose here, yet when applied (as teenage girls must) it only served to heighten, not hinder, her heaven blessed pulchritude.

Whilst at school, she displayed an aptitude for learning that was beyond her years and it came as no surprise to her high school teachers when she attained excellent grades in her final exams and secured a place in one of the top colleges. Yet, despite her academic prowess and model looks, she retained an innocent modesty that seemed to enhance her personality and thus, make her a very popular and approachable young lady. She was, on the surface, a happy go lucky girl who gave the impression that her life, for the most part, was carefree. What people didn't see, was the secret torment she had harboured since her pre-teen years as she yearned to have the same level of interest from her parents as they had shown towards her brother Liam. Though she loved her sibling dearly and wouldn't have changed him for the world, she couldn't help but feel a little jealous of the fuss that was made over the slightest of his achievements. When she herself had done something that merited praise, she would simply be told 'well done' or 'we expected nothing less' only then to be asked the usual anticlimactic question of, 'can you help me with tea?' However, with Liam's conquests, it was normally hugs and kisses all round with an unprecedented amount of accolades, usually followed by the statement, 'you deserve a special tea for that!' It was petty, she knew, but she also felt it was unfair. Not that she was decrying Liam's ability, but it appeared that he was rewarded more for his efforts, with her parents always going overboard with their plaudits. Maybe she was just being over sensitive but as much as she tried, she couldn't help but notice the extra little considerations shown towards Liam. One particular example she would often recall, with some bitterness, was the time when a family holiday had been arranged and her dad was unable to go. The fact that he wasn't there was disheartening enough for Margaret, but whilst she would only have the company of her mum to seek solace from, Liam had been allowed to take his fat, *eat all* friend along with him, something she would never have been permitted to do. Now how was that fair?

The ancestral tradition of the Connor family had not been one of liberalism and for generations, any female members of this particular clan had always known their role; that of homemaker. They cooked, cleaned, tended to their offspring and saw to it that their husbands were well cared for. Though Bridie and Michael Connor did not conform to this antiquated way of life, preferring and maintaining that their marriage was an equal partnership, they did remain steadfast on one thing; that their daughter Margaret (though allowed to have friends and ultimately attend college) would be discouraged from any close association or intimacy with boys until she was of an age where neither parent could stop her. This had naturally caused some heated arguments during Margaret's early teen years and had led, on more than one occasion, to testosterone fuelled suitors finding a less than warm welcome if they ever dared to visit the Connor household in search of her company.

"They're all the bloody same," her dad had once said whilst watching a dejected sixteen year old boy heading off quickly down the garden path. "Only after one thing!"

"They're not *all* like that dad," Margaret had disagreed. "And come away from the window, it's embarrassing enough as it is!" Michael turned away from the window, but he wasn't finished with his speech just yet. He was well and truly up on his soap box, as Margaret used to think, though she had learnt that it was usually best to let him have his say and move swiftly on.

"Oh believe me sweetheart," Michael continued, "they most certainly are ... just like that spotty little upstart a few months ago. All over you like the rash on his bloody face he was. What was his silly name? ... Jane?"

"It was Gene, dad, as in Gene Kelly!" Margaret corrected. "And he wasn't all over me at all. He's actually the other way, everybody knows that!"

"Oh they tell you that," Michael quickly pointed out as if a great authority on the subject. "They will lure you into a false sense of security, claiming to like your clothes and stuff and then, BAM! They've had their way, got you pregnant and have left you to pick up the pieces!" He turned to take one final look out of the window and in a tone barely loud enough to be heard added. "He's no more a puff than I am, the bloody liar!"

Though the strict rules on boyfriends and the imposed curfew of 8pm on a school or college night, 9pm on a weekend, had served to ensure the chastity of Margaret (and no doubt the outstanding exam grades) it also had a knock on effect of preserving her naivety and making her a little less '*streetwise*' than other youths her own age. It was a trait that would prove to have an unforeseen yet devastating effect in the future.

On the day the Police raided her home, Margaret saw a side of life that she would never have imagined even existed. It was a side of life that caused a deep fear at the time and one that would leave her mentally scarred with anguish and torment for many years to come. Up until that day, she had seen the Police as protectors of the public, keepers of the peace, not as a violent establishment determined to ruin the lives of others with their lies and bullying tactics. On that day, she had heard them accuse her father of all sorts of treachery (something she would never accept) and witnessed them physically assault her mum and brother to the point of Liam's unconsciousness. She herself had suffered untold humiliation as the rough and groping hands of a smirking policeman had subjected her to a *body search* under the guise of checking for hidden weapons.

Already threatened with arrest, she concluded that any form of protest would be futile. So, with tears of unwilling submission falling slowly down her cheeks, she had offered no resistance to the farce. What they had expected to find on a frightened teenage girl wearing nothing but a nightdress was beyond Margaret.

She had cried all that day, wanting her dad to come home, hold her and tell her that everything would be alright. That particular hope was not to be and as her mum tended to an injured Liam, she found herself (for the main part) alone in her room with nothing but her harrowed mind for company. Later that evening, as she continued to try and make sense of the horrors of the day, she left the house and unexpectedly found comfort. Not from her friends, as she thought she would, but from her first experience of vodka; a temporarily soothing liquid that she would forge an unhealthy bond with.

Later that week, Margaret was taken out of her college lecture and given the devastating news that her father had died. She remembered little of the journey to Ireland or indeed the first few weeks of her residency there as the gates of her own personal abyss opened up and consumed her with unprecedented feelings of grief, guilt and resentment. As the months passed by, Margaret remained unable to find closure on her loss as it seemed that nobody wanted to talk about the death of her dad. And though she learned the basic circumstances from overheard conversation and rumours, she felt ostracised from the truth, driving her deeper into depression.

After two and a half years of arriving in Ireland and by now a regular (though still secretive) Vodka drinker, Margaret crossed her own boundaries and entered a pub for the first time. She had had a particularly bad day and had made the decision to go into the pub with no regard to what anybody might think, say or do if she was caught. In reality, she didn't even care anymore.

The Volunteer Public House was a small, run down establishment in a less affluent part of Ardboe. Its clientele were more likely to be the local wannabe hoodlums and ladies of the night rather than an attractive, well presented girl such as Margaret Connor. From the moment she entered, she was hit by the stench of stale beer and sweat and began to cough as she inhaled the yellow sea of tobacco smoke that hung in the air like a Victorian London smog. Being the early afternoon, only a dozen or so hardened drinkers were present, most of them huddled over their drinks as if in silent reflection. One or two looked up at Margaret, disapprovingly shaking their heads. This was their sanctuary, however grey and ugly and the intrusion of a newcomer, especially one so pretty, would only serve to make them dwell on just how miserable their own lives really were.

"Bit young for a stripper isn't she Seamus?" somebody shouted to the landlord who was stood behind his bar studying the female stranger with some bewilderment.

"Aye, but better looking than the usual shite he puts on!" somebody else added, causing a burst of laughter around the room.

"Hold your tongues now boys, will ya?" the landlord asked his patrons, before adding. "She's obviously lost and thinks we're a fekkin' Wetherspoons!" The small crowd erupted once more with the inclusion of a loud cheer that made Margaret jump slightly. At any other time, she would have quickly turned around and left, chastising herself for being so stupid. But this was now and the savage lure of the Eastern European tipple was proving far greater than a feeble memory of dignity. "Did you want something Miss?" the landlord asked Margaret as she reached the bar. "Only I'm pretty shite at cocktails y'see!"

"Vodka," Margaret replied quietly, causing the Landlord to lean forward and cock his head to one side.

"Sorry, you'll have to speak..."

"Vodka!" she repeated loudly before adding. "A double ... please!"

The landlord looked at Margaret as she bowed her head and he felt an unexpected surge of pity towards her. This wasn't where she belonged, he could see that and he knew, that whatever her circumstances, she was better than this place. He put down the glass he was drying and leant over the bar, gently touching Margaret's arm to get her attention. When she looked up, he could see a sadness in her eyes that was normally only reserved for recent widows, a sadness that bore deep into the heart and soul and would take an age to tame let alone conquer. Here was a girl no older than his own daughter, twenty maybe twenty one, who appeared to be carrying the weight of the world on her unsubstantial shoulders, a girl who fitted into this shit hole of a pub as much as a square peg fitted into a round hole. Through her drawn and tired features, Seamus could see that she was an attractive girl and it concerned him that within only a couple of hours, his hostelry would be filling up with adolescent male scum eager to make her their trophy if she stayed here. He smiled kindly and spoke in a low tone as he made a suggestion that went well against the grain of his profit margins. "Look Miss," he started. "Why don't you just go on home and forget the drink. It's for the best, believe me!"

For a few moments, Margaret stared at him blankly, her thoughts temporarily elsewhere. And then, as if suddenly realising her own foolishness, she smiled slightly, gave Seamus a small nod of acknowledgement and turned around intending to leave. She had taken less than three steps towards the exit when the pub doors opened sharply and loudly, announcing the arrival of Bernie Fitzpatrick; a tall yet skinny male in his early twenties who sported a mullet of unkempt black hair and wore a distressed leather jacket over a tight fitting, *Fred Perry* polo shirt that did nothing to mask his prematurely developing beer gut. His wrists and fingers dripped with a quarry of jewellery that he truly believed gave him the look of being a successful and important man. In reality, it only accentuated his status as being on a par with that of the cheap and tasteless gold he displayed. Bernie looked slowly around the pub, smirking, as if expecting some kind of fanfare, but no other punter even bothered to look up. In his deluded mind of self importance, he put this down to their fear of him and nodded smugly. In reality, nobody found him interesting enough to break away from their own silent worlds. His gaze finally rested on the surprisingly pleasant addition to an otherwise dire drinking house.

Margaret stopped in her tracks when Bernie entered the pub, whilst the landlord cursed under his breath at the man's arrival, silently willing the girl to carry on and leave without so much as a glance towards him. Seamus didn't care for this boy in the slightest. He was a trouble causer, a thief and above all else, a low life, minor league drug dealer. He sold his wares on behalf of much bigger fish in the town and had been known to supply anything from cannabis right up to heroin. He'd even had the nerve, on one occasion, to peddle his filth right here in the pub, an act which had led to an altercation between him and Seamus. The landlord, not himself a small man, had easily ejected Fitzpatrick from his premises on that day, barring him in the process. But it wasn't long before a few broken windows, threats of violence and some *quiet* words of advice from Bernie's family, had seen the bar lifted and the man allowed to return to The Volunteer Public House. Seamus wasn't intimidated by it all but he wasn't a fool either. He knew that any prolonged acts of violence against him or the pub would undoubtedly see off any decent customers that he had and eventually lead to his financial ruin. As such, he had agreed to waive the ban but only after assurances were given by his brothers that no more drugs were to be sold in his establishment. Incredibly, the assurances had been honoured, though Fitzpatrick was arrogant in his victory. "No hard feelings Shay?" he had offered on his first night back after reinstatement, thrusting his hand across the bar. Seamus reluctantly took hold of it and nodded as Bernie added. "And to show it, I'll even let you buy me my first pint!"

"Don't be pushing it now Son!" the landlord warned, pulling his hand back sharply and gesturing towards the front entrance. "Those doors open outwards too, as well you know!" he said, before glaring at Bernie intensely.

Fitzpatrick held up his hands and stepped back slightly. "Whoa big man!" he said laughingly. "I'm only having a little joke wit ya. Relax man!"

Seamus didn't relax. Not then and not as long as this arse hole was gracing the pub with his presence. Unbeknown to Shay, Bernie had seen the look in the landlord's eyes that night and as a result, the subject of free drinks was never raised again.

Margaret put her head down and set off again towards the exit only to be prevented from gaining much ground by Bernie stepping deliberately into her path. She quickly looked up and saw the grinning face of Fitzpatrick looking right back at her. Margaret did not return the smile but scowled at Bernie as she was slightly irritated by the unnecessary obstruction. "Is there something you wanted?" she asked shortly. "Only I'm in a bit of a rush!"

"Ah well now," Bernie replied. "Is it not true that a thing of beauty should never be rushed?"

"Smooth, very smooth," Margaret scoffed and shook her head slightly. "Now, if you'll excuse me?"

Bernie hesitated for a moment before moving aside in a motion of mock gallantry, waving her on and bowing his head slightly as she walked by. "Can I at least know your name?"

205

he called after her, causing Margaret to stop yet again and turn around.

"It's Margaret Connor. Why?" she replied in a slightly offhanded manner, though Bernie merely smiled, raised the palms of his hands and looked up to the ceiling as if giving thanks to the Lord above.

"Ah. Saint Margaret. Most Patron Saint of Beauty!" he said before gazing back at her.

"Of pregnant women actually!" Margaret corrected. "There isn't one of beauty!"

"There is from where I'm standing!" Bernie added grinning widely.

Margaret raised her eyes then frowned in dismay. "And these are your best lines are they?" she asked sarcastically.

"To be honest Margaret Connor," Bernie replied, glancing around the pub, "there's not much call for any better in a dump like this. No offence Seamus!"

Behind Fitzpatrick the landlord remained silent, watching the girl, still hoping she would leave before the conversation went any further. He knew it wasn't to be, especially when he saw a faint smile appear on Margaret's face. "Well I'm sure *somebody* will appreciate them!" she said encouragingly.

"Just not you?" Bernie suggested. Margaret shook her head and was about to say something more before Bernie added. "Well can I at least buy you a drink before you go, only to apologise for my terrible blarney you understand?" Margaret remained silent, unsure of what to do. Yes, she wanted a drink, badly, but did she want to be bought one by a stranger? Would it be seen as an open invitation for this man to become over friendly and want more than just a drink? But it's just one drink, surely there's no harm in that, is there? She glanced towards the door and then back to Bernie, biting her lip as she considered his offer.

"I think she's just wanting to go Bernie!" Seamus called from behind the bar, hoping this would spur her on to leave.

206

"It's funny!" Bernie shouted back, frowning, without turning to face the landlord. "I thought you were just a barman Seamus, not some kind of psychic as well!" He looked pleadingly at Margaret and continued. "Surely, one drink can't do any harm Margaret Connor and who knows, y'might even enjoy it!" Margaret shrugged her shoulders and then, having made her decision, started walking back towards him. "Ah good on ya," Bernie said triumphantly as he joined Margaret's side for the last few remaining steps to the bar. "But I bet you drink those trendy *Spritzers* don't ya?"

"No!" Margaret replied sharply. "Vodka!" She smirked a little before adding. "And doubles at that!" Bernie stared at her with a look of both mild shock and some respect before he too smirked. He bowed his head again in submissive acknowledgment then turned towards a silently disgruntled landlord and ordered the drinks.

As the early afternoon faded like an old photograph into the sepia tones of an Autumn evening, one drink had become several with neither Bernie nor Margaret seeming to notice or even care. Margaret was surprised at how easy she had found herself opening up to this stranger and how well he appeared to listen without ever judging her; he actually seemed to care. Bernie was surprised at how much she'd drunk without it having had much effect, other than on his wallet. When she finally looked at her watch and decided it was time to leave, Bernie escorted her onto the street to say his goodbyes. "Well. It's been a pleasure Margaret Connor!" he said and held out his hand. Margaret responded and placed her hand into his, shaking it gently.

"Yes, thank you," she said. "And thank you for listening. I know I must have gone on a bit!"

"Not at all," Bernie replied lying. "It sounded like you needed to get it off your chest!"

Margaret smiled and nodded looking deeply into Bernie's eyes. When he leant in to kiss her, she turned away slightly and offered up her cheek, momentarily confusing Bernie who had obviously misread the signals of the day and was hoping for a full on joining of lips. Despite this setback, he pecked her on the cheek then released her hand to allow her to be on her way. "Will I see you again Margaret?" he asked as she began to set off.

"That depends now!" she replied smiling.

"On what?" Bernie enquired frowning slightly.

"On whether you're in there tomorrow or not!" she answered and nodded towards the pub. Bernie smiled as he watched Margaret turn back around and walk away. As she rounded the corner, he turned to go back into the pub but hesitated as he took time to check the contents of his wallet.

"Shit!" he exclaimed when he saw how his funds had depleted. He replaced the wallet into one pocket of his jacket and then put his hand into another, bringing out a number of small plastic snap bags containing an array of illegal substances. "Better go make me some punts!" he sighed, before walking away in search of needy customers.

Margaret stopped just outside her front door and breathed into her cupped hands, analysing the odour. When she was convinced that the *Sharps Extra Strong* mints had masked any trace of alcohol, she went into the house.

"Is that you Margaret?" Bridie called from the lounge. Margaret sighed and raised her eyes feeling a wave of renewed depression wash over her. Her mum suddenly appeared in the hallway, a look of anger on her face. "Where the hell have you been till this time?" she questioned loudly.

"Out!" Margaret replied.

"Obviously out," Bridie snapped. "But out where exactly? I was expecting you back hours ago!"

"Just out!" Margaret spat back. "Why does it matter where. I just ..."

"It matters to me Margaret!" Bridie interrupted. "I've been worried sick, not knowing if ..." She suddenly stopped talking and appeared to be studying her daughter more closely. "Have you been drinking?" she asked sharply, but as Margaret opened her mouth to speak, her mum continued with her own conclusions. "You have, haven't you? I can see it in your eyes!"

"So what if I have?" Margaret retorted. "I'm old enough aren't I? And before you ask, I went into a pub to buy it!" Bridie held up her hands to her mouth in utter shock. She may well have just been told that her daughter had murdered the local Priest, such was her reaction.

"Lord Jesus!" Bridie exclaimed in disbelief. "Have ya no morals Margaret? Girls like you shouldn't be going into those places!"

"Why? What makes me so special that I can't enjoy myself or have a normal life like anyone else?"

"Normal!" Bridie repeated angrily. "You think hanging around pubs like some common whore is *normal* do you? My God, what would your father say? And what would Liam think about his sister becoming a drunk?"

"For one thing, I'm not a drunk!" Margaret said bitterly. "And for another, you may not have noticed, but my Dad is dead!" Her voice broke slightly before she added. "And who gives a fuck what your precious Liam thinks!"

Bridie moved forward and grabbed her daughter by the wrist, holding on to it tightly. "You mind you're filthy tongue and remember whose house this is!" she growled. "I won't have you talking like that under my roof, do y'hear me Margaret!"

Margaret yanked her arm away from her Mum's grasp and glared at her through tear filled eyes. "Then maybe I should go somewhere else, 'cause we can't be upsetting the golden boy can we?"

"What in God's name are you talking about girl?" Bridie asked as Margaret headed back towards the front door. "Margaret? Margaret, where are you going?" she shouted. "Margaret, don't you leave this ...!" Bridie flinched slightly as the heavy slamming of the front door cut her off mid sentence. She remained fixated on the back of the door for a few moments wondering if she should go after her daughter or just leave her to calm down and return of her own free will. Deciding that the latter would probably be for the best, she sat wearily on a chair in the hallway and sighed. "What am I to do with her Michael?" she asked softly as if her late husband was present. "What am I to do?"

###

Chapter 27

31st July 1994

The portly woman looked into the mirror and started to apply her lipstick before averting her eyes to the reflection of the door as it opened. She saw a waif of a girl dressed in ill fitting clothes enter the ladies toilets and silently wondered when she had last had a good meal. The girl's dark ringed eyes were highlighted by her deathly white complexion and she noticed, not without disdain, that her jet black hair appeared to be screaming out for the introduction of a brush. The lady looked back at herself in the mirror and continued to freshen her lips, conscious of the girl who she could sense hovering directly behind her. When she turned around, she gasped slightly as she suddenly recognised the girl that moments earlier, she would have put money on being a gypsy. "Oh!" the lady exclaimed, unsuccessfully trying to disguise her grimace with a smile, resulting in a brief uneasy silence between the two. "It's a lovely do Margaret," the woman continued in a forced chirpy voice. "And you must be very proud of that brother of yours?"

"Oh yes!" Margaret answered sarcastically with an equally forced trill and an overly false grin. "We're all so very, very proud. In fact we're so proud, we're thinking of putting him forward for canonisation!" The large woman's smile faltered slightly as she became unsure of whether Margaret's comment was said in mere jest or bitterness. "Now if you'll excuse me," Margaret continued before the woman had reached her conclusion. "I really must pee!" She stood to one side and glared at the woman, as if giving her a cue to leave; it was taken without another moment's thought.

Once the woman had left, Margaret quickly checked that the three cubicles in the room were empty, before occupying the one furthest away from the main entrance. Locking the door behind her, she sat on the seat and began searching hastily through her handbag, removing various items from within and placing them on the toilet cistern. Moments later, she glanced at the objects, mentally checking that she had everything she needed. Satisfied, she picked up a small clear packet containing a brownish coloured powder and emptied the contents carefully onto a bent and blackened spoon. Using a cigarette lighter, she held a flame under the spoon causing the powder to melt, transforming it into a bubbling liquid of golden brown, a liquid she then transferred into the body of a hypodermic needle. Then, holding the syringe between her teeth to momentarily free up her hands, she pulled up her left sleeve, revealing a track of small, dark puncture wounds along the bottom of her forearm and applied a makeshift tourniquet around her bicep. Feeling her arm throb as the blood struggled to flow its course, she administered a couple of hard slaps to it trying to encourage the vein to swell and become visible beneath her skin, a task that was proving more and more difficult to achieve as time went by. "Jesus, come on!" she hissed impatiently through gritted teeth, slapping her arm for a third time and knowing that every minute she was absent from the party was an extra minute she would be missed. Her family seemed to be watching her like hawks just lately which was probably not surprising, given her association with Bernie Fitzpatrick. '*They never liked him!*' she thought bitterly. As she listened to the rapturous chorus of *For He's a Jolly Good Fellow* ringing out for the umpteenth time in the church hall, Margaret smirked slightly at the appearance of a pleasingly swollen artery in her arm. 'To you Bernie,' she thought sardonically as she offered up the needle to her vein.

November 1992

After storming defiantly out of the house, following the argument with her mum, Margaret had wandered aimlessly around the darkened streets of Ardboe trying to clear her head and put the relationship with her family into some kind of perspective. She had regretted walking out of the house the moment she'd slammed the front door behind her, but her inherent stubbornness had negated her immediate return, instead, spurring her on to stomp away in tears. After what appeared to be an age, she suddenly broke from her thoughts and found herself directly across the road from The Volunteer Public House. She shook her head and smiled at the irony of where her subconscious tracking device had taken her. A cool breeze wrapped itself around her body making her shiver and it was only then that she realised, in her haste to leave the house, she had forgotten to bring her coat. Without money or protection from the onset of a cold night, she decided that now would be a good time to return to the warmth and safety of her own home.

"Well now," a voice cried from behind her, making her jump. "If it isn't Saint Margaret!" She turned around and for the second time that day, saw the grinning face of Bernie Fitzpatrick looking right back at her. "What's wrong," he continued with some arrogance. "Couldn't wait another day before you saw me again, eh?"

"Yeah, something like that," Margaret replied. "But I was just about to go home again!" They stood and looked at each other for a few moments, silent but smiling. "So," Margaret continued. "You gonna buy your favourite Saint a drink then?"

Bernie looked genuinely shocked. "Jesus Mary and Joseph!" he exclaimed. "Y'surely can't be wanting another drink after what you downed in there this afternoon, can ya?"

"Mister Fitzpatrick!" Margaret falsely gasped, holding a hand up to her heart. "I sincerely hope you're not implying that I'm some sort of drunken lush are you?"

"God forbid," Bernie replied. "But your taste for the Vodka did put a wee dent in my wallet. Not that I ..."

"Oh God," Margaret interjected, suddenly looking embarrassed. "I'm so sorry. I didn't mean to ... I didn't know I ... Oh God!"

"Hey relax," Bernie said. "I was jus' jokin' wit' ya. And anyway, it was my pleasure to share a drink, or many, with a real live Saint!" Margaret smiled meekly and then shivered again as a fresh breeze whipped through the air. "You look freezin'," Bernie remarked before removing his jacket and wrapping it around Margaret. "There now," he continued. "And don't you look a treat?"

"Thanks," Margaret said quietly. "Though maybe I should head back home after all!"

"What?" Bernie asked with surprise. "And turn down a drink from your new friend?"

"I think you've spent enough!" replied Margaret still feeling a little embarrassed.

"Ah," Bernie said, holding up his finger. "But who said anything about buying it?" Margaret looked at him confused as he held out his hand and added. "C'mon, follow me."

"Where to?" Margaret asked frowning.

"Trust me," Bernie replied. "It's cheap, warm and free. You'll love it!" Margaret hesitated, switching her gaze from his outstretched hand to his grinning face and then back again. After a few moments, she decided to throw caution to the wind and placed her hand into his, allowing herself to be led away to who knew where.

###

214

Bernie's flat was the smallest home that Margaret had ever seen and probably one of the untidiest. It consisted of one lounge that appeared to be doubling up as a bedroom, a cramped kitchen area and a bathroom that had no door on it. To the left of the bathroom was another room, although Margaret was unable to see into it as the door was securely locked with three padlocks. "Is that where you keep all your money?" she joked, pointing to the room, though Bernie simply tapped his nose and said nothing. In the lounge, there was a settee with an open sleeping bag on it and an old coffee table playing host to an overflowing ashtray, numerous empty cans of beer and an array of half full and empty drinking vessels. In the corner of the room, atop a spindle backed chair, sat a portable television with a wire coat hanger attached to it, acting as a makeshift ariel. The drawn curtains looked as though they hadn't benefited from a clean in a good number of years and hung unevenly as some of the plastic rings holding them up had broken but never been replaced. *'This'll never feature in Home and Gardens'* Margaret thought before smiling politely at a watchful Bernie.

As if sensing disapproval, Bernie leapt to the settee and quickly folded up the sleeping bag before inviting Margaret to sit down. "I must apologise for the mess," he said light heartedly. "But my cleaner's ill at the moment!"

"Must be quite serious!" Margaret exclaimed, carefully sitting down, whilst Bernie set about scooping up the empty cans to take into the kitchen.

"Months she's been off," replied Bernie. "And I think she's robbed half me furniture as well!"

Margaret chuckled as she watched Bernie scurry around trying to make the place look half way presentable. One thing he was right about, Margaret mused, was the warmth. So warm in fact, that she found herself removing his jacket within minutes of arriving. The other thing she noticed, was the smell. Not an unpleasant smell, but a distinct smell nonetheless. It reminded her of a damp forest undergrowth, slowly drying out as it struggled to catch the intermittent offerings of heat from the sun's rays breaking through the tree tops; sweet yet musty at the same time.

"So tell me," Bernie started as he came back into the lounge from the kitchen. "Why *were* you standing back outside the ale house, looking all sorry for yourself?" He sat down next to Margaret, searched the pockets of his jacket that she had discarded and produced an old looking tobacco tin from one of them. From inside the tin, he pulled out a rather strange looking cigarette that made Margaret frown a little. "Oh," Bernie said, noticing her look and holding up the cigarette. "You don't mind do you?"

"No, no not at all," replied Margaret. "It just looks a bit weird. The shape I mean!"

"Ah," said Bernie. "That will be me rolling it when I was a bit the worse for wear. Still, until they legalise joints and sell them in packs, this will just have to do!" He laughed slightly at his own joke and then lit the cannabis filled cigarette, watched open mouthed by a mildly shocked Margaret. "Would you like some?" he asked in a tone that sounded like he was losing his voice and offered the fiercely smoking roll up to Margaret.

As the heavy fumes drifted over to her, Margaret realised that this was what she could smell when she had entered the flat. She found herself feeling strangely excited, yet nervous at the same time. She had heard about *dope smokers* but never once imagined that she would be sitting in the same room as one. And he seemed kind of normal, not like the horror stories she had been told by her parents about *pot* users losing their minds and becoming mental cases. "I ..." she began. "I've never tried ... y'know ... marijuana!"

"Then you don't know what you're missing Margaret Connor, for this is the chosen blend of the Gods, believe me. Go on, have a little drag, it won't kill ya!"

With an inexplicable lack of hesitation, Margaret did. As she drew on the joint, the burning smoke hit the back of her throat like a freight train, causing her to cough violently and tears to stream from her eyes. As she eventually regained her composure, she looked up and saw that Bernie was grinning widely. "That wasn't funny!" she rasped, as her vocal chords tried to recover from the assault.

"It's always like that the first time," Bernie reassured her whilst chuckling. "Here. Have another blast, but slowly this time. Try not to take too much in at once." Again, Margaret succumbed and though she did cough again, it wasn't nearly as traumatic as the first attempt. "Tell you what," Bernie said, getting up from the settee, "you keep that one and finish it off."

"What about you?" Margaret asked, still sporting a husky voice.

"Don't you go worrying yourself," Bernie replied as he started to undo the padlocks on the door next to the bathroom. "I've got plenty in here to be going on with!" As he opened the door, Margaret blinked as she was temporarily dazed by the brightest light she had ever seen, omitting from the room. Once she had focused and could see clearly again, she gasped at the vast amount of plants occupying what should have been a bedroom, obviously in the process of being cultivated. She also now knew why it was so warm in the flat as a heavy, damp heat radiated into the lounge, no doubt caused by the high intensity spotlights that had been erected in the room. Fans whirred and oscillated around the plants, whilst large silver venting pipes ran across, then up, into the ceiling. Margaret thought that it looked like a large scientific indoor greenhouse which, Bernie proudly pointed out, it was, kind of. When she asked what he was going to do with so much cannabis, he simply replied, "sell it of course!" Margaret knew that she should have been horrified. After all, had Bernie not just admitted to being a drug dealer? Wasn't this the point where she was supposed to quickly leave? The answers were probably yes, but she found herself not only intrigued, but in a state of mind where she couldn't actually care less. The effects of her first *joint* had already started to kick in, putting her on a very happy, yet very giddy plain. For the first time in many, many months, her troubled thoughts seem to evaporate and the more she smoked, the more she felt ready to take on anything life could throw at her. Anything that happened that night, whether funny or not, always resulted in Margaret laughing. In fact she laughed so much, she could feel her stomach muscles and ribs ache, which bizarrely, made her laugh even more. When she eventually arrived home later that night and was lying in her bed, Margaret was thankful for two things. The first was the fact that her mum hadn't confronted her again when she had gotten in and the second, was the chance meeting of Bernie and the amusing introduction to his stash of marijuana. Margaret saw the makings of a good friend in Bernie. Bernie, however, saw the makings of a good customer in Margaret.

###

Over the next eighteen months, Bernie proved himself to be (in Margaret's eyes) a very good and reliable friend. Whenever she was down, which was becoming more often these days, Bernie was always there to offer a smile and a little *pick me up* and never once complained whenever she turned up at his flat unannounced; unlike her mother who was always moaning about her going out so much and seemed to be on her back twenty four seven. When Margaret told Bernie that her family were obviously against her seeing him, he simply smiled and hugged her. "They're only looking out for you," he had said reassuringly. "But maybe we should stop seeing each other for a while, only to get them off your case!"

"No way!" Margaret said. "I'm old enough to do what the fuck I want and if they don't like it, then tough!" Margaret bowed her head before adding. "And you're the one good friend that I have. In fact, the *only* friend that I have!"

"That's nice to know," Bernie smirked. "And as a good friend, may I tempt you with one of these?" He produced a joint from his tobacco tin and offered it to Margaret.

Margaret looked up at the gift and then into Bernie's eyes. "Thanks," she sighed, taking it from his hand. "Though I can't see the point of these anymore 'cause they don't seem to calm me down like they used to!" She lit the joint, took a deep drag and exhaled hard, before frowning at Bernie. "Maybe I'm immune!" she added sullenly. "Or too fucked up to feel the effects anymore ... What d' you think?"

Bernie secretly rejoiced. Not because she sounded like she might give up the cannabis and therefore stop scrounging his *stash*, but after months of nurturing this pathetic, immature girl, he had finally been rewarded with an opportunity to take this *friendship* to the next level; a level that would see a nice flow of easy cash, whether begged, borrowed or stolen, line the pockets of Bernie Fitzpatrick. Predictably, Margaret had allowed herself to be led. She had fallen for the smooth yet shallow words of Bernie, translating them into caring and considerate advice and was very quickly transformed from having the status of being his friend into that of being his dependant. The dark world of habitual drug use consumed Margaret without a fight and it wasn't long before her physical appearance was deteriorating as rapidly as her self esteem. She craved the high that her first experience with cannabis had brought all those months ago, ridding her mind of worry and grief and though she continued to assault her body with an array of various narcotics, it was a quest that was never to be conquered. Margaret's family had watched her demise with horror and sadness, attempting to intervene on several occasions yet failing to understand the reasons for such blatant self destruction. They had even invited the Parish Priest round to talk with her privately in the hope of making her see sense, such was their naivety in these matters. Uncle Joe had decided that only tried and tested methods would help the situation and had made a personal visit to Bernie to offer him some *man to man* advice. Though Bernie had heeded the warning to the letter (which he would have done even without the inflicted violence) it was an act that proved to be too little too late as predator dealers, smelling the stench of opportunity, were swift to move in and ply their wares to Margaret.

Two weeks before her brother's twenty first birthday, Margaret was taken ill and confined to her bed through sheer exhaustion. The effects of her habit had seen her immune system plummet so that even the slightest chill caught, rendered her dramatically unwell. In a twisted sense, this pleased her mum Bridie, no end. It was an ideal opportunity to wait on her hand and foot, smother her with kindness and love and hopefully show her that the path she was on would only lead to a very bad place. Remarkably, Margaret appeared to respond favourably to Bridie's compassion and on the day before Liam's birthday, after many tears and much hugging, Margaret promised her Mum that she would seek help for her habit just as soon as the weekend was over. Bridie was elated and in her joy, not only agreed, but positively encouraged her daughter's suggestion of getting up and going for a walk. "Will you be ok though sweetheart?" she asked with genuine concern.

"I'll be fine," Margaret replied. "I just need to clear out the cobwebs before Liam's big day tomorrow. I don't want to feel all groggy for that, do I?"

"Well as long as you will be alright, that's all that matters. And it's a lovely day outside, so that should lift your spirits!" Bridie smiled at her daughter, gave her another hug and left the room to allow her to get dressed, secretly thanking God for his interjection. Margaret's smile lasted until her mum had closed the bedroom door behind her. Getting quickly dressed, she began rummaging in the top of her wardrobe and retrieved a handful of screwed up bank notes which she shoved into her pocket. Before leaving her room, she glanced in the mirror and saw an unrecognisable girl staring back at her. She sighed heavily as she attempted to fashion her hair into a half way decent style, eventually deciding on a simple and quick pony tail. She shook her head in dismay at the spectacle she had become before pondering on the promise she had just made to her mum. "Just one more hit," she said to her reflection as if it had offered its disapproving council. "Just one more!"

31st July 1994

As soon as the tourniquet was released, the heroin surged through Margaret's veins with an uncharacteristic burning sensation, causing pain to rush through her body at a rapid pace. Dropping the dispensed needle to the ground, Margaret immediately knew that something was wrong and though she tried to get up, the near immediate onset of violent shaking throughout her fragile frame, caused her to slump back against the cubicle wall. Within seconds, her breathing became laboured and control of her bodily functions was lost, resulting in her involuntarily soiling herself. Her heart pumped hard and fast in her chest trying desperately to regulate the flow of contaminated blood whilst her stomach aggressively rejected its contents. Drenched in sweat, she began to choke on regurgitated mucus and vomit and found that the ability to call for help had deserted her. Panic and fear enveloped Margaret and with one final attempt to move, she fell from the toilet and collapsed onto the floor, writhing in renewed agony, crying unheard tears.

And then, just as abruptly as it had begun, the pain, the shaking and the fear had gone, replaced instead by a comforting warmth as though a thick blanket had been wrapped around her. In this newly acquired haven of safety and contentment, she heard her name being softly called from somewhere in the distance and though confused, she wept as she immediately recognised the familiar voice. Through her glazed eyes, she looked up and saw a kind and forgiving face smiling lovingly back at her. "I'm so sorry," she whispered, as her daddy reached down, picked her up and placed her gently onto his knee. As he wrapped his arms around her, she was suddenly eight years old again and this was their moment; nothing else mattered anymore.

On August 10th 1994, just ten days after Liam's twenty first birthday celebrations, Margaret Connor, twenty three, was laid to rest in the grounds of the English Martyrs Church, immediately next to her father.

###

Chapter 28

With information that Bernie hadn't been seen for some time, together with a raft of complaints about a pungent smell, two Police Officers forced entry into a flat known to be his home. Like so many low lifes, Fitzpatrick was no stranger to visits from the Garda of Ardboe. They knew of him and of the lifestyle that he led and they had no time for his kind whatsoever. Scum, who flaunted every law in the book as if they were untouchable.

"So what if he has gone missing?" Brett, one of the older Officers at the station, had remarked. "Good fuckin' riddance to bad blood is what I say!" His Sergeant had quietly agreed though it hadn't prevented him from allocating the job to Brett as a reminder to stay professional at all times.

As Brett watched his less experienced and more youthful looking counterpart attempt to force the flat door open, he joked that it always seemed to be the night time when they did these kind of jobs and the occupants were nearly always dead and rotting. "Although he'll probably just be his usual pissed or drugged up self!" he quickly added, noticing that his colleague was now looking a tad anxious.

When the door finally gave way, Brett was the first to enter the dark flat, much to the delight of the younger Officer who was being to feel a little uneasy. When Brett first caught sight of Bernie, at the end of his torch beam, he was sat upright on his settee with his head leaning slightly back as if he was asleep. He was surrounded by an array of drug paraphernalia strewn across the couch and floor, giving the Officer the initial impression that he was, in fact, *wasted* on a concoction of narcotics.

"Oi, Bernie!" Brett shouted, holding the motionless body in the torch's yellow glow whilst the other Officer searched for the light switch on the flat's wall. "Wakey wakey, you drunken bastard!" He approached Fitzpatrick, kicking his feet as he got close to him. "C'mon you eejit, let's be ... Oh fuck!" The Officer stared at Bernie open-mouthed, suddenly lost for words. When his colleague finally found the light switch and illuminated the room with a forty watt overhead bulb, he too approached Bernie. The colour instantly drained from the young Officer's face when he saw the man close up and he quickly put his hand to his mouth as he found himself wanting to wretch at the sight. Bernie was most definitely not in a drink or drug induced state of sleep but quite clearly, dead. Packed into his mouth, as though he had tried to hurriedly consume them, were literally dozens of small, plastic snap bags, some of which contained a cocktail of illegal powders and pills. The Officers noticed that whoever had put them there had, in an effort to force more bags in, purposely sliced either side of Bernie's mouth and broken his jaw to allow it to be opened to an otherwise impossible size, giving Bernie the look of a snake devouring its prey. What concerned the Officers the most, is that it was clearly evident from the congealed sick and mucus in and around Bernie's mouth and nostrils, that this barbaric act had probably been carried out whilst he was still alive. Though they imagined that this must have been agonising in its own right, it was in fact only the prequel to death, not the cause of it; the single bullet that had removed Bernie's left eye and ripped through the back of his skull, splattering the wall beyond with fragments of shattered bone and brain, certainly was.

Just over a week later, the local paper reported on the murder of Bernie Fitzpatrick, a known drug dealer that had obviously been the victim of a gangland style execution. The

Police had no positive leads and with resources already stretched, coupled with the lack of witnesses willing to come forward (no doubt from fear of reprisals) they didn't expect the investigation to continue for any length of time and the case would more than likely be closed and remain unsolved.

A faint smile appeared on Liam's face after he'd read the article that had only made page five of the local rag. For some, the murder of Bernie Fitzpatrick was seen as a fitting end to a life intent on destroying the lives of others, yet for Liam, it wasn't enough. The untimely death of his sister had not only upset him greatly but had fuelled an anger that had spurred him on to exact an immediate form of retribution. Hence, he had visited Mr. Fitzpatrick three weeks previously and held trial in the closed, makeshift courtroom that was Bernie's flat. He had listened with zero interest as a sorry and shallow defence speech from Fitzpatrick, quickly manifested itself into a pathetic display of grovelling for redemption as the verdict of guilty was announced and the sentence personally carried out.

But now, as then, Liam felt that there was another party equally guilty of Margaret's death. The same people in fact, responsible for the murder of his father; namely, the British Government. Without their oppressive and intrusive stands against the people of Ireland, his dad might never have been in the IRA and might never have been shot. They wouldn't have had to move to Ireland, leaving their home and friends behind, and Margaret would never have met the man instrumental in her subsequent death.

So, when he was invited by his superiors to participate in a campaign that was to see the detonation of the largest device ever used on the UK mainland, he embraced the opportunity with an unprecedented enthusiasm. As with Fitzpatrick, Liam would again become both Judge and Jury, though in this greater trial, he would preside over the citizens of Manchester.

###

Chapter 29

15th June 1996

From the back of a black car, Joseph Connor stared impatiently down the Manchester street towards his nephew. He checked his watch for the fifth time in as many minutes and scowled when a group of six or seven people walked past the waiting vehicle, giving it a little more than a casual glance as they did. The city was coming alive, slowly but surely and Joseph knew that before long, it would be teaming with workers and shoppers alike, scurrying around like soldier ants in a disturbed nest. The longer they stayed there, the more they were likely to be noticed thus compromising the whole operation. "What the fuck is he doing for Jesus' sake?" he growled to himself. "Has he forgotten why he's here or does he think it's a fuckin' sightseeing tour?" The driver turned around and looked out of the window to where Liam was standing. He merely sighed and shook head as Joe continued. "And who the fuck is that he's talking to?" he said angrily, turning a shade of red in his irritation. "He might as well carry a fucking banner advertising the fact that we're here!" Joe and the driver continued to watch Liam, mentally willing him to turn around and head towards the car. When, after a couple more minutes, Liam showed no sign of ending his little *tete a tete* with the unknown male, Joseph announced that he would have to take a risk and go and get the little shite.

"Wait, wait. Look!" the driver advised hastily as Joe opened the rear door and began to step out. Joseph glanced back over his shoulder towards Liam and let out a long relieved sigh, thankful that at last, his nephew had shaken hands with the male to whom he was talking and was now finally walking towards the car.

"Jesus Liam," Joe began as soon as his nephew was in the front seat of the car. "Did y'not understand the instructions given man? They couldn't have been any fuckin' clearer ... 'deliver the package and get out'... *immediately*!"

"No matter now," Liam replied without turning round. "It's sorted!"

"No matter?" Joe repeated slightly bemused. "Do you remember why we're here Liam or is it something..."

"I said it's sorted!" Liam snapped, turning around to glare at his uncle. Joe saw a fierce look in his nephew's eyes that appeared as though they were daring him to make one more comment. He aired on the side of caution and decided not to press Liam further. Shaking his head, Joe tapped the driver on his shoulder directing him to drive on. As the vehicle pulled slowly away, joining the growing traffic of the city centre, Liam turned slowly back round and stared out of the window.

"Who was he anyway?" Joseph asked casually after a few moments.

"Just an old friend from school," Liam replied quietly before adding, "Sean Bevan."

"What?" Joe asked sounding mildly shocked. "Sean? ... the lad who was always at your house? ... bit chubby but good at football?"

"Aye," Liam replied. "That would be him!"

Joseph frowned and quickly glanced out of the rear window eager to see if this unforeseen anomaly was still standing there, watching the departing car perhaps, wondering where his old school chum Liam was headed. When Sean was nowhere to be seen, Joseph wanted to smile and feel some sort of relief, but he didn't. He wanted to put the '*chance*' meeting and the fact that good old Seanny was in exactly the same vicinity at exactly the same time as Liam, down to pure coincidence, but he couldn't. Joseph Connor didn't believe in coincidences. *'So why the fuck was he there?'"* he thought to himself. *'And what the hell did they talk about?'* His mind was working overtime as anguish began to cut into his logic. Was it possible that Liam had given up some vital information that would stop the campaign in its tracks or was it just an innocent exchange of pleasantries? Worse still, was Sean now working for an agency that had turned Liam, making him become a grass? *'No, that's not possible!'* Joe considered. *'Not Liam!'*

'Would you not have said the same about Robbie?' his taunting conscience suggested. *'And look what happened to him!'* Joseph sighed and shook his head, refusing to accept that Liam was anything like his deceased uncle. So what was it and why did Liam look so on edge? He wanted to ask him outright but had already witnessed the mood Liam was in when he had gotten into the car. Joseph rubbed his eyes wondering if he was over analysing the situation. *'Stay calm Joseph!'* he thought, mentally checking his rising panic. *'Maybe it was the shock of seeing Sean again that has thrown him slightly. Yeah, that will be it. After all, didn't Michael always say that they were thick as thieves?'*

Joseph nodded, feeling like he could afford himself a small contented moment. But then, as if some invisible power was determined to keep the wheels of his torment turning, another possibility entered his mind. What if seeing Sean again had opened some deep emotional Pandora's Box, rekindling Liam's own conscience and giving him a reason to think about the consequences of his actions? What if Liam now decided he actually wanted to do something about it, what then? It didn't help that he was sitting there so quietly, immersed in his own thoughts that only he and God were privy to. Joe felt helpless as his stared intensely at Liam, his glare burning into the back of his nephew's head searching for answers. He needed to get Liam talking again and find out where he stood in the closing scenes of this epic drama. Did he still crave the adulation and applause from his superiors and followers that this job would bring, or would he *'exit stage left'* before the final curtain fell?

"You alright son?" Joe eventually managed but silently chastised himself knowing that his opening gambit was, at best, pathetically weak.

"Fine!" Liam replied, though this had been a lie. In truth, he was far from fine. He had just parked up a lorry in the middle of Manchester that contained an explosive device so large, it would, when detonated, have a hugely catastrophic effect on the city and its occupants. What's more, his oldest and former best friend, the man he once classed as family, could possibly be killed by it. And, not only was Sean at risk of losing his life, but his fiancée Louise Duffy, another good friend from past times, also had the odds of survival stacked against her as she was scheduled to be in the city to meet Sean this very day. *'What right have you to be their executioner?'* his mind demanded angrily, but as much as he searched for the rationale to justify an answer, he knew there was none. Oh, he could harp on about the oppressive, underhanded British Government and the fight for Ireland's freedom all day long, but what did Sean or Louise know of such things and in reality, would they even care? These were his friends, people that he knew and had loved like kin. There was a time when they would have trusted each other with their lives, without question. So why should it be any different now and who was he to destroy that unwritten law? Who was he to determine their fate? It wasn't right. "Stop the car!" Liam suddenly shouted, startling both the driver and his uncle Joe.

"What? ... why?" the driver said sharply. "Stopping isn't part of the plan!"

"No it's not!" Joe agreed angrily. "Liam. What the fuck are ..."

"Stop the fucking car, NOW!" Liam demanded, suddenly producing a small handgun and pointing it towards the driver's head. Without the need for further instruction, the driver pulled over immediately and screeched to a halt.

"Have you lost your fuckin' mind Liam?" Joseph spat at his nephew.

"No Joe," he replied calmly, "I've just found it ... and I won't murder my friends!" He put the firearm back into his jacket pocket and reached for the handle that would open his door and allow him to get out of the car. Without a second thought, Joe quickly leaned forward, grabbed Liam's jacket at the shoulder and viciously dragged him back into his seat. Liam's face was now so close to Joseph's, he could almost taste the remnants of whisky on the man's tainted breath as he exhaled. When his uncle spoke, it was with a menace that Liam had heard so many times before, though never once been on the receiving end of. It was a tone that conveyed both extreme anger and deep discontent, yet remained calm and controlled so as not to be misunderstood by the listener in any way. For many, it had been the one and only time they had heard the voice of their killer.

"Now listen to me Liam and listen well," he began. "If you leave this car and jeopardise the operation for the sake of your re-enlightened conscience, then I cannot, and will not, guarantee your safety within this organisation. Do y'understand what I'm sayin' comrade?" Liam yanked his shoulder free from Joe's grasp but remained seated and silent. Joseph sighed heavily and sat back in his own seat before continuing. "Is it worth your life to save a couple of meaningless people you knew a long time ago, people who have no idea who you really are or what you have become and would probably despise you even if they knew? Think about it Liam. These people aren't your friends, anymore than they are mine. They are friends of the British Government, followers of the same parasites that we are fighting hard to rid our country of and if they are destined to become casualties in the war against this oppressive nation, then so be it!" Joseph paused for a moment to allow his words to saturate Liam's mind before going on. "Consider this," he said, "and consider it hard and long. If these so called *friends* knew what you knew, if they had the privilege of being in your position, would they do the same for you or would they be smart and save their own necks? If you're honest with yourself, I think you already know the answer to that!" Joseph moved forward again and placed his hand onto Liam's shoulder, his voice now sounding like a parent bestowing logic on a child. "You go out of that door Son and you will become one of them ... a Brit, an enemy of the Irish Republican Army. You'll be like a dead man walking, always looking over your shoulder, forever running. Is that what you really want?" Liam remained silent leaving Joseph to continue with a last ditched attempt at re-educating his nephew. "Leave them to their destiny Liam, to the inevitability that each and every one of us has to face one day or another. In the memory of your father, would you truly want to sacrifice yourself to save them, or should you leave them to their fate so that our great nation might at last be freed? Heroes are for comic books son, not our world!"

Liam had listened intently until he guessed that his Uncle Joe had finally finished talking. Each and every word had been digested, analysed and disseminated between the logic of his brain and the caring of his heart. He sighed heavily and looked out of the car window, temporarily rendered speechless as his mind raced with a thousand different thoughts. Thoughts of his old friends and of the good times they shared. Thoughts of his first love, Jeanette and of how, after all this time, he still felt a warmth whenever he remembered their moments together. Thoughts of his beloved Ireland and of his family, or what was left of it. Of his mother, still loving and caring despite her exposure to so much adversity. Of his sister, lost so young to the cancer of habitual drug abuse and of his dad, his heroic and revered father, slain at the merciless hands of the British soldiers.

Liam quickly wiped unexpected tears from his cheeks as his glazed eyes re-focused on the city outside of the car. He heard his uncle mutter something from behind but felt no urge to ask or even care about what was said; his only pressing consideration was whether to leave the car or not. A few moments later, as if enlightened by a sudden interlude of pure clarity, Liam had made his decision.

###

Chapter 30

It had been one of the hospital's busiest days to date and though most of the seriously injured had been attended to, there was still an incredible number of walking wounded waiting to be seen and treated. Doctors, nurses, ambulance staff, porters, receptionists and even cleaners had been retained on duty or recalled from their days off when news of the explosion, that had decimated parts of the city, first came in.

The television and radio news bulletins running constantly throughout the day, informed the nation that the IRA had claimed responsibility for what was being described by the Government as, '*a cowardly act of terrorism*'.

Disturbing images of the bomb's aftermath were beamed around the country showing the viewers how once proud structures of the city had been reduced to smouldering effigies of carnage. From historical buildings such as The Corn Exchange, that had stood the test of time for many decades, to the less impressive, yellow bricked, modernist construction of the Arndale Centre, nothing within fifteen hundred meters of the blast site, had escaped the wrath of this terrorist device. Broadcasting live, a news reporter was standing in front of blue and white Police tape that surrounded a vista of twisted metal, rubble and shattered glass. He informed Ms Lucy Meacock back in the Granada TV studio, that behind him, was the prominent yet now unrecognisable Marks and Spencer store, where it was believed that the three thousand pound bomb, hidden inside a white Ford lorry, had been detonated at

233

approximately eleven fifteen hours that morning; a precise yet merciless act knowing that, at that time of day and with Father's Day looming, this particular area of the city would have been teaming with shoppers and workers alike, innocently going about their business.

Eminent figures of the United Kingdom, from Police Chiefs and Home Office representatives' right up to the official spokesperson on behalf of the Sovereign, had all made their public statements decrying the outrageous event whilst sending their thoughts and well wishes to the residents of Manchester. For the umpteenth time that day, Prime Minister John Major was assuring the people of Great Britain, that they would stop at nothing to bring the perpetrators of this vicious attack to justice and would continue to fight the war against terrorism no matter how long it took.

An injured male lay in his hospital bed watching the constant loop of the day's news on the ageing television set in the corner of his room. It was a day that would certainly go down in the history books, he mused, as he began to switch between all four channels with the remote, hoping for a fresh update to the now repetitive recorded broadcasts. Sighing, he eventually settled on BBC1 before laying down the remote and glancing impatiently around the room. He had never been in hospital before, other than to visit a dying relative and couldn't understand why he had been placed into a private room thus negating the opportunity to converse with others and break his feeling of solitude. He also couldn't see the necessity for such an array of monitors, tubes and other medical sundries that, he deduced, was far too much equipment for what he needed. But what did he know? Maybe he should care less about hospital logistics and start thanking his lucky stars that he had not been housed in that part of the building reserved only for family identification and post-mortems. Maybe he should share the sentiments of the Doctor who had visited him that afternoon and appreciate just how close he had actually been to meeting his maker.

"Had that stranger not stopped and attended to your leg," the Doctor had pointed out, "then you simply would have bled to death and we wouldn't be having this conversation now. Fortunately for you, he seemed to know what he was doing and has quite probably saved your life!" The patient had frowned though the Doctor had smiled. A warm yet practiced smile that said, '*all is looking well but you're not out of the woods just yet!*'

Doctor Jeffries, as his name tag announced, had then proceeded to ask about the events of that morning in the city centre and appeared genuinely concerned as he took a seat on the edge of the bed to listen to his patient's experience.

The injured male began to tell him as much as he could remember, though most of it was clouded by a sort of surreal haze, as if it had all been a strange and bad dream that he was expecting to wake up from at any moment. The Doctor had pointed out that some of that might be due to the effects of the anaesthetic he had been given, coupled with some mild concussion, as it appeared that he had also injured his head slightly during the incident. Suddenly aware of a dull ache coming from the back of his skull, the injured man had reached up and felt his head, grimacing when he happened upon a lump that he hadn't even known was there; he didn't remember receiving that. He told the Doctor that he had been in the city that day to buy a birthday present for his wife and was on Cross Street heading towards Marks and Spencer. "Always good for gift ideas, Marks and Sparks!" he had pointed out but had no idea why he felt he needed to share that little snippet of information. Nonetheless, the Doctor had surprisingly murmured his agreement.

He recalled either a Police Officer or Security Guard stopping him in the street and telling him to evacuate the area immediately because of a bomb that had been planted nearby and remembered feeling slightly annoyed at the inconvenience of it all. "It meant I would have had to go to Kendal's you see and it's not cheap that place!" He saw the doctor raise an eyebrow and found himself apologising for adding such irrelevancies. "I'm just trying to piece it all together in my own head," he said quietly. "I'm normally good with details, but it's all just ..."

"Don't worry too much," the Doctor had assured him. "It will all realign itself eventually. Just give it time!" And there was that smile again.

There was, what felt like an eternal moment of awkward silence in the room before the Doctor finally (and thankfully) spoke again. "Can you remember where you were when it went off?" he asked.

The man shook his head slightly, a thoughtful yet puzzled look on his face. "I have absolutely no idea," he replied. "Though I can remember the deafening bang it made when it did!" The man fixed his stare on the ceiling above him as if trying to focus his thoughts. "Loudest thing I've ever heard," he added, almost inaudibly. He paused for a few moments, looking as though he was trying to quantify the scale of the resonance in his own mind. "But what was strange," he suddenly continued, "was the uncanny silence immediately after it, almost deathly, as if everybody and everything around had been muted by its sheer ferocity ... no shouts, no screams, nothing. Not even the sound of breaking glass ... weird! But then, it was like somebody had flicked on a switch and turned the volume up to full ... it's hard to describe really!" The man closed his eyes, feeling like he needed to sleep for a very long time. *'But that would be rude,'* he thought to himself. *'Especially when the Doctor's listening to you!'* With what seemed like a tremendous effort, the patient opened his eyes, turned his head slightly and focused on the Doctor, who he could see was jotting something down on a clipboard.

"Please, go on," the Doctor encouraged, looking up. "I was just updating your notes!" He hung the clipboard on the end of the bed and placed his pen into the breast pocket of his surgical coat. The man really didn't have much more to say. The only things he could remember was an incredible searing pain in the bottom of his right leg, being on his back and some young man leaning over him telling him to lie still. "I take it you didn't know the man?" the Doctor asked.

"Well, no," the man answered vaguely. "But you know when you get that feeling that you've seen somebody before?"

"All the time in my job," the Doctor answered with a small chuckle. "And usually on a Saturday night when the pubs have closed!" Both men shared a smile as the Doctor got up and went to the end of the bed. Underneath the blankets, positioned over the patient's right leg, was a metal frame designed to keep the weight of the linen off his injury and stop any contact with the bandage. He carefully lifted the sheets, studied the leg for a while and then nodded approvingly. "Good," he remarked before replacing the bed covers. "Though it will probably need re-dressing in a couple of hours or so!" He looked up and smiled at his patient. He guessed the man would have asked him for a prognosis, had he not fallen asleep.

When the same footage was shown for the fifth time in ten minutes, the man decided that enough was enough and turned the television off. He looked at his watch and wondered why his wife hadn't been in to see him yet. *'Maybe she has and I was asleep,'* he thought. *'But where is she now?'* He began to worry that she might not even know he was in hospital and was sitting at home panicking after watching recent events on the news. As he himself began to feel a little anxious, he looked around his bed to see if there might be a call button he could press to get somebody's attention. Seeing one just above his head, he reached up to press it but as he twisted his body, felt a bolt of excruciating pain shoot from his right knee all the way down to his toes. He shouted out in agony causing a nurse to rush into the room and come to his assistance.

"You need to try and keep as still as possible," she advised more clinically than caring, readjusting his pillows. "That leg of yours can do without any sudden movements!"

"Don't I know it," he replied irritably. "It was like somebody had hit my shin with a bloody hammer. What happened to it anyway?"

The nurse looked at him with a slight frown before saying. "The Doctor will be along shortly to see you again and he can tell you all you need to know. He's only at the other end of the ward so he won't be too long. Now, is there anything I can get for you?"

"A wife would be a start!" he replied shortly but saw a confused look on the nurse's face. "My wife," he repeated. "Can you see if she's here or if she has at least been informed I'm here? I've not seen her all day!"

"Oh right," the nurse answered. "Yes, yes of course I can. I'll go and check the waiting room. But in the meantime, keep that leg of yours still!"

"Yes Matron" the man jested compliantly. She smiled before she turned around and walked out of the room. Had the dwindling but still present pain in his leg not negated it, he would have smiled back.

Around twenty minutes later, the Doctor he had been speaking to earlier that afternoon, entered the room, followed by another male with *difficult* hair wearing casual but unkempt clothing; a look that reminded the injured male of Art Garfunkel in *The Graduate*. He was introduced as Simon Phillips, one of the hospital's Psychiatrists, who was there to '*help in any way he could.*' The patient imagined that this man would be very busy, given the traumas of the day.

"So what exactly happened to my leg Doctor?" the man enquired. "I was going to ask you earlier, but must have fallen asleep!"

"You did," the Doctor replied. "And as sleep can be the best medicine, I decided to let you rest!" He smiled at the patient before continuing. "Your leg, or more the bottom half of it, was actually hit by a large piece of plate glass that had broken away from a shop window during the blast. It not only managed to shatter the shin bone in several places, but also put a sizeable nick in one of the main arteries, causing quite a heavy bleed!"

"Jesus!" the man exclaimed. "That sounds serious!"

"Oh believe me," the Doctor went on, "it was *very* serious. Like I said to you earlier, the man who first found you was either extensively trained in first aid or was himself in the medical profession as he managed to stem the flow of blood long enough for the ambulance crew to arrive and take over. He basically kept you alive!"

The patient looked noticeably shocked as he stared open mouthed at the Doctor and his colleague. "But, I'll be okay now, won't I Doctor?" he asked warily. "I mean, apart from the pain in my shin, I feel fine, just a little tired. But my leg will be ok, won't it?" The Doctor looked at Mr.Phillips and then back at his patient with an anguished expression. "What?" the man asked, noticing an obvious hesitancy. "What's wrong?"

"Like I've said," the Doctor went on a little apprehensively. "The shin bone was completely shattered and, what with that part of the artery being so badly damaged and with such a loss of blood, we really had no other option!"

"Option?" the man asked sharply. "What option? What do you mean?" He glared at the Doctor waiting for an answer he hoped wouldn't confirm what he was now dreading. Lady Luck was not about to shine twice.

"We had to amputate part of your leg, from the knee down, otherwise you might ..."

"NO! ... NO!" the patient interjected loudly, looked down at his bed and suddenly grabbed his blankets, yanking them off the metal frame over his leg. He looked down in horror, as he saw that the area around his knee was heavily bandaged where the bottom half of his leg had once been joined. Beyond that, he saw nothing but the bed sheet. "Why, for fucks sake?" he growled, looking up at the Doctor, tears now forming in his eyes. "Surely you could have tried something else and saved it?"

"We tried everything we could," the Doctor answered sternly. "But in the end, we had to make a choice. Either lose a leg or lose a life ... I chose your leg!"

The man slumped back against his pillows and put his hands on his head. "Jesus! Jesus! no no no!" he cried. "You've turned me into a fucking cripple!"

"No, we have saved your life!" the Doctor replied shortly. "It was those cowards out there, the ones who destroyed our city, that have given you your injury!" He paused for a moment whilst he regained his own professional composure and then walked over to the patient's side, putting a hand on his shoulder. "I take no pleasure from this sort of surgery, but I make no apologies for the decision I made!" The injured man put his hands down and looked at the Doctor, his eyes full of torment, hate and sadness. He opened his mouth to say something, but no words came out allowing the Doctor to continue. "Though it is no consolation and probably not what you want to hear right now, there have been great developments in the field of prosthetics and with time and our continued help, there's no reason why you can't continue to live a full and active life!"

"You're right Doctor," the man said with a grimace of angst on his face, "I don't want to hear it right now. So why don't you and the silent shrink over there just leave me alone!"

The Doctor considered the situation for a few moments before nodding his head. "Very well," he agreed. "A little time alone, to gather your thoughts, is probably a good idea given the circumstances!" He gestured to his colleague who nodded and walked out of the room. As the Doctor also started to leave the room, he stopped and glanced back towards his patient who was now staring intensely at the ceiling, seemingly lost in his own turbulent world. He shook his head, silently damning the day's events. "I'll get a nurse to give you something to help you sleep," he offered quietly. As expected, he got no response.

A short time later, the patient felt the effects of the sedative start to kick in and wondered if he would be blessed with an untroubled slumber; given the day he'd had, he felt that he should be allowed that at least.

As his body relaxed and his eyes became heavier, his mind gave out sporadic flashbacks as if summarising the events of 15th June 1996. Kissing his wife goodbye that morning, walking the streets of Manchester, the Police Officer, the blast, the pain, the man ... Yes, that man. Where did he know him from? Whoever he was, he *'saved your life,'* or so the Doctor had pointed out. The Doctor, ha! What a good old boy! The man who cut off my lower leg ... God, my leg! ... The nurse with a needle ... *'This won't hurt!!'*

Through half open eyes he watched the hazy figure of the nurse pottering around his room, seemingly making ready to leave. When she eventually went to the door, she turned around and spoke. Though her image was now lost behind his shuttered vision, he heard her voice with unfathomable clarity, tuning in to every word she said. "I couldn't seem to find your wife," he heard her say almost matter-of-factly. "But don't worry Mr.Roach, I'll look for her again later. You get some sleep for now, ok?"

'What was that?' he thought feeling a little confused and wondering if he had heard correctly. *'Did she say Roach?'* He replayed her statement back in his mind and then, eager to fight the lure of the impending sleep, quickly yet forcibly, opened his eyes. "Wait!" he cried out to the departing nurse. She turned around and stared at him quizzically before he

continued. "Who the fuck is Mr.Roach? That's not my name!"

"No?" the nurse replied with a slightly patronising tone. "Well that's what it says in your wallet there!" She smiled and gestured towards the bedside table causing the man to slowly turn his head and look. Using every last reserve of strength he could call upon, the patient was able to inform the officious woman that the wallet was actually not his and that he, was most definitely not, Mr.Roach. With a final satisfied sigh, he was thankful that he had also managed to reveal his true identity, just before the power of the sedative had reigned supreme throughout his body and mind.

The nurse looked on aghast as the man finally fell into the blackness of sleep. Through his drug induced ramblings and slurred speech, he had managed to utter a startling revelation that definitely warranted some immediate attention. When the ambulance staff had brought him in earlier that day and handed over a wallet that they found lying next to him at the scene, everybody naturally assumed that it belonged to the patient and that he was, in fact, a Mr.David Roach. *'No wonder we couldn't trace his wife!'* the nurse thought as she hurried out of the room with a great sense of urgency, hoping that now, for everybody's sake, it wouldn't take too long to discover the whereabouts of the man's spouse.

###

Chapter 31

2200hrs 15th June 1996

A little over two miles away from the hospital, in a small room of a run-down Bed and Breakfast, Liam Connor sat in darkness listening intensely to the news updates on a cheap radio alarm clock next to his bed. It was bad enough that he could only tune in to one local station, but when they constantly broke off from the bulletins to play current chart toppers or run adverts from the best *double glazing* or *car insurance* companies in the region, he would sigh, get up and pace the room impatiently. He was hoping to hear a particular announcement, a certain piece of information that he was sure would help ease his mind and perhaps bring some closure on the day's events. Without it, Liam knew that the decision he took would have been worthless.

Half a day earlier and despite his strong words of advice, Joseph Connor had watched his nephew get out of the car and disappear into the growing swell of the city's crowd.

The compromised position that he now found himself in should have evoked feelings of anger in what would be seen as an act of betrayal by his superiors. But Joe felt nothing but sadness. Yes, he thought Liam was making the wrong decision, but he knew that it had not been made without serious consideration and silently admired him for displaying a virtue that was otherwise extinct in their organisation; that of compassion.

The driver had turned to Joe demanding that the Commanders be informed of this outrageous display immediately. "This changes things dramatically," he'd said irritably "And you need to start letting people know!"

Joe turned from the window and glared at the driver intensely. "Firstly," he began calmly. "This changes absolutely nothing. The operation will continue as normal and you will drive us to our rendezvous point as planned. Secondly, I will inform our Superiors about this minor inconvenience as and when is necessary, as I really don't feel that they need be troubled with the confused emotions of a man who can do nothing to prevent what is soon to be. And thirdly, but more importantly." Joe paused and leant forward slightly before continuing, a stark tone of warning in his voice. "Don't ever dictate to me what needs to be done, or it will be the last living thing you ever do. Do you understand me son?" The driver bowed his head, realising that he had overstepped the mark. Joe held him in his stare for a few moments longer before adding, "Now, don't we have somewhere to be?"

The driver turned back round and for the second time that day, joined the steady flow of traffic. Joe looked out of the window and sighed. '*I only hope you know what you're doing Liam!*' he thought to himself, as the black car suddenly picked up speed and headed out of the City.

###

Liam had watched the car leave from the cover of a doorway before he himself set off on foot. His idea was simple but he feared that it might prove impossible to carry out, especially as the city was filling up so rapidly with people. There was a slight moment when he wondered if he had actually made the right decision and should instead make his way immediately to the meeting point. But that thought was quickly dismissed as he told himself why he had gotten out of the car; to save the life of his best friend, Sean.

He stood by the spot where he had spoken to his friend less than half an hour previously, conscious of the lorry and its deadly load being only twenty yards away from his current position. "Think man," he muttered to himself, as he tried to remember if Sean had mentioned where he worked or where he was headed. He tried to recall what Sean was wearing to see if that would give him any idea as to where his friend might be employed, but he could remember nothing other than the look on his face. *'He was meeting Louise,'* Liam thought. *'And they were going for a drink.'* He glanced at his watch and mentally sighed. *'But that's not for ages and by then it'll be too late!'*... "Shit!" he exclaimed, loud enough for a passing woman to overhear and cast him a disapproving look. He needed to move.

He quickly scanned the area before his eyes settled on The Sherlock Holmes Public House. Was that the place where Sean was meeting Louise? Should he go in and wait in a dark corner hoping that his friend would appear? He dismissed that idea as soon as he had thought of it, cursing himself for such a stupid approach. He couldn't rely on supposition and he certainly couldn't assume that they would go into that particular pub either, especially as there must have been at least four or five in that area alone. No, he would have to come up with a better plan than that if he was to find Sean. But what? He shook his head in despair trying to focus on his next move before looking around his surroundings again. And then he saw it, like a beacon of hope shining brightly in last chance city. He paused for a while weighing up the alternatives and even though what he now had in mind probably wasn't an advisable option, it seemed to be his only one. *'Fuck it!'* he thought to himself and within seconds, was standing back inside the same telephone kiosk he had used earlier, dialling a number he had remembered since his childhood.

A few minutes later, Liam had slammed the receiver down on Sean's mum, angry and frustrated by his complete lack of judgement. From his brief conversation with a very surprised yet tired sounding Mrs. Bevan, Liam had discovered that Sean didn't actually work in the city centre and being a Saturday, wouldn't be in work today anyway. "You stupid fuckin' idiot!" Liam snapped at himself, bringing his clenched fist down on the telephone with each angry word; in desperation to achieve his aim, he had assumed too much and gained absolutely nothing. There was nothing else for it. He would have to walk the streets and hope, beyond all hope, that he'd be lucky enough to find his friend. The risk of being in the open and exposed to potential eye witnesses didn't matter anymore to Liam, he had made his decision and was damned if he was going to give up without trying.

In what seemed like no time at all, Liam found himself standing on the approach road to Piccadilly train station, a good way from his starting point. His initial brisk walk had developed into a near run as he had tried to cover as much area as possible, but it had been useless. He had peered into numerous shop windows and cafes, been up and down side streets and carefully studied random groups of people hoping to see Sean. But as timed moved on and frustration set in, every young male that he saw had started to look like his friend. The reality of finding one person in amongst a growing crowd was proving impossible, but Liam refused to be beaten. In a mind consumed with vengeance, sounding the death knell on the people of Manchester had once seemed justifiable, but seeing Sean again, however brief it had been, had made him realise that his fight was with the British Government and not the innocent. Though he could do nothing to stop the attack, he could at least listen to his re-emerging conscience.

Breathing heavily, he wiped the sweat from his forehead and looked at his watch again. "Fuck, no!" he cried in disbelief as the timepiece told him that the planned detonation was almost at its inception. In his endeavour to locate one man, he had failed to notice how the minutes had quickly led to more

246

than an hour. He had become oblivious to anything other than his new objective, even failing to see the police cordons that had now been put in place and how the egress of shoppers and workers alike, directed away from the suspected bomb site, was already well under way. He looked back towards the city and to his horror, saw a tide of people heading towards him, fast and menacing like the swell of an impending tsunami. In his own panic, he began to run. Not away from the city, but towards it, his mind racing with thoughts of how his oldest friend might soon be a casualty of a war he had no part in.

Liam's leg muscles burned with pain as he sprinted back towards the main street, thankful at least that the crowd of pedestrians was thinning dramatically the closer he got. He stopped within a hundred yards of the first cordon he saw, frowning at the blue and white tape manned by two Police Officers, the white lorry looming in the background some three hundred yards beyond them. Army personnel were standing inside the cordon methodically inspecting the suspect vehicle by using a remote control bomb disposal robot, no doubt with the intention of carrying out a controlled explosion. Liam shook his head. "You're too fuckin' close!" he whispered to himself but knew he could do nothing about it.

As he frantically looked around, he was shocked to see a handful of individuals still loitering, making no attempt to flee the area. *'What the hell are they waiting for?'* he thought to himself, confused yet angry. *'Why don't they leave?'* He wanted to shout out and tell them. Tell them that they could die through their own stupid curiosity and needed to go, now. But he couldn't. Finding some solace in the fact that none of the steadfast onlookers appeared to be Sean, Liam finally made the decision to leave. With one more glance around the area, he began to move.

He had walked only a few steps when suddenly, a strange yet uncontrollable urge came over him. An urge that was void of any logical rhyme or reason but one that caused him to stop in his tracks and slowly turn back around. He put a hand across his forehead to shield his eyes from the brightness of the sun and stared intensely down the street, his vision inexplicably drawn towards the deadly package. Like a three dimensional picture, the lorry stood out from the flat grey of its surroundings, eerily glowing as its white body reflected the light. Liam frowned. He knew that the urgency to leave was paramount, but like a hypnotist's subject unable to follow his own rationale, he seemed to be held in a trance as if waiting for a spoken word that would command him to return to reality. In a moment of shocked realisation, Liam closed his eyes as that command came, voiced by the ferocity of the lorry's demise.

2315hrs 15th June 1996

Liam peered out towards the road that ran adjacent to the Bed and Breakfast, thankful that it appeared to be empty of traffic and pedestrians. Despite opting for the secrecy of the dark, he found himself being illuminated every few seconds as a tired neon light that hung precariously on the wall just outside his window, saturated his room with intermittent hues of lust red, whilst announcing to the world that the hotel was eloquently named *The Starlight*.

When he first came across it, Liam sensed that '*The Starlight*' would not be featured in any glossy travel brochures nor would it be the hotel of choice for high flying executives. To describe it as bordering on seedy would actually be doing it a service as Liam imagined that its guests would be more akin to travelling motorway '*navvies*' in need of cheap and temporary accommodation or working girls entertaining their clients for a few private hours. It was dark and uninviting with a presence that literally encouraged people to walk on by and try elsewhere. To Liam, it was perfect.

He had checked in under the pseudonym of Eamon Andrews and could have kicked himself for his stupidity the moment he'd said it. Fortunately, a disinterested landlord with greased back hair, a half open shirt and a heavy odour of stale sweat mingled with *Old Spice* after shave, had merely raised a sardonic eyebrow before insisting that the ten pounds nightly rate be paid in cash, in advance. "No offence mate," he'd offered, whilst carefully examining the note passed to him by Liam. "But I've had hundreds of '*celebrities*' staying here, from Marilyn Monroe to Donald Duck!" He smiled disdainfully and slipped the cash into his shirt pocket. "And you know what?" he added rhetorically, as he took a room key off a board behind him and handed it to Liam. "Every last one of them would fuck off without paying, given half the chance!" Liam remained silent as he took the key from the man's nicotine stained hand and waited, holding his stare. "Was there something else?" the landlord asked frowning.

"Directions to my room would be good!" Liam replied with a slight tone of sarcasm.

"Top of the stairs, turn left and it's on the right!" the man answered sharply, not approving of the Paddy's smart mouth. Liam nodded and left the counter feeling the eyes of his host burning into the back of his head. He didn't look back.

The landlord shook his head as he watched Liam climb the stairs, heading for his allocated room. "Another one with an attitude!" he sighed, before disappearing eagerly into a small side office to attend to more pressing business. He pulled back the tab on a fresh can of lager he had retrieved from a small fridge and grinned at the images on the video case that lay on his desk. He pressed play on his vcr and slumped into a worn leatherette chair hoping to enjoy the film without further interruption. "If only *Debbie 'did' Manchester!*" he quietly mused.

Liam moved away from his window and headed towards the bathroom, deciding to take yet another shower. He had been caked in brick dust and dried blood as a result of events in the city centre earlier that day and though he had managed to use the facilities of a nearby burger bar shortly after, he had only been able to clean a small proportion of it from his hands and face. His clothes, hair and bodily orifices had remained matted with congealed dirt and sweat and it was no small mercy that the Bed and Breakfast he now took refuge in, had at least offered a plentiful supply of hot water. Despite his initial vigorous attempts, he could not seem to remove the overwhelming dank stench that oozed from his pours and so, for the third time that afternoon, he stood beneath a hot stream of water, watching the remnants of grit and blood from his own weeping wounds, being washed from his body into a swirling pool around his feet. As the warmth of the shower caressed his neck, he closed his eyes and once again, thought back to earlier that day.

He sensed what was about to happen a few seconds before it actually did. One moment he was standing there, inscrutably fixated, the next, he was being thrown backwards by the force of a deafening blast as the device, planted by him just two hours previously, suddenly detonated, uncontrolled.

Liam landed heavily on the ground behind him, temporarily winded and stunned as his head made contact with the hard concrete of the floor. Tired and blackened buildings, that once stood proud and strong along Corporation Street, crumbled and fell unwittingly as if in forced homage to the might of the explosion. Within the blink of an eye, a thick and menacing cloud of masonry, glass and aged pollution was heading towards Liam, consuming breathable air and natural light as it seemingly engulfed the world around it. Despite a sharp pain in his head, Liam quickly turned onto his side away from the approaching dust storm, closed his eyes tightly and covered his head. For what seemed like an age, he was subjected to sharp pieces of debris slamming painfully into his body as the shock wave catapulted rubble in all directions. But then, as quickly as it had begun, the nightmare had ceased. Liam opened his eyes and lay still, finding himself in a surreal moment of silence that was only broken by the sound of building alarms echoing dutifully under a blanket of manufactured smog. His ears rang from the enhanced acoustics of the blast whilst his body felt as though it had been systematically tortured. For Liam, this was good; it meant that he was still alive.

After methodically checking movement in all his limbs for signs of any breakages, Liam eventually sat up, coughing heavily as the damp and grit-sodden air made it difficult to breathe. Though his eyes streamed with tears, caused by the irritation of dirt particles, he looked around trying to get his bearings, suddenly aware of all the noises around him that he hadn't noticed before. People crying out for help, sirens of emergency service vehicles wailing as they raced to the scene, the hissing of water as fractured utility pipes spewed their contents onto the street and the occasional rumble of loose brickwork or shattered glass falling from now condemned structures.

Within minutes, Paramedics, Fire Fighters and Police Officers were flooding the street, much to the disquiet of Liam. "Christ Almighty!" he growled to himself, as he frantically scanned the area looking for his quickest exit, fearing that the longer he stayed, the more people might start asking him questions; how he was, what he had witnessed and no doubt, what his name was. Despite the pain from the cuts and bruises about his body, Liam rose to his knees, the necessity to leave eventually pushing him to his feet. He squinted in the settling but still present fallout trying to figure out a direction of travel. An arduous task, as landmarks, that may have helped him before the explosion, had now changed beyond recognition or disappeared completely, leaving Liam at a loss as to where his route of escape may lie.

He decided that a side street, some fifty yards ahead of him, was probably his best option and as the Officials got closer, he quickly made his move. Stepping over mounds of bricks, timber and cables, Liam travelled swiftly but carefully, conscious that any wrong footing could send him immediately back down into the dirt. Though his body ached, he forged on with adrenaline fuelled agility, mentally prioritising what he needed to do as he moved. First, he needed to find somewhere to check and clean his wounds. Then, he would make to the outskirts of the city, away from the dangers of inquisition and identification and find somewhere to hold out for a few hours. He figured that *his* people would start to look for him in no more than forty eight hours, eager to establish where his true loyalties lay; an inquisition he was keen to avoid for as long as was humanly possible. He knew that the air and ferry ports of Great Britain would now be highly policed (negating any thought of leaving the country just yet) as the security level of the country jumped retrospectively to high alert; an action that immediately brought the words *barn door*, *horse* and *bolted* to Liam's mind.

As he finally entered the street, he was surprised to see just how many people lay on the ground both shocked and injured and couldn't comprehend why it was they had actually stayed, despite the warnings. It was as though they had wanted to encourage the Grim Reaper himself to pay them a visit. Just ahead of him, he saw a yellow coated security guard, kneeling down, attending to a distraught and injured pregnant woman as best he could. As Liam passed, he heard the man offering her words of comfort, telling her not to worry and that help was close by. Liam kept his head down, making sure that he avoided any eye contact with the man. It wasn't enough. "'Ere Mate!" he heard the man shout after him. "Can you give us a hand?" Liam grimaced and slowed slightly, wanting to ignore the guard and continue walking. But the man persisted. "Hey! You! Come on mate, I need your help! Please!"

Liam stopped and turned around to face the man. He was about to give a raft of excuses why he couldn't help, but the security guard was quick off the mark. "Nice one pal," he said, sounding genuinely relieved and then gestured towards an adjacent side street. "It's him over there!" he continued with some concern. "He looks in a pretty shit way!" Liam looked and saw a man lying in the dirt, one hand across his face, the other gripping his left leg. He was writhing and moaning in obvious pain and Liam could see that his left shin appeared to be trapped under debris from a collapsed shop front.

Liam glanced up and down the street, hoping to see other potential helpers approaching so that he himself could leave. But there was nobody on hand to fill that post. He looked back at the injured man and then towards the security guard who was still staring at him with pleading, yet suspicious eyes. The past words of a respected comrade, who had trained Liam in the area of battlefield injuries, came flooding back into his mind as though he was being watched by the man himself.

'In the aftermath of Battle, there will be many casualties. Casualties that will rely on your expertise. But remember this. Should circumstances dictate, we help who we can, even if that casualty is the enemy. We are soldiers gentlemen, not barbarians!'

At the time, Liam had filed those particular sentiments under the *unlikely to be used* section of his memory bank, never once thinking that he would find himself in such a compromising situation. How wrong he had been.

He hesitated for a few moments longer before cursing to himself and walking over to the injured male. Within seconds, Liam had pulled away enough rubble to expose the male's shin, gasping at the extent of the injury now revealed. He could see shattered bone that had ripped through the skin and now sat at an acute angle to the rest of the man's leg. Added to this, a steady flow of blood was pumping from the wound, causing a pool of deep red to form in the dirt around him.

'*This is not good!*' Liam thought, guessing that the fragment of razor sharp glass that lay next to the shin, had sliced through muscle and tissue like a hot knife through butter and in turn, caught an artery. He needed to act fast if he had any hope of saving the man's life. With great skill and speed, Liam tore strips of cloth from the man's trouser leg and using pieces of damaged wood that lay scattered about the ground, fashioned a temporary splint that he then bound to the shin. The injured male screamed in agony and began to thrash about as Liam tied it tight. Without looking up, Liam shouted at the man to try and keep still, whilst he continued feverishly with his work. Once the splint was in place, Liam elevated the leg slightly, reached up to the man's groin and applied heavy pressure to the muscle, attempting to compress the femoral artery within. Liam watched, with some relief, as the flow of blood from the open wound began to subside to a mere trickle. He then looked up towards the man's face. "Help will be here soon friend," he said, trying to offer assurance on a subject he had no idea about. When the man eventually took his hands away from his face to utter a pained reply, Liam looked on with horror as he immediately recognised the man whose life he was trying to save. Though he was covered in thick dirt and was obviously older, there was absolutely no doubt that it was him. Liam's mind was racing beyond all control as adrenaline pumped hard and fast through his veins. Shock turned to anger and anger turned to hatred, as Liam remembered the last time they had met. He pushed the man's leg higher in reaction to his own frustration, causing the male to cry out in agony. Was it not for the sudden and unexpected arrival of two paramedics, Liam would have gladly released the man's leg altogether and watched him suffer to his death.

As though he was held in a trance, Liam glared at the injured male, oblivious to the paramedics releasing him from his position and taking over. He didn't even register them congratulating his efforts as they eventually began to stretcher the man away. It was something that he really wouldn't have wanted to hear anyway. For all Liam cared, the bastard could have died. As ironic and as bitter as it was for Liam, it appeared that nobody would be mourning the death of former Superintendent Peter Gale just yet.

2355hrs 15th June 1996

Liam lay on his bed feeling physically drained. He planned to sleep for a few hours, leave the Bed and Breakfast early the next morning and find a telephone. He would need to contact certain colleagues and call in a few overdue favours if he was to disappear for the foreseeable future.

As his eyes became heavier, he tried to concentrate on the sounds of the radio still playing next to his bed. The DJ had just announced who'd performed the last single and was now handing over to the news desk for the latest updates on the bombing of Manchester. Liam turned his head to the radio, mentally urging them to relay the news he needed to hear. Without it, he had no way of knowing if Sean was dead or alive or if his last minute decision to look out for his best mate had been in vain. He could have phoned the hospitals or he could have phoned Sean's family, but he didn't. Not because of the obvious risks to his identity, but because he was scared. Scared of what he might find out, scared that he had possibly ended the life of his oldest friend.

It seemed that fate was to play a cruel game with Liam's conscience a little while longer, as the news report extended far beyond his ability to resist the call of sleep. Had he managed to stay awake, he would have heard, with undoubted relief, the newscaster's final words.

"Yet, despite the sheer scale of the explosion and the injuries it has caused to many people, officials have now confirmed that, miraculously, there have been no fatalities reported ... a great comfort at the end of a daunting yet historic day!"

Chapter 32

Ten years later.

Somewhere in Belfast.

The three men sat silently in the room, looking intensely at an older male who would ultimately be responsible for organising the task, a man who never envisaged that this time would actually materialise; not in his lifetime anyway.

A year earlier on 28th July 2005, the IRA Army Council had publicly announced an end to its armed campaigns, stating that, '*it would work to achieve its aims using purely political and democratic programmes through exclusively peaceful means!*'

Politicians worldwide had breathed a cautious sigh of relief, though the man had been quietly advised that there would be no immediate disarmament or withdrawing of comrades from other countries just yet. He had been instructed to hold back on that particular activity for a year, just to see '*how the land lay.*' In truth, he never expected the promise of peace to last much longer than two months let alone a year. It seems he was wrong.

Despite his own personal feelings, he had to be seen to be doing what was in the best interests of the country he served and if that meant recalling, then disbanding, members of the Irish Republican Army that were scattered secretly around Europe, then so be it. He had to admit that these peaceful times had brought new opportunities to Belfast and had watched the regeneration of the city with great pride. Ironically, he had even managed to profit from that growth himself, a feat that would never have been thought possible two years previously. It seemed that the time for change really was upon them and it would be foolish of him to ignore that change or indeed his superiors, who had suddenly become overnight politicians and business men.

"It would appear gentlemen," he said to the three men watching him, "that these are times for quick talkers and fancy suits, both of which, I'm sure you'll agree, I am not!" The three men chuckled slightly as the man continued. "What I am comrades, is a protagonist, a man who firmly believes that actions speak a lot louder than smart words, which is why I, like yourselves, have dedicated my whole life to The Cause!" The three men nodded, murmuring their agreement and understanding of their host's sentiments. "But," he continued sombrely, "we have to be realists and if our superiors have decided that we are to follow the path of deals and political back scratching, then follow it we must!"

"It's total bullshit if you ask me!" one of the men spat bitterly. "Bringing every one of our soldiers home leaves us wide open and vulnerable ... fuckin' madness!"

The older man raised his hand gesturing for his colleague to remain calm. "Don't you think I know that Pat?" he replied quietly. "Which is why, it has been decided to bring only a percentage of them home!" He paused and glanced at the other men as if studying their reaction.

"And what about the rest?" one of them asked frowning.

"The remainder," answered the older man, "will be left in which ever part of Europe they are currently in, with instructions to lead as normal an existence as is possible. They will be given new identities, found new jobs and even receive a little cash bonus to help them out in their new lives. In short, their services will be dispensed with and any connection they have with the Irish Republican Army, dissolved!" The man turned to Pat and smiled. "But if this current process of peace should suddenly change its course Patrick, as we know it can, then we will ..."

"Wake them up again!" Pat finished quietly, now returning the smile.

"What?" another man questioned eagerly, as if suddenly grasping the idea. "And keep them as *sleepers* you mean?"

"Aye Francis," the older man answered. "That's exactly what I mean. This way, if it all goes tits up, we at least have somebody to call upon that is in an ideal position to re-engage if necessary and give us a strong advantage!" The three men smiled and nodded their approval, whilst their host leaned forward and raised a pointed finger. "But this is to remain amongst ourselves gentlemen," he warned sternly. "And not disseminated to the fools who wish to share tea and sympathy with the puppeteers of Whitehall. We keep our mouths shut and our options open and that way, we get to keep an ace card very firmly up our sleeves!" The man slowly scanned each of the three men, looking for signs of total agreement. When he was satisfied that he had it, he nodded contently and leant back into his chair, raising the glass he was holding in a toast to Ireland. The other men quickly followed suit.

Less than half a day later, the man had managed to orchestrate the majority of his comrades into returning home, leaving only a select few in situ under the guise of indefinite leave. He wondered how his immediate superiors would have felt if they ever discovered the plan to leave *sleepers* throughout Europe and the United Kingdom without their knowledge or consultation. He smiled faintly when he thought about the look on their faces if they ever discovered that it was in fact *their* superior who had suggested it in the first place.

"Frankly," the Commander had said to him during a recent private meeting, "I don't feel that the rest of the Council would be so open to our views, which is why I have no intention of informing them of my plans!" The Commander removed his glasses and began to clean them, a thin sardonic smile appearing on his lips. "So," he continued. "I shall leave them in ignorant bliss to carry on jumping through the sycophantic hoops of the Blair Regime!" He paused as he replaced his spectacles and returned a handkerchief to the breast pocket of his jacket. He then clasped his hands together, resting them on his lap and looked directly at the man. "Whilst I, Joseph," he added unenthused, "will of course continue to publicly affirm our declaration of peace and maintain the status quo ... for now!"

As he had done so many times in the past few hours, Joseph Connor picked up the telephone and dialled a mobile number that he knew, after this conversation, would no longer be obtainable.

"I think it's past your bedtime son!" is all he said to a silent recipient on the other end of the line. He paused for a moment, noticing the quiet breathing of the listener and smiled. He wanted to say more but couldn't, fearing that idle chat might compromise his position. Reluctantly, he disconnected the call and sighed, "Sleep well comrade!"

In a crowded city centre somewhere in England, a man listened carefully to a familiar voice on his mobile phone. As was expected, he offered nothing in reply to the instruction given to him, though he sensed an unusual pause before the line eventually clicked and went dead. In a strange way, he instinctively knew that the caller, like he, had wanted to say more, but it was a protocol that couldn't be broken. In a gesture of quiet understanding, the man smiled slightly and nodded his head. *'Silence speaks volumes!'* he thought to himself, as he closed his phone and placed it into his pocket.

Fastening up his jacket against the unexpected onset of a summer shower, Liam Connor set off along the busy street, soon lost amongst the bustling ocean of oblivious people.

Epilogue

At approximately 11.15 hrs on Saturday 15th June 1996, a 3000 pound bomb, hidden inside a white Ford Cargo Lorry, exploded on Corporation Street, Manchester, England; the largest device to have been detonated on the mainland of Britain since the Second World War. The Irish Republican Army was to claim culpability.

With only one hour before detonation, after the coded message was received, it was the responsibility of a mere twelve Police Officers from Bootle Street Police station, together a handful of Security Guards, to orchestrate the evacuation of some seventy five to eighty thousand people from the City Centre streets and save them from the wrath of an explosion that was to cause an estimated £700 million in structural damage. Though the resultant carnage left over 200 citizens injured, it was down to the actions and sheer determination of the people tasked with their evacuation that miraculously, there was no loss of life.

Despite an extensive investigation to try and bring the perpetrators of the Manchester bombing to justice, it is relatively sardonic that, as of this day, the only people to have been arrested in connection with this crime were a Police Officer and a Journalist for allegedly leaking and reporting on, information regarding the identity of a possible suspect. Though both were cleared of any charges, the case against the one and only suspect was rendered inadmissible in court, subsequently closed and still remains, for now, unsolved.

Many people, both in and out of Manchester, have been heard to say that, in terms of the regeneration that followed, the IRA bombing was probably the best thing that could ever have happened to the City as, like a Phoenix rising from the ashes of destruction, it has become one of Europe's most cultural and modernistic centres. Though the sheer power of the explosion on that fateful day had indiscriminately destroyed aged buildings and cleared the way for the birth of a new and modern City, it is ironic that the one item within the immediate epicentre of the blast that survived relatively unscathed, was constructed during the reign of Edward VII. And to this day, like a beacon of defiance shining brightly against a world of adversity, the red Letterbox still remains in situ on Corporation Street, Manchester, England.

THE END

Lightning Source UK Ltd.
Milton Keynes UK
UKOW031620191112

202325UK00010B/5/P